PENGUIN BOOKS

# The Burning

Sue Walker is a television journalist. She started out in her native Edinburgh, eventually moving to London to work in BBC TV's News and Current Affairs Department. For the past sixteen years, Sue has concentrated on documentaries specializing in crime investigative work and miscarriages of justice, mainly for Channel 4. She now lives on the Sussex coast.

*The Burning* is her fourth novel, following *The Reunion*, *The Reckoning* and *The Dead Pool* (all available in Penguin paperback).

www.sue-walker.com

# The Burning

SUE WALKER

PENGUIN BOOKS

PENGUIN BOOKS

Published by the Penguin Group
Penguin Books Ltd, 80 Strand, London WC2R ORL, England
Penguin Group (USA) Inc., 375 Hudson Street, New York, New York 10014, USA
Penguin Group (Canada), 90 Eglinton Avenue East, Suite 700, Toronto, Ontario, Canada M4P 2Y3
(a division of Pearson Penguin Canada Inc.)
Penguin Ireland, 25 St Stephen's Green, Dublin 2, Ireland
(a division of Penguin Books Ltd)
Penguin Group (Australia), 250 Camberwell Road, Camberwell,
Victoria 3124, Australia (a division of Pearson Australia Group Pty Ltd)
Penguin Books India Pvt Ltd, 11 Community Centre, Panchsheel Park, New Delhi – 110 017, India
Penguin Group (NZ), 67 Apollo Drive, Rosedale, North Shore 0632, New Zealand
(a division of Pearson New Zealand Ltd)
Penguin Books (South Africa) (Pty) Ltd, 24 Sturdee Avenue,
Rosebank, Johannesburg 2196, South Africa

Penguin Books Ltd, Registered Offices: 80 Strand, London WC2R ORL, England

www.penguin.com

First published 2009
1

Copyright © Sue Walker, 2009
All rights reserved

The moral right of the author has been asserted

Set in 11.75/14pt Garamond MT
Typeset by Palimpsest Book Production Limited, Grangemouth, Stirlingshire
Printed in England by Clays Ltd, St Ives plc

ISBN: 978-0-141-02568-1

www.greenpenguin.co.uk

Penguin Books is committed to a sustainable future
for our business, our readers and our planet.
The book in your hands is made from paper
certified by the Forest Stewardship Council.

For
Annie, Tom and Finn
&
Ilka, Sam, Liam and Isla

Not really worlds apart

Great thanks to my editor, Beverley Cousins,
and to my agent, Teresa Chris.

## Funeral Days

There are so many kinds of funerals.
Raw funerals. Calm funerals. Empty funerals.
I don't like funerals.
My first one was my grandmother's.
I've always remembered the coffin being lowered,
And the bright brass nameplate on the lid.
It shone so brightly in the winter sunshine, almost
    blinding me.
I was very young but old enough to remember.
To remember how I felt.
I imagined my name being on that brass plate.
I still do, at every funeral I attend.
And I've attended one or two.
Not surprising really.
Since I cause the funerals.

# Prologue

*London, June*

**FOR SALE: UNIQUE OPPORTUNITY.
EARLY VIEWING RECOMMENDED.**

St Margaret's House is a six-bedroomed family villa in the Scots Baronial style, dating from 1860. Thought to have been designed by the renowned architect David Bryce, the house is situated in the heart of ancient Corstorphine, one of Edinburgh's most sought-after 'village' locations, only three miles from the city centre. The property comes with additional attic rooms and a large secluded garden. Set on a quiet lane with a few other select properties, it enjoys the benefit of being near the popular Dovecot School. The historic medieval parish church of St Margaret's stands opposite the property.

'Is that the post?'

Murray Shaw looked up quickly. His wife, Rowan, was standing at the top of the stairs, a bath towel wrapped tightly round her slim torso. She was frowning down at him, her dark hair trailing over the banister as she waited for an answer.

He offered her a weak smile to hide his mild

irritation. Much of her mail was still arriving bearing her unmarried name. 'Oh, just junk mail for recycling,' he said. 'Nothing for either of us today.'

He kept his smile frozen in place until she moved away and he could hear the pad of her fading footsteps retreating to the bedroom. Then, silently, he eased open the envelope. He knew the scribble of handwriting on the front only too well.

Dear Murray,

As discussed on the phone, here's the blurb I've put together on the house sale. By the way, are you absolutely sure you don't mind living in a house with such – how can I put it – <u>dark</u> connections? If you're sure, then I'll let you know more when we meet. Hope it won't put you off when it comes to it – it was all a long time ago. The house will be yours, I'm sure. You're a determined man. When can you make it up from London?

Best,
Ian

Murray edged the letter carefully back into its envelope and looked up again. He could hear the rattle of the wardrobe door upstairs – Rowan selecting her outfit for the day. In half an hour his wife would be out the door and off to work. Then *he* could get to work. To beg, borrow or steal that house. It was going to be his. And the estate agent's concern was unnecessary.

Of course he didn't care that St Margaret's House had dark connections.

That was why he wanted it.

Murray waited until his wife was on the street and walking towards her car. He tracked her tall figure, elegant in a thin summer dress, her hair billowing out in the breeze. As she paused at the car, he thought for a moment that she was going to glance up at the flat. Instinctively, he stepped away from the window. When he looked back, the car was gone. He was alone.

He wandered into his tiny windowless office and fumbled in the pocket of his jeans. The filing cabinet key fell from his grasp. *Don't be nervous today. There's so much to do.* He unlocked the cabinet. The drawer slid open with a metallic rumble and he reached deep inside, pulling out an envelope. Staring at it, he moved to his desk, switching on the nearby lamp. With trembling fingers, he pulled out the pages and began scanning the fine script written in blue ink. His eyes settled on the familiar, pleading passage:

*I don't know what answer, if any, lies in that house. But, for my sake, for your sake, if you can find out, then all our minds, more importantly all our <u>souls</u>, will be at rest. Or in perpetual torment.*

# One

*Edinburgh, five months later*

Shelagh Kerr looked down at the startling white page, the black lettering holding her gaze until the words blurred out of focus.

'Shelagh, have you managed to look at the order of service I've prepared? Is everything okay?'

With difficulty, Shelagh tried to pull herself away from the text to answer, but her eyes were locked on the words in front of her.

A Service of Remembrance to Celebrate the Short
but Joyful Life of
**PETER DANIEL NICOLSON** (1999–2009)
*St Margaret's Parish Church, Corstorphine*
Service conducted by the Revd Dr Shelagh Kerr

'Shelagh? Is everything okay?' The voice of her assistant was both pleading and worried.

Curtly, the Reverend Kerr handed the slim booklet back to him. 'It's fine, Sandy, just fine. I checked through it earlier when you were out.' She took a step away from him and opened the vestry door. 'But I won't be officiating. I've got some urgent family business to deal with tomorrow.'

She caught his look of alarm and held up a hand. 'Don't worry. I've spoken to the family. David Menteith from St John's is going to stand in for me. He's visiting the family as we speak, trying to find out a bit about them and get a sense of what the boy was like. After all, they weren't churchgoers.' She sighed, shaking her head very slightly. 'It doesn't really matter who officiates. As long as it's done appropriately. They're fortunate that one of the child's forebears *had* been a churchgoer and secured an extra burial plot that was never used. We're so very short of room.'

She turned to go and and heard Sandy shuffle his feet awkwardly. 'Yes, but it's such a shame what we do have will be filled by a child.'

Without answering, she walked towards the heavy wooden front door, her assistant's look of concern burning into her back. She quickened her pace, relieved that her face was hidden just as her mask of control started to shatter.

Shelagh rose earlier than usual the next morning. Peering out of her bedroom window on the first floor of the three-storey manse, she could see that the November day was going to be grey, overcast and chilly – perfectly in keeping for the funeral of a child. Craning her neck further to the left, she noticed that the SOLD sign at the entrance to St Margaret's House was gone. It had still been there yesterday. Had the the new owners moved in, or had the stormy winds blown it down in the night?

Slowly, she turned from the window. She was glad her husband was away. She didn't want Gordon to see her today. She needed to be alone.

Twenty minutes later she was showered, dressed and wrapped up against the cold. Slipping out the back door of the manse, she made for the entrance to St Margaret's House a few yards away, across the lane. The sign had indeed been taken down, not felled by the night's strong winds. Using the right-hand stone pillar at the driveway's entrance for cover, she scanned through the wintry gloom. The front of the house seemed alive again. The tail end of a Volvo estate could be seen through the open garage door. There were new curtains drawn across the ground-floor windows. Two windows in the upper storey had wooden blinds – an office or a study? They too were drawn. Not a light to be seen. But she knew someone was there. The house was inhabited again. She shivered, huddling further into her coat. Moving away quickly, she made for the safety of the manse. But she hadn't been fast enough.

'Shelagh!'

Sandy's young frame, willowy in an oversized suit, was straining forward into the wind. He scuttled across the lane, tripping on the ruts made by the wheels of occasional cars. Clutching his briefcase to his chest, he blurted out nervously, 'Shelagh, what are you doing here? I thought you were seeing your father. You said urgent *family* business and I . . . I presumed it was your father and . . .'

She let him tail off. 'Yes, you're right. The nursing home wants me to visit. I'll be taking the train and be back tonight. There's no need to stay on after the funeral. If you can just help David Menteith with whatever he needs.' She turned to go but stopped, trying to force a smile. 'And, Sandy? Don't worry about the funeral. It's not your job. Just be there to . . . to *support*.'

With a brief nod, she hurried round the back of the manse and marched into the welcome warmth of her kitchen. Refilling her coffee mug for the third time since waking, she locked the back door, then the front one. Checking the hooks above the hall table she saw that the two sets of spare manse keys were there, not in the church office building a few yards away. She felt a wave of relief; no one was welcome here today.

At the top of the house, she made for one of the guest rooms at the back. Sipping coffee, she pushed gently at the door, expecting its faint creaking. But as she entered, the full-length mirror stopped her short, coffee slopping over the side of the mug on to the carpet. Her own solemn image was reflected back at her. She scrutinized it, aware that her heart was racing and her limbs trembling slightly. *Shape up, woman. Too much coffee, but today of all days you can forgive yourself for being so nervy.* She breathed in deeply and slowly, squinting at herself in the dim light seeping through the closed curtains. Tall, slim – no, gaunt, she had lost even more weight – and, what with the shaking, the drawn features, the tired sunken eyes, she looked terrible.

She swivelled the mirror to face the wall and approached the windows, parting the curtains just enough to peer through. The view was perfect. She could see the entrance to the church and graveyard, or rather the part of the graveyard that she needed to. Settling down in a well-used easy chair, coffee mug warming her palms, she prepared herself. To wait and watch.

# Two

Rowan Shaw twisted in the uncomfortable sofa, half smiling as her editor offered his now-familiar lecture. 'I know I've said this a hundred times, Rowan, and I'll say it again. You're going to be a great loss to this newspaper and to me. We're all going to miss you. I can't believe it. You've turned down every incentive to stay I can think of. Why? Why Edinburgh? Why poacher-turned-gamekeeper? I mean, media relations executive for the Scottish Parliament? You'll be lying to your fellow journalists for a living – that's what "media relations" means. Have you no shame!'

'Come on, Ben. We've had this one out too many times already. I intend to run an ethical show up there. And you *know* why I'm leaving. It's a new start. There's nowhere else I can go in the paper, at least for the foreseeable future. I'd like *your* job, but I suspect you'll be in that chair for many years to come. You're not much older than me, not even middle-aged yet, let alone close to retiring.' She smiled more fully and spread her arms as if to encompass the room. 'Yes, I'll miss all this, but Murray and I need security. I need to feel I have a life, a *home* life. My new contract is very specific. I'll be at home more. I owe that to Elliot at least. I've missed the first fifteen years of his life and he's suffered for it. I'm not going to miss any more. Not because of my career.'

Rowan watched Ben as he pushed his glasses back on to his face and stared over them sceptically. As usual, his expensive shirt looked as if it had never seen an iron. 'And dragging your son four hundred miles from London to somewhere where he's got no mates is going to help?'

She could forgive her boss his impertinence. He was a friend as well as her editor. They went way back. 'Look, Ben. None of this is easy. You know very well that Elliot's been going off the rails this past year or so.'

'I know, but it's not *that* bad. Elliot's just frustrated at the minute. It's only a phase, Rowan, he'll come through. Don't you remember being fifteen? I do, and once was enough. But if you move him away, well . . . is it wise?'

She was beginning to feel defensive. 'Yes, it *is* wise. I just don't know who he keeps company with now. I can only hope the change will do him good. Eventually. Of course he doesn't want to go. But we have to. Murray can't get a job down here.'

Ben offered up one of his doubtful sneers. 'Yeah, well, I find that hard to believe. Murray's pretty well thought of in his field, isn't he? Widely published and all of that. I'm surprised they made him redundant and with so little warning.'

Rowan sighed with exasperation. 'Yes, it was a shock. But all the universities, or rather all the ones worth working for, are cutting back. He's not the only academic out on the street down here. It's tough, really tough, even for the good ones. But Edinburgh may be more fruitful for him. In the meantime, someone's got to earn the big bucks and that someone is me. Much bigger bucks than you could ever pay me. Besides, Murray's found us a place near to where he was brought up.'

'Have you been up there before?' Ben asked.

'To Edinburgh? Yes, but not to this part. His parents ended up living outside Edinburgh when they were older and Murray never got round to taking me to his childhood haunts. But he's found us the dream home.'

'Dream home?' Ben looked unconvinced.

She smiled. 'Yes. I only viewed it a couple of times. I managed to coincide the viewings with my interviews for the new job, so it was all a bit rushed. But I *loved* the place. I think, grudgingly, Elliot did too. He can have triple the space he's got down here. My flat's pretty big by London standards, but it can still feel poky when we're all in it. The new house is huge, and so's the garden. Murray's up there right now getting the place ready.' She laughed lightly. 'Actually, from what I could see, there's not a great deal to be done. The place is in great nick. But I suppose Murray wants everything to be perfect. So, I'm letting him get on with it.'

She grew serious again. 'It's a quality of life issue,

Ben. Simple as that. I don't have any other ties. Mum and Dad are long gone. I'm free to do what I want. And it's time to move out of this unforgiving city and start a new life.'

Her editor leaned forward. 'New home, new job, new husband, and you're all off to live happily ever after? I'm not convinced. You like people, you have friends here. Aren't you just a *bit* scared of being alone? Of being isolated?'

This bald statement, outlining perhaps her greatest fear, caught her off-guard and she felt the first prick-lings of tears. In a gesture of reassurance, she reached out and patted his hand. 'Don't worry about that, Ben. I'll make friends in my own time. Anyway, my flat's sold. I've got to go.' She stood up, forcing a smile, determined to deflect any further discussion. 'But until then I'm still working my notice. Let's see if we can get me a juicy story, eh? So I can go out with a flourish!'

The phone was ringing as she approached her desk. Murray's mobile number came up on caller display and she picked up the receiver. 'I'm in, Rowan!' he said, before she had time to say anything. 'Not a stick of bloody furniture to speak of except the few bits and pieces I said I'd bring up from storage. But it's brilliant! Brilliant!' He sounded overexcited. 'So, how are you?'

She sighed quietly, fiddling with her pencil. 'Wow, that's the first time you've asked me that in weeks. I'm okay. Just had some gentle grief from Ben again, about moving.'

'God, he's like a stuck record. Course he wants you to stay. You deliver great stories. And you're the love of his life he could never have.'

She sighed more heavily this time. *Not this again.* 'That's rubbish and you know it. I wish you'd drop this obsession with Ben.' Before Murray had time to remonstrate, she talked on, not stopping for breath. 'Do you think you're going to get everything done in a couple of weeks? Do you need me up there at the weekends? If so, I need to organize Elliot an–'

'No, no, it's okay. I don't need any help. It's just project-managing the trades folk. I'll be fine. You stay where you are until it's all sorted. Anyway, you've got your flat to organize. Packing up is a major job.'

For a moment Rowan thought she detected a hint of . . . what? Overeagerness that she and Elliot should stay away? She knew Murray was a perfectionist. He'd want everything to be just so when she pulled up with the removal van. Rowan stopped fiddling with the pencil and rotated her chair to look out at the rain staining the drab building opposite. Yes, there were better places on earth to earn a living than gloomy London.

'Listen, Murray, I . . . I *am* looking forward to being up there. I've got my head round it. Honestly. Even the new job. It'll be good to work less and earn more. It's going to be fine.' She wondered if he could hear the pleading in her voice. Who was she trying to convince – Murray or herself?

He cleared his throat. 'I know it's going to be okay. We can't help but be happy in this fantastic house. It's going to be great. But I'm still worried about Elliot.'

*Join the club*, Rowan thought. Elliot had been sullen and uncommunicative again at breakfast, and she knew he had no intention of going to school today. It was his skirmishes – although thank God that's all they were as far as she knew – with soft drugs, drinking, fighting and truancy that had decided her. The move to Scotland had to be better than this. A father who was somewhere on the other side of the world, and who didn't seem to care a damn about his son, had made things very difficult for Elliot, and he was most resolutely *not* accepting Murray as a replacement. Things had run smoothly during their first year or so together, until the announcement of their marriage plans. Since then, Elliot had most definitely turned against Murray. It had been a slow process, one she hadn't noticed for a while.

'Rowan? You still there? I said I'm worried about Elliot.'

She shook herself out of her reverie. 'Ah . . . he'll be okay. The other phone's going, I've got to go. Call me tonight. Bye.'

She hung up and stared at the other, silent phone. The familiar tug of anxiety had returned.

Murray threw his mobile on to the broad windowsill and gazed out at the quiet lane. One solitary old man, paper thrust into his coat pocket, was braving the cold – on his journey back from the newsagents, presumably. He watched the elderly, hunched figure disappear out of sight, and turned his thoughts back to the phone call. Rowan would come round to the idea of living here, he was sure. He knew she was putting on a show – a good one at that – of being happy about the move. After months of countless arguments and open hostility to his suggestion that they move, she had run out of steam and capitulated. He also knew why. She saw the proposed move as good for one reason: Elliot's salvation, his survival even. But how could that be, when the boy's main problem – his stepfather – was still going to be around?

Murray shook his head and turned back to look at the splendour of the room. He remembered it as it once was. Where he was standing had been the sitting room. But now it had been knocked through to what had originally been a large kitchen, making the main ground-floor room vast. He hadn't been allowed in the sitting room when he was a child; he had only managed the odd glimpse through an open door. Angus's parents, like so many of their generation and social class, had kept it pristine, unused. It was only for special visitors – when the minister was doing his pastoral rounds, or the occasional relative stopped by. Murray walked towards the centre of the room. How hard it must have been to receive the police officers that day. Caps in hands, bearing their hellish news.

He shut his eyes tight for a moment, willing the intruding image to disappear. Turning back to the window, his open eyes caught sight of an all-too-real image that nearly felled him, catapulting his memory back through the decades. Moving along the lane, as if in slow motion, was a horse-drawn hearse, carrying a small white coffin.

# Three

Shelagh Kerr risked parting the curtains in the guest room a bit further. It was safe now. Directly below, she could see Sandy, his lanky figure oddly foreshortened by the angle of her view. He looked pale and nervous. This was going to be an ordeal for him, but he'd cope. His heart was in the right place. He'd make a good, solid parish minister one day. Of farming parents, somewhere outside Elgin, he had had a sheltered childhood, and though this area wasn't exactly a tough urban one, it did offer him a gentle introduction to city parish life.

With some relief she saw David Menteith approaching in his ecclesiastical garb, the picture of calmness as he stood beside Sandy. She inched the window open to try to catch what they were saying. Both were staring over at the church. She could hear David's clear voice floating up to her as he put a hand on Sandy's shoulder.

'Is the burial plot ready?' Sandy nodded and David went on. 'It's time we were getting over there.'

But Sandy was hesitating. 'David, do you think

everything is all right with Shelagh? She seems . . . not herself at the moment.'

David was obviously surprised by the question. 'Shelagh? Oh, don't worry about her. She *has* got some worries with her father. He's really not well. But she's very strong. Come on, we need to go.'

They began walking away and their voices faded. Silently Shelagh closed the window, pondering David's last words. Strong she might be, but could she withstand this? She continued watching as David whispered something to Sandy and then moved away towards . . . *yes, there it was*. The cortège came slowly into view. Shelagh gasped. She hadn't expected a horse-drawn hearse. Through the glass walls, she saw it: the small white coffin, afloat in a sea of equally luminous white lilies. Her jaw tightened as she felt the first acid tug of nausea. Thank God she'd stayed away from officiating. It was going to be worse than she had imagined. Uncannily, the scene below was a carbon copy of the one on that darkest of days some forty years before.

Shelagh watched as the black-clothed figures unloaded the coffin and the grieving relatives filed on to the path. The mother, veiled and stumbling, was also a throwback to forty years ago, to the burial of a child whose remains lay a few short steps behind the church. The gravestone's inscription, weathered but still clear, was chiselled into Shelagh's memory.

She stood up and walked over to the teak bureau standing against the back wall. Fingers trembling, she opened the small top drawer and eased the rectangle of yellowing newsprint on to the bureau's surface, smoothing it out under her palm.

# FIRE TRAGEDY – SCHOOL BLAZE KILLS TEACHER AND PUPIL

Fire swept through part of the Dovecot Primary School in Corstorphine yesterday afternoon, leaving a teacher and pupil dead. Angus Gillan, 10, and Lavinia Crombie, 26, were in a second-floor classroom in the school's north wing when the blaze began. Initial reports suggest that the fire started in the corridor outside the classroom, blocking their escape. In a disturbing development, police sources have indicated that both bodies showed signs of head injuries. A spokesman commented, 'There is evidence that the victims were beaten before the fire took hold.'

The school's headmaster Brian Macpherson said, 'The tragedy is made worse by the fact that the entire school was enjoying itself at the annual Friday sports day in Corstorphine Park, totally unaware of what was happening. Our thoughts are with the families of Angus and Miss Crombie.' Mr Macpherson went on to explain that Angus had been in detention and was going to be released at 3 o'clock so that he could attend part of the sports day.

*Full story, pages 2–3*

Without warning, the sobs took hold, wracking her thin body. Quietly she shushed herself, fearing irrationally that someone from outside might hear her. Hurriedly she returned the news cutting to the bureau. Then, staggering to the stairs, she made her way slowly down to the ground floor. What to do? Stranded in the darkened hallway, she spun round, her sense of feeling trapped growing with every second. Grabbing her coat and handbag, she moved through to the kitchen, silently letting herself out through the back door into the bitter cold morning, before scurrying down the lane. To escape the punishment she had so deliberately just put herself through.

# Four

Elliot lay back on his bed, fingering the now-worn sheet of paper: 'FOR SALE: UNIQUE OPPORTUNITY. EARLY VIEWING RECOMMENDED'. Was his mother out of her mind? *Yes, go on, Murray, put an offer in! Yes, go on, uproot Elliot from everything he knows, to go and rattle about in a fucking mausoleum of a house!* He tossed the paper aside and reached for his cigarettes, not even bothering to open the window. His mother would be late as usual and, with Murray at the other end of the country fussing around in the mausoleum, the flat was his all day. There was no one to check whether he went to school or not, so he wasn't going to make the effort. What difference did it make? He was leaving anyway. The school probably wouldn't bother enquiring about his absence today. No, they would be only too relieved to see him gone.

He took a long, satisfying drag and glanced back down at the estate agent's advert. There was something weird going on with Murray and this new house. His mother hadn't noticed, she was too busy working. But *he* had. Murray had been secretive and shifty over the purchase. He kept all the papers about it *locked up*. Elliot's eyes narrowed. He'd gradually become aware that everything Murray received about the house purchase was sent in his name and ended up in his study in the second drawer of a locked filing cabinet. All except this stupid bit of overblown blurb. Cigarette clamped between his teeth, Elliot crumpled the estate agent's paper into a ball with one hand and batted it away with his other.

It made no sense. When his mother had sold her old place and bought this one a few years ago, it was a straightforward process. Stressful yes, but not mysterious. So why the secrecy? And then there was Murray's relationship with the estate agent. Elliot thought back to the secretive telephone conversations that had ended quickly when anyone else entered the room. The ones he'd managed to eavesdrop on were too ... friendly, overfamiliar. In fact, if the estate agent had been a woman, he'd have seriously considered whether Murray was having an affair. But that was unthinkable. Anyone lucky enough to be married to his mother wouldn't look elsewhere. So what the hell *had* been going on?

Suddenly, Elliot leapt up. *Idiot! Why didn't you think of this before?* He marched through to the tiny box-room that was Murray's study and then stopped, staring at the filing cabinet. He was going to pick the lock. If it proved tricky, no matter – he could take all day. And if he didn't succeed, he knew a mate who would give it a good go. Whatever happened, he had to make sure he left no evidence; no scratches, dents, nothing. He peered closer. *Hang on a minute.* He switched on the overhead light and a wide beaming smile spread across his face. *No, surely not!* At the top right-hand side of the filing cabinet the key was stuck firmly in the lock. *The fool. Murray's forgotten to lock up!* Once more gripping the glowing cigarette in his teeth, eyes squinting from the smoke, Elliot pounced on the cabinet, tugging at the second drawer. With a grunt of delight, he wrenched it open.

Empty.

The drawer had been cleared out. He rifled through the other drawers, but he could see from the neat filing system that he wouldn't find anything about the house in these. As if not trusting his eyes, he tugged at the second drawer again. Still nothing. Defeated, he withdrew to his bedroom, flinging himself on the bed.

Reaching for the cigarette packet again, Elliot fiddled with the box, turning it round and round in one hand, his thoughts straying to other problems he'd been trying not to think about. But he had to face it: his father had pretty much disowned him now. These past three years the presents, the invitations to visit him in Japan, had faded into nothingness. Some money every birthday and Christmas and that was that. Was his father dishing out some sort of retaliation? Not to him but to his mother? There was no escaping the fact that his pulling away had coincided with his mother and Murray getting together.

Elliot blocked the thought and for a few minutes lay with his mind blank. Then, bored with being in his room, he made his way to the light, airy kitchen. Grabbing a carton of milk from the fridge, he settled down at the table and drank. The only beacon of hope about the move was that he had an old school friend living in

Glasgow. One who had moved for pretty much the same reason: his mother had remarried and the new husband had taken up a job in Scotland. Glasgow was only forty-odd miles from Edinburgh. Maybe they could meet up at weekends? He gulped the cold milk as thoughts of Murray forced their way back into his mind.

Apart from his father pulling away, he couldn't put his finger on why he had changed his mind over Murray. He had seemed all right at first. But over the past year or two he'd begun to see him in a different light. Murray's mother and father had both died in pretty quick succession and that had left him gloomy, especially after his father's death. His mother had told him that Murray had gone into a 'deep depression'. But there were other things. Like Murray's clumsy attempt at trying to impose some discipline on him soon after marrying his mother. It had been a bad mistake, though Murray had tried to rescue the situation. *'I know I'm not your father, I don't expect you to call me Dad or anything. I just want us to get along.'*

Elliot finished off the milk in a final gulp. But what about the stuff he'd never told his mother? Like the two big fights Murray had got into when he'd taken him to see the rugby? Murray had begged and practically bribed him to keep quiet about those, and he'd agreed. After all, he'd been younger then, easier to control. But he wouldn't take any more from Murray now if he started up again.

He glanced up at the far wall. The photograph of

the three of them on the shores of Lake Windermere had been lovingly framed in expensive wood by his mother. They'd asked an elderly passer-by to take the photo and she'd done a pretty good job. She had made them all laugh, and the dramatic scenery formed a great backdrop. It was a happy picture. The trip had been an attempt at cheering everyone up after Murray's redundancy. The loss of his job had come out of the blue just a few months ago. At first Elliot had felt sorry for Murray and tried to bury his doubts. But then he began noticing what his mother hadn't. The truth was that Murray hadn't been looking very hard for a new job. He'd heard him and his mother talking at night – Murray saying he'd done this, done that, called this contact or that friend. *'There doesn't seem to be anything for a history lecturer in or around commuting distance of London at any of the decent universities.'* But he knew just how little Murray had been on the phone or online. He'd even overheard him turn down the offer of an interview that a friend had set up for him at the LSE. *'Er . . . yeah, thanks, but I think our plans are changing. Looks like Rowan and I may be in for a big move . . .'*

Elliot shrugged on his jacket and opened the front door. He hadn't a clue what that remark had meant at the time. He did now. The funny thing was that Murray had made it before there had been any decision to buy a house in Scotland. So how had he known what was going to happen?

Unless he had planned it that way.

# Five

Murray thought back to the eerie sight of the child's funeral. It had been a few hours ago, but still he felt shaken. He had wandered aimlessly about the house, wasting precious time. Now he needed to get out. Thankfully the day had brightened from its grey start; it was still cold, but crisp and sunny. He knew where he wanted to begin his walk. Corstorphine Park was a welcome relief from the London green spaces he had been used to for so long. Two large areas of well-tended grass lay either side of a tree-lined central path, running north to south, and there would be no rowdy drunks or graffiti to mar his enjoyment.

The park was empty, save for a couple of dog-walkers in the distance, heads bent towards each other deep in conversation, and a young mother wheeling a buggy along the path. The small, enclosed play area to his right was deserted. He strolled over to the swings. The place was unrecognizable from his childhood. Everything was painted in bright blue and red. The swings and climbing frame were modern, as was the slide. The roundabout looked familiar, but that had to be an illusion. It was already an ancient contraption when he and Angus used to twirl themselves dizzy on it. He lifted his gaze from the play area and smiled wistfully. The distant view of the Pentland Hills that had so captivated them as children was still there. Nothing could change that.

He strolled on down the central path. Everything seemed so much smaller than in his childhood. He paused to look back. It had been the area on his left where the sports day had taken place. There had been many sports days in this park, but never one like that. For a moment he could almost hear the gaggle of cheering voices – both parents and children – as various races began and ended. Prizes won, prizes lost. A child lost . . .

Murray closed his eyes for a moment, trying to shake off the memory. He felt the mobile vibrate; his estate agent was calling. He'd been expecting him.

'Ian, hi. Thanks for calling back. How are you doing?'

'I got your message. I was wondering how *you* were doing. Still happy with your purchase, I hope? No ghosts?' His tone was light and jocular.

'I'm absolutely fine, Ian. Look . . . I wanted to talk to you just to make sure that our private purchase will remain *confidential*. I'd prefer it that way.'

Ian laughed. 'Hey, you paid top dollar for the house. Both myself and the previous owners made a bundle. I'm not interested in telling anyone. As for the vendors, they moved out of the area. I think they're thanking their lucky stars! Don't worry. Now, gotta go. Got money to make!'

With that he was gone. Murray felt relieved. He

continued walking to the end of the path and found himself on Dovecot Road. To his left was the sixteenth-century dovecot that the road was named after. The place had fascinated him as a child. Nearby, and set back from the road behind railings, was the school. The welcome board looked new.

Welcome to the Dovecot Primary School
Founded 1823
Head teacher: Ms Fiona Muir

But the buildings looked just as he remembered them. The fire-damaged north wing was complete again, of course. The restoration job had stood the test of time. He recalled those weeks and months during his last year at the school when the entire area had been cordoned off. From time to time mysterious, solemn-faced men in suits could be spotted entering and leaving the site. Murray grasped the railings in both hands and thrust his nose through the gap, staring at the building. For a moment he imagined himself aged ten, the stench of burnt wood still hanging in the air and invading his nostrils. It was barely believable how, in the space of one hot summer's day, so many lives had been altered – including his own – and two of them lost.

Strangely, the death of the young teacher had been forgotten almost immediately, subsumed by the very public grieving over the loss of a child. How had her loved ones felt about that? he wondered. And hadn't a pupil at the school been related to her? He tried to think back. He hadn't known the teacher, but he thought he remembered hearing that she had come from somewhere in rural Aberdeenshire. Presumably her parents must have been devastated. Still, he couldn't recall much discussion about her among his family and friends.

But with Angus? That was an altogether different affair. From initial stirrings of numbed shock, local feeling about his death had soon been transformed into a deafening clamour for answers and retribution. The question *why did it happen* had never been answered.

Murray released the railings, and headed for the library.

The library search hadn't taken long. He'd known exactly what he was looking for. Despite the cold day, he sat on a churchyard bench nearest to Angus's grave and settled down to examine the clutch of photocopies harvested from the library. He studied the gravestone and surrounding area. Someone looked after this grave. Unlike many of the others – some ancient, some not so old – the grass and vegetation had been tamed and neatened. The stonemason's lettering was still clear, despite four decades of the worst that Edinburgh weather could throw at it. Angus's memory lived on in someone, it seemed. But this couldn't be the work of his nearest and dearest. They had left long ago.

Murray leafed through the archive stories from the local paper. The grainy black-and-white image of the burnt-out classroom stared back at him from one of the pages. He flicked through to the next photocopy: Angus's school photograph. He smiled. The tie was, as always, slightly askew, and the short curly hair unruly, despite his mother having repeatedly raked a comb through it before he sat in front of the camera. Murray leafed through several more articles. The newspapers had reported on the story for weeks.

## HUNT CONTINUES FOR SCHOOL ARSONIST – JANITOR RELEASED

The chief suspect in the hunt for the arsonist and murderer of a teacher and pupil at the Dovecot Primary School in Corstorphine has been released. James Atholl, 53, a janitor at the school, was released without charge yesterday. Mr Atholl said, 'I have been put through hell – all because I'd had a disagreement with Miss Crombie and was unable to provide an alibi for that Friday. I had taken the day off and was fishing alone in the Borders, on the River Tweed. The disagreement, which happened weeks before the fire, was a simple misunderstanding. To suggest that I would deliberately set a fire to get back at her is ridiculous. I am a respectable citizen who was decorated for valour in the war. I am innocent.'

A couple of weeks later, a new line of enquiry had turned up.

## CHILD WITNESS

The search continues for a child, thought to be a boy, who was seen running from the back of the school on the afternoon of the fire. The child was wearing shorts and was carrying what may have been a cricket bat. Police are concerned that this child could be a vital witness, possibly a school pupil, who is afraid to come forward. Teachers and parents are being invited to encourage their children to admit if they were in the school that day.

Finally, the unsolved case disappeared from the front pages. This one was buried inside the local paper.

## FAMILY LEAVE – FORMER HOME IS 'TAINTED BY TRAGEDY'

The family of 10-year-old arson victim Angus Gillan have asked for privacy in their time of grief. A close friend, who refused to be named, has let it be known that the family have moved away from the area. He said, 'Their whereabouts will remain secret as they wish to grieve in private. They are satisfied that Angus is buried in the place where he was happiest. However, the village of Corstorphine now holds too much sadness for his parents and older sister. They had to move on. In particular, St Margaret's House, once the home of a fine and decent family, has become tainted by tragedy.'

Murray turned to another of the photocopies, taken from a broadsheet's magazine supplement dated years after the deaths. He assumed that it must have been a slow news weekend for the magazine to have dug this story up after so long. The only accompanying photograph was a long shot of three unidentifiable figures walking away from the camera in what looked like a Highlands landscape, silhouetted by a setting sun. The shot was captioned 'Angus's mother, father and sister contemplate the police's failure to find his killer.' He skim-read the uninformative piece and flicked through the remaining cuttings.

The final piece was accorded only a few lines in the local paper:

# FIRE VICTIM'S MOTHER DIES AT FORMER FAMILY HOME

Ruth Gillan, 41, mother of Angus Gillan, the 10-year-old boy who died in an unsolved arson attack at the Dovecot Primary School almost six years ago, was found dead yesterday in the grounds of the family's former home, St Margaret House. Mrs Gillan's body was discovered in a summerhouse to the rear of the property. She is thought to have died from an overdose of prescription medicines. The owners of the property, a mental health charity, said that the house had been empty for several weeks due to refurbishment.

Murray shivered. He looked at his watch; he'd been sitting here for longer than he'd imagined. The cold had seeped inside him. But it was far more than the weather that had chilled him. Slamming a hand down on top of the cuttings, he stood up and walked away through the wintry morning air.

# Six

Shelagh checked her mobile phone as she stepped off the bus and into the darkness of the quiet lane leading down to the church. Nothing new on voicemail. Sandy had left a faltering message hours ago, saying that the funeral had gone as planned. She'd felt no guilt, only tremendous relief that it was over.

Walking briskly down the road, huddled into her coat against the attacking wind, she thought back over the day. It *had* crossed her mind to visit her father in the nursing home. The journey by train over the Forth Bridge to the Fife coast had tempted her as she'd hurried away from the funeral scene. But not for long. These days, who knew whether her father would even recognize her? Betting on his lucidity was a fool's game. Instead, aimlessly, she'd taken a bus ride to the other side of Edinburgh, trying to obliterate the morning's images. But she knew that she'd had no choice. Watching that harsh reminder of Angus's funeral had been a deliberate act of penance.

Surprisingly, she'd found herself enjoying the warmth of the bus as she surveyed parts of the city she hadn't seen in years. By midday it was time to get off. After a long lunch, she'd made for a multiplex in the city centre and watched two unmemorable films one after another, feeling safe and cocooned in the gloom of the cinema. By the time she'd emerged into the early evening, she had felt ready to return.

As expected, the church was in darkness, but the porch light of the manse was glowing gently and re-assuringly. She must have left it on since the early morning, and was grateful for its welcome. Pausing at the front door, she turned to look over at St Margaret's House. A faint light on the ground floor was the only indication that it was occupied. The garage door at the left of the property was open, but there was no sign of the Volvo she had spotted earlier. As she entered the manse's hallway, she stepped on half a dozen letters. She flicked through them before tossing all but one on to the hall table. She knew what it was. *They haven't stopped. They won't stop unless . . .* She tore at the envelope and glanced at the single page of lined note-paper.

*Please answer me. Answer my calls. Don't make me turn up on your doorstep.*

She stuffed the piece of paper into her coat pocket, a reply to the unwelcome note whimpering inside her. *Stop it! I want it to end now.* Hesitating, she looked at the row of keys on the wall above, and selected a hefty bunch. Then she turned and made her way towards the church. As she crossed the graveyard path, she heard some quiet rustling in the nearby undergrowth and stopped for a moment. Nothing. Merely the rising wind. She moved on and stopped again. The plot with the new grave was in the far corner behind the church. She wished she'd brought a torch, but that was unnecessary. She knew every square centimetre of this graveyard. Her head bent against the wind, she noticed the lilies first, their luminous white petals gleaming in the moonlight.

Once at the grave, she found herself in a quiet oasis, the wall and trees providing a protective nook away from the wind. There were fewer flowers, cards or other symbols of grief than might be expected, but there'd been a specific request for family flowers only. She understood. Hadn't her own parents made that same request forty years ago? With a heavy sigh, she bowed her head in a quiet benediction for the dead child before turning away.

It was as if the gale was sucking her towards Angus's grave over in the opposite corner of the churchyard. No, she couldn't go there tonight. In truth, apart from maintenance duties to tidy up the plot, she'd avoided the grave as much as she could since returning to this place. *Stop! Don't think about that tonight. Just don't. Don't think about anything tonight.*

She veered away towards the church and unlocked its ancient door, fully prepared for the loud creak as she pushed it wide. The vestibule smelled wonderful. The vase of flowers that always stood on the small table, along with various church-related leaflets, had been renewed and their fresh scent was a pleasing jolt to her senses. She unlocked the inner door. Shelter and silence at last. To her right lay an array of switches and she selected two of them. The wall lights gave out the subtlest glow, just enough to see by. She chose a pew halfway down the aisle on her right and prepared herself for a short prayer. As she knelt, she saw it, nestling under the pew in front. The single white lily must have fallen from the coffin during its journey towards the front of the church.

She picked up the bloom and sat back, examining the flower's delicate stamens and stroking the soft, fleshy petals. She choked back a sob. There would be no attempt at prayer tonight. As she rose to go, a gust of icy air invaded the small church. Foolishly, she had left both doors unlocked and the wind must have blown them open. Keys jangling in one hand, she almost ran back down the aisle and, after locking the inner door, she stood in the vestibule. Then, her long fingers stained orange from the bloom's pollen, she gently placed the single lily in with the vase of fresh flowers.

Another gust of wind attacked her as she heaved the heavy outer door shut. Head down again, she began striding towards the the manse and its welcome warmth. The slam of a door brought her up short. Someone had just gone into St Margaret's House. The Volvo was back in the garage. She glanced at her watch: quarter to eight. Not too late to visit, surely? It would be an ideal distraction. She hurried back into the manse, grabbed a bottle of decent red wine from the kitchen, gave her hair a quick brush at the hallway mirror and ran through the wind to greet her new neighbour.

# Seven

Murray felt an overwhelming weariness as he dumped the carrier bag from the off-licence on to the kitchen worktop. He really needed to be in bed. But would he be able to sleep? All the wandering about had left him exhausted. The bed he'd brought out of storage after two years, along with all the other bits and pieces from his old flat, was still serviceable. So often since selling his flat and moving in with Rowan, he'd thought of flogging the lot off wholesale. But he knew they'd move, knew one day they would have more room. He fell into one of his old kitchen chairs, bottle and cork-screw in hand. Rowan was working late; maybe that was just as well. He'd text her to say that he was turning in early. He didn't want to reveal just how little he'd achieved today as far as readying the house was concerned – although, in truth, there was little to be done. But there was so much else to do.

Popping the cork on the wine bottle, he glanced down at the bulging file of papers the solicitor had sent him. It was definite, then: the only building work carried out on the house in the past forty years had been the knocking through of the ground floor to combine kitchen and sitting room. The charity that had once owned the house had wanted an open-plan office with a recessed kitchen area, and had vacated the premises for the duration of the work. Murray's thoughts turned to Ruth Gillan. *And then she had made her way in and killed herself . . .*

A rat-a-tat on the front door sounded through the empty house. He marched along the hallway; a slim silhouette was visible through the stained glass of the door. As he opened it, a blast of bitter wind caught him full in the face. He took a pace back, trying to regain his balance. Under the brightness of the outside light, he saw a middle-aged woman beaming up at him from the bottom step. She was brandishing a bottle of wine. 'It's getting stormier by the minute. I do hope it's not too late to say hello. I'm Shelagh, Shelagh Kerr. We're neighbours.' She tilted her head backwards. 'I'm the minister at St Margaret's over there.'

Murray tried to smile in return. This was the last visitor he'd expected: a minister *and* a woman. He stood back. 'Please, come in. Very good to meet you.' He held out a hand. 'I'm Murray Sh—' The mobile rang unnaturally loudly in the almost empty room. 'Excuse me. Please come through to the kitchen and take a seat.'

Jogging ahead of her, he grabbed the phone from the table and answered it. He saw who was calling. 'Hi, Rowan, I thought you were working late? Look . . . I've got someone here. A new neighbour, can I ring you back?'

Shelagh lowered herself on to a chair, placed her bottle of wine on the table and studied the man before her. He'd stepped away a little to deal with the phone call. She judged him to be mid to late forties, dark, good-looking, with a middle-class Edinburgh accent. She wondered where he'd moved from. Another part of the city?

In a moment he was back. 'Sorry about that. My wife. Now, as you can see I've just opened a bottle. Will you join me? We do, at least, have something to drink from.'

'Thank you, I'd love to.' Shelagh began unbuttoning her coat. 'I was surprised to see the house sold. I only realized it had been for sale when I saw the previous owners move out and the board go up.' She laughed softly. 'I didn't get to know them. They were disapproving of religion, so I'm told.'

Murray passed her a glass of wine. 'Oh . . . right. Yes, it was a quick sale really. I heard about it through an estate agent I know and put an offer in straight away. It was accepted. The owners wanted to be gone quickly, I think.'

His visitor looked thoughtful for a moment. 'That's funny. I got the impression that they were well settled here. Or at least so I heard through the grapevine. Anyway, where have you come from? Another part of Edinburgh?'

He sipped at his drink. 'No. Actually we're moving up from London.'

'Oh, I thought . . . with your accent.'

He laughed, taking a chair opposite her. 'Twenty-odd years in London, but I've never lost my accent. I

41

think only those who want to lose their accents do. I'm proud of mine.' He lifted his glass. 'Your very good health and I'm ... *we're* going to be very happy here, I'm sure. My wife and stepson will be here in just over a week. I'm the advance party, as it were.'

Shelagh toasted him in return. 'And your very good health.' She paused to taste the wine and then placed her glass carefully back on the kitchen table, looking around the room as she spoke. 'Twenty-odd years in London. *Bravo*. It's not my kind of city. I can barely spend a day there without wanting to run away.' She smiled and reached for her glass. 'Tell me, what brings you home?'

'Well ... I've been working as a university lecturer for a good many years, but I was made redundant quite recently. Jobs are thin on the ground down south, so I'm trying my luck up here.' He began to stand up. 'Sorry, rude of me – shall I take your coat?'

She shook her head. 'No, really, I only wanted to pop in for few minutes. I've got a very early start tomorrow. Lots of catching up to do.'

'Were you officiating at the child's funeral today? I ... I couldn't help but see the cortège.'

She shook her head twice and looked down at the floor. 'No, no. I had to do something else today. Very urgent.' He watched her; she appeared momentarily disorientated but then seemed to rally, lifting her head with a smile. 'Tell me, what's your subject? What do you lecture in?'

Glad to move away from the topic of children's funerals, he replied, 'Er ... history, modern history.'

'Ah, well, my husband Gordon will be very keen to meet you. He read history. Both world wars were his thing. He's a senior archivist now for the National Library of Scotland.' She smiled. 'He's away in France for a few days on a wine-tasting course. It's his other passion, after history. But I'll introduce you soon. Maybe you'd like to come over for dinner when you're all settled in?' She caught the look of mild apprehension and smiled again. 'Don't worry, you don't have to be a churchgoer to come to dinner at the manse, believe me.' She stood, pushing her half-drunk glass to one side. 'I must be off now. I think we're both pretty weary.'

Murray got up, ready to escort her to the door. 'Well, it's good to meet you, and thanks for the wine. Much appreciated.'

Slowly they made their way out of the kitchen and into the hallway. Murray noticed her studying the room again and hesitate before reaching the front door. She offered him a firm handshake as he let her out. 'Thank you for the drink and for seeing me on this cold night.' She hesitated once more, her voice almost a whisper. 'It was good to see inside the house again.'

'Again?'

His visitor seemed almost to drift away as she answered. 'I knew this house as a child.' Then she appeared to rouse herself. 'But it was a very long time ago. I believe it's had various owners since then.' She smiled wistfully, more to herself than at him. 'It's looking lovely. This place is very like the manse in many ways – they shared the same architect. But I'm

43

so happy that a family is going to live here. This house should know happiness.'

As he stood holding the open door, he could feel himself sway as the rush of memory hit him. Was it something about her eyes: deep, almost black with their over-large pupils? They were features that would never change. 'Shelagh,' he said a little too loudly, 'your last name – is it your married name?'

She took a step down, alarmed by his raised voice. He had gone pale and she could detect a trembling in the hand grasping the door. She frowned at him. 'Are you okay?'

'What's your last name?' He practically shouted the question at her.

'My . . . my married name is Kerr, but I was christened Gillan.'

He was blinking rapidly. 'No. No! I never thought . . . don't you know me? I'm Murray, Murray Shaw.' He didn't wait for her response. 'I was Angus's best friend.'

She took the last two steps backwards, almost tripping on to the driveway, ignoring the wind as it tore through her open coat. 'I . . . no . . .'

He moved down towards her and took her arm. 'Look, I'm sorry, I never dreamed anyone from Angus's family would still be here. You . . . you all went away. I'm so sorry, but I . . . I love this house. Always have. Please, I'm so sorr–'

Shaking her head, she pulled away from him. 'It's all right, really. I . . . I must go. *Please!*'

As she stumbled blindly into the lane, a car screeched to avoid her and then revved away, the angry driver blaring his horn repeatedly.

Murray cupped cold, rigid hands to his mouth. 'Shelagh! Wait! Shelagh!'

Through the darkness, he watched as she raced towards the manse, the harsh slam of her front door echoing back towards him on the wind.

# Eight

*'Hi, it's me. I . . . I've decided to have an early night. So . . . speak in the morning. Okay?'* Rowan stopped the message and replayed it. There was no mistake. Murray sounded odd: hesitant, unsure, worried? Should she call him to see what was up? No, it was late. If she woke him it would only make matters worse. She stood staring down at the phone. He'd seemed fine earlier when he said there was a neighbour visiting.

She poured herself a whisky before collapsing on to the sofa with the bundle of post Elliot had left piled on the sideboard. Roaming through the TV channels, the volume low, she stopped at the news and then flicked back to an old black-and-white film. Slowly she waded her way through the post: junk, junk, bill, bank statement. Staring blankly at the television screen, she ripped open the statement, dropping her head to look over the figures. Confused, she sat up; the numbers made no sense. Then she understood. She had opened Murray's quarterly statement by mistake. She was about to put it back into the envelope but then paused. *'What?* Where's all the money gone?' she whispered to herself.

She stared at the bald figures: five cash withdrawals of £5,000 each. All in the space of six weeks. *What on earth?* He could only have withdrawn that amount of cash at a branch. But why? Why cash, and why so much money? All the financial transactions for the house had been dealt with through their joint account. Any bills that were to be paid to tradespeople would come from there too. But this statement was for Murray's savings account, holding the money he had inherited from his father. Or at least the bit that was left after buying the house in Edinburgh. It just didn't make sense.

The worry that had first kicked in with the hesitant telephone message was growing as the fatigue of a long working day hit her. Ben's continuing scepticism about her decision to move had made a home in her, leaving feelings of vulnerability and doubt about the future. Was it just that the moment of change was fast approaching? She'd be gone from this flat, this city, her job, in two weeks. The changes were going to be monumental. By deciding to work her notice until just before the move *and* organize the removals from her own flat, she'd been left with no time to really face up to the upheaval she was about to undergo. Yes, she'd weighed up the decision carefully. Yes, her prime concerns were Elliot and then Murray. But what about herself?

'Hi, Mum.'

She spun round to see a bleary-eyed Elliot in T-shirt and shorts, rubbing his eyes. 'Hi, darling. She glanced over at the answering machine. Were you in when Murray called?'

He shook his tousled head. 'I ignored the phone tonight. Was watching a movie in my room. Why, what's up?'

She smiled again, trying to keep the concern out of her voice. 'Oh, nothing, nothing at all. He just said he was off to have an early night. Probably been working hard on the house.'

Elliot looked doubtful. 'You said there wasn't that much to do on the place.' He turned to go. 'Anyway, g'night, Mum.'

She took a step forward. 'Elliot, darling. Have you been okay today?' She wasn't going to ask him about school because she knew the answer and didn't want to force him into a lie.

'I'm fine, Mum, just fine. See you.'

She watched him saunter away, and then looked down at the torn envelope resting in her lap and half smiled to herself. She was doing what she always did: letting in the demons of self-doubt. Despite her confident, at times over-assertive exterior – especially in the workplace, where it was essential to wear that suit of armour – she frequently felt weak and exposed. No wonder that right now, of all times, she was at a low ebb. She swigged the last of her drink and stood up. It was time to get some sleep. She'd feel stronger in the morning. *What you're doing is right – scary but right. Stick with it.* Throwing the post back on to the sideboard, she moved through to the kitchen and rinsed her glass. Then she made her way to bed, hoping for deep, dreamless sleep.

On the other side of the flat, Elliot waited. He blew some smoke rings through the open bedroom window and then checked his watch. His mother would be out for the count soon. He could see the reflection of her bedroom light on the trees by her window. When that went out, he knew there wasn't long to wait before he could find out what was troubling her. Earlier, on his way to greet her, he'd been stopped in his tracks in the hallway outside the living room by her whisper about money. She was reading something, something that was obviously worrying her. He needed to find out what.

Ten minutes later he padded through to the living room, walked to the hallway on the other side and stopped. There wasn't a sound from his mother's bedroom. Turning round, he scanned the room. The pile of opened post lay on the table. But first he wanted to listen to the answering machine. Reducing the volume to its lowest level and bending down with his ear to the speaker, he listened to Murray's faltering voice. He sounded nervous and tense. Elliot turned his attention to the post. Immediately he saw what his mother had done: opened Murray's mail by mistake. Gently he slid the bank statement out, ran his eye over the figures and blew a silent whistle.

Carefully leaving the post as he'd found it, Elliot padded back to his room. The disquiet he felt about the future was taking a permanent hold now. For himself. But mostly for his mother.

# Nine

The concerned expression on her assistant's face irritated Shelagh. 'What is it, Sandy?' She knew her tone was abrupt, but the last place she wanted to be was here, in the church office, going through dreary church business.

'I was just thinking that you look tired, Shelagh.' Sandy coughed nervously. 'Are . . . are you okay?'

Momentarily, she ignored him. Her eyes kept straying to the window, over the road towards St Margaret's House. The Volvo was still in the open garage. Was he at home? What was he thinking? How was he feeling?

'Shelagh?'

Sandy's raised voice dragged her attention back to him. 'What? Oh, yes. Look, I *am* a bit tired. I may be coming down with something. Can you do the hospital visits today? Let's leave the paperwork. I need to have a lie-down. I must be well for the services on Sunday.'

She stood up awkwardly and her assistant moved swiftly to open the door. 'Okay. You have a rest. See you later.'

Without answering she waved her hand in farewell and walked briskly out of the building, heading for the manse. With the same urgency and stealth as the day before, she began sealing up the house against intruders. Once this was achieved, she made her way up to her bedroom and looked out over the road. She was feeling faintly light-headed with exhaustion. She had tossed and turned all night, managing only a few periods of fitful, troubled sleep, endless questions flying through her mind.

Why had Murray Shaw bought the house, *that* house? There could be no mistake – it had been a deliberate act. He'd admitted as much, shouting out at her as she broke from his grasp. *'I'm so sorry, but I . . . I love this house. Always have.'* Was that reason enough? The entire episode seemed surreal now. She would never have recognized him, not after all those years.

Shelagh backed away from the window and sat on the edge of the bed, nervously clasping and unclasping her hands. What was she going to do? What could she do? People were free to buy property where they wanted. She lay back on the bed, transfixed by the white ceiling rose above, her eyes repeatedly tracing its contours until she felt giddy. She had to think more rationally, despite her exhaustion. While, on the face of it, his move into the house seemed distasteful, Murray Shaw had been a very young child when Angus died, and his protestations last night that he hadn't expected anyone from the family to still be around were reasonable.

If he truly did love the house, then was it so bad that he and his family move in? And there was another thing. His warm feelings about the house seemed, now that she considered it, surprising. The house, certainly when her father had been around, had been gloomy, the atmosphere repressed. But of course friends weren't allowed to visit when their father had been at home. So maybe his affection for it was more understandable. After all, her mother had always been delighted to see him. Yes, Murray had been lucky. The house, beautiful in its grand Victorian splendour, had been a very different place without her father there. She could see its strong attractions for a ten-year-old boy.

Shelagh swallowed nervously. So why did Murray's presence over there make her feel so uncomfortable and exposed? The answer was simple: it brought those terrible events too close. Coming back here under her own control, for her own very private reasons, was one thing, now that she had changed her life around. All she wanted was to be left in peace. To be near enough to her father so that she could deal with him when necessary, and to be close to Angus. But Murray's arrival was quite another thing.

Suddenly, she sat bolt upright, her tired mind clearing at last. *You must get to know Murray Shaw and his family. Make friends with them. Find out what memories of that day he has. Be sure. That way you'll be safe.*

# Ten

Murray stood hidden behind the blind of a top-floor window, thinking over what he'd seen a few minutes earlier. Shelagh Kerr had been scuttling through a grey morning mist, heading from the office building in the direction of the manse. She'd kept her head firmly fixed towards the ground, but he'd bet that she'd been looking over at his house whenever she could get the chance.

He turned away and sat down on a paint-spattered wooden stool. How long had she been awake? he wondered. Most of the night, like him? Thoughts of having to sell the house immediately and think up some plausible – plausible! – excuse for Rowan had tormented him as the night wore on. Repeatedly during the early hours he'd cursed his folly. Yes, he had considered it a possibility that people from that time might still be living in the area. But he had never dreamed there would be anyone from Angus's family. The implications of Shelagh's presence were enormous, sickeningly so. *And* she had serious religious beliefs. Somehow that made it worse. But, most worrying of all, what was he going to tell Rowan? He'd let all her calls this morning go to voicemail. But that couldn't continue.

A few minutes later he made his way down the

stairs. Pausing at the first-floor landing window, a movement caught his eye. There was Shelagh Kerr again, trying to wrench on a heavy winter coat as she hurried to her car. Her face was pinched with cold and something else perhaps. Anxiety? Fear? He heard the rev of an engine and, with a jolt, she sped off. After a few moments he saw a tall young man in a clerical collar and baggy dark suit emerge from the office building, peering down the lane after her. His expression was unmistakable: worried, very worried.

At the bottom of the stairs, Murray lifted his jacket from the newel post and opened the front door. The wind had died down but the air was still freezing, his breath clouding in front of him. He checked in his jeans pocket for house keys and gently closed the door behind him. An enveloping haar had been drifting in from the coast all morning. The surrounding streets seemed unusually quiet for a Friday morning, every sound deadened by the mist. He recalled those ghostly haars from childhood: creepy but exciting. Taking a deep breath, he headed for the park.

Yet again only a few distant dog-walkers lay in sight. The mist seemed to be thickening by the minute, transforming them into ghostly stick-figure silhouettes. In the far distance, the usually uplifting view of the Pentland Hills was completely obscured. In a moment of near panic, he found that he had lost his bearings. He looked down; his feet were on grass now, not the path that led directly across the park from one exit gate to another. Turning through three hundred and sixty degrees, his eyes frantically searching the greyness, he struggled to find a familiar landmark. *There.* The play area seemed to float into view, the bright blue and red roundabout offering him a welcome anchor point.

He moved past the playground towards the south gate. *Stupid. You're only in a public park. Calm down.* The wrought-iron gates, painted a dark green, loomed out of the mist in front of him. He turned left and found himself outside the school again. All was quiet. One hand on the school railings, he glanced at his watch: nine-thirty. Classes would be well under-way.

He looked up, frowning. Suddenly he could hear the scraping of footsteps. Then, out of the greyness, he saw a young woman dressed in a heavy sweater and smart trousers, carrying a folder. She seemed to be heading round the side of the school building, but as she glanced in his direction, her pace slowed. Murray watched as she peered through the mist and then began walking across the playground before coming to a stop.

'Excuse me, can I help you?' she asked, standing a carefully judged distance away on the other side of the railings. She was clearly suspicious. 'I'm the school sec-retary. My office is over there on the ground floor. I think I saw you yesterday. At this very same spot . . .' She let the sentence tail off. A deliberate tactic, he thought. She was waiting for an answer. Of course, he under-stood what she was doing. These days, all schools had to be alert to the attentions of strange men who hung around the gates.

He was momentarily struck dumb, but finally found his voice. 'I'm so sorry. Let me introduce myself. My name's Murray Shaw. I've just moved here ... well, *back* here. I was brought up in Corstorphine. Went to this very school. I've just been going back in time, if you know what I mean ... old memories. Me, my wife and ... and stepson are moving up from London.' He ended his explanation with the most reassuring smile he could muster.

She squinted, tilting her head almost imperceptibly. 'Where have you moved to?'

'Oh, not far from here.' He pointed behind him. 'Back there. St Margaret's House, opposite the church.'

'Very nice. Tell me, when were you at the school?'

'Oh ... I was here in the late sixties.' He tried his smile again. 'I'm pretty old, you see.'

It seemed like an age before she responded. Then she surprised him by taking a step forward and offering the hint of a smile in return. 'I see. What were you hoping for? To see round the place?'

He was struggling to answer. What *did* he want? 'Er ... I ... yes, that would have been interesting but I'm sure it's not possible.' He began to back away. 'Look, I'm sorry to have worried you. I'll go now.'

The woman turned to her right, indicating the school welcome board. 'You should call the head. See if she'll let you come round. She's very nice. I'm sure she will. The contact number's on our website.' She began to turn away. 'Just don't go prowling around without permission. You might get arrested.'

With that she vanished back into the mist, her footsteps fading into the distance.

# Eleven

'Reverend Kerr, please take a seat.'

Shelagh sat in the carefully positioned chair, facing the two most senior staff at her father's nursing home, but she wasn't going to remain compliant for much longer. 'Look. You told me to get here as soon as I could but not to worry. You can't have it both ways. I *am* here and I *am* worried. Just what exactly has been going on and what's this ... this "episode" that you said my father has had? And why can't I see him yet?'

The home's matron, a former NHS nursing sister, looked to her colleague for an answer. The GP retained by the home was an old-fashioned but highly experienced family doctor, nearing retirement. Shelagh had thought him a good choice for a place like this.

He smiled. 'As we told you on the phone, your father has been in some distress today. So much so that I've administered a sedative. That's why you can't see him at the moment. He's still sleeping and I would like him to wake up naturally.' The doctor took a quick glance at his watch. 'He'll be awake soon. No doubt he'll be wanting some lunch.' The reassuring smile was back again. 'And he'll seem more lucid, easier to get through to.'

Shelagh shifted in her chair. 'I see. But what *exactly* made him so distressed?'

The matron held Shelagh's gaze. 'We had a fire here. In the early hours.' She held up her hand. 'Don't worry. It was in an outbuilding. The gardener's hut, as it happens, nowhere near the main premises. The fire brigade and police were called. They suspect that it was started by some of the local youths having "a laugh". We're going to look at access to the grounds and see what else we can do to make it secure. We don't have CCTV around the perimeter, but we may have to reassess that situation.'

Shelagh was beginning to feel sick. 'But . . . my father, what did he have to do with . . .' She tailed off, uncertain what to ask.

The GP answered. 'Your father was the one who raised the alarm. He saw the fire from his window. Amazingly, given his physical infirmity, he managed to pull on some outdoor clothing and tried to run towards the blaze.' The doctor paused. 'He was shouting uncontrollably.'

'Shouting?'

'Yes. Shouting for Angus. I'm sorry.'

Shelagh took a deep breath, but before she could respond the matron spoke up. 'As you know, we view your father's condition as complicated. He's wrestled with severe mental health problems and depression so long now, and old age hasn't made things better. Quite the reverse. There are indications of incipient dementia, and his increasing physical infirmity has led to a deeper depression.' She sighed before continuing. 'Surprisingly or not, since coming in here your father hasn't mentioned Angus at all. Locking it all away has, of course, been a major part of his problems. But the fire ... I think we can all understand how such an event could have led to his distress.'

It was the GP's turn again. 'Reverend Kerr? On your most recent visits has your father talked to you about Angus, about that day?'

Shaking her head, Shelagh turned her hands palms upwards in an all-too-familiar gesture of despair. 'As I told you before he moved in, he hadn't mentioned Angus for years. But then, as his illness worsened, he started talking about him again. Not very coherently and not regularly, and not *that* recently. I think the most recent time was last June.' She paused before going on. 'The fortieth anniversary of Angus's death.'

Shelagh stood outside her father's room. The last hour had been spent in the matron's office, drinking over-stewed tea and forcing down a sandwich that might as well have been made of cardboard. Eventually, the GP had returned to announce that her father was awake and able to receive visitors. Her hand hovered over the door handle. Part of her wanted to turn on her heels and flee. The other part wanted, *needed*, to know what was going on in her father's head.

She knocked gently and, without waiting for an answer, slowly turned the handle, pushing the door wide. He was sitting in his armchair by the window, thin hands clasped tightly in his lap, staring out at the distant Fife coast. The pose was familiar. His near catatonic rigidity and brooding air already had her longing to be away from this place. Looking at him closely, she saw that he was well turned out, dressed in a clean shirt, brown corduroy trousers and woollen cardigan. His white hair, though still too long, had been trimmed. It looked neater than usual, and he'd had a recent shave. The staff were to be thanked for all that. They were exceptionally good at the personal details.

'Dad?'

He didn't turn to greet her. She tried again. 'Dad? How are you?'

This time, he responded. But only with his head, which swivelled to take in her tall figure. The rest of his body remained resolutely turned away from her, facing the remote headland, grey sky and sea. She knew very well that he'd rather be out there enjoying the fresh sea air than be cooped up in here.

'You shouldn't have come,' he said finally. 'I'm fine. Don't you have church matters to attend to? Doesn't your flock need you?' He turned back to face the window again.

His voice was unusually gruff, even by his standards, but the doctor had been right: her father was clearly in a lucid, engaged state. That was something at least. She moved fully into the room and shut the door quietly behind her. Should she sit down or wait to be asked? Eventually she opted to perch on the armrest of the other chair. 'The home called me, Dad.

They asked me to come in. They told me about the fire here last night.'

He remained looking out at the view as he answered. 'Well, they had no business calling you. I don't know what they're complaining about. I saved the bloody day. The whole place could've been burn–' He didn't seem to want to say the word. 'Could have been destroyed. There are a lot of disabled people in here, you know. They wouldn't exactly be able to dash to the fire rallying points.'

'No one's complaining, Dad. They were worried about you.'

He gave a curt shrug of the shoulders. 'Pah! Worried? Interferers more like. I'm sick of this place. Sick of it. I want to go home.'

She sighed inwardly. *Not this again, please. This is home. Your old homes are gone, sold. St Margaret's and that godforsaken Highlands hole we ended up in after . . .*

She thought back to that last family home. After her mother's suicide she had fled the place, going late to university and then straight into various undemanding administrative jobs located as far away from her father as possible. She had been sorely tempted to become permanently estranged from him – and almost had, for years, apart from her terse replies to his occasional self-pitying letters. After all, it was only because of her mother that she'd hung around. But that had changed in recent years. Now, at this stage of her life, working in the Church – like her father but in such a different role – she had made it her duty to be within travelling distance of him, regardless of how difficult she found his moods and his mental deterioration.

She tried again. 'Dad, please. It's nice here. You know it is.' Why did she always feel like a small child when she visited him, terrified of saying what she had to? Enough. Today was going to be different. She was a grown-up and she was going to behave like one. 'You can't look after yourself, Dad. You need to be here.'

This time his head whipped round, his wizened features set in a vicious grimace. 'Need, *need*? What do you know about what I need? I want my life back! *That's what I bloody well need!*'

Usually, when he was in one of these moods, she would make her excuses and leave quickly. Then, the next time they met, he'd be either monosyllabic and surly, nursing his perceived grievance, or in a manically good mood, overly polite. But she wasn't going to run away this time. Moving to a nearby footstool, she sat down and leaned towards him. 'Dad, they said that . . . you . . . were talking about Ang–' She coughed, his name literally stuck in her throat. 'You've been talking about Angus.'

The movement, when it came, was at lightning speed. Standing over her, swaying, her wrist gripped agonizingly tightly in one of his claw-like fists, he hissed, 'Never, *never*. I did not. Whoever said so is lying. They're a bunch of liars in here!'

She could see that his sudden burst of energy had left him badly weakened and, trying to remain calm, she half lifted, half shoved him back into his chair. Defeated, he looked away again to the outside.

'All right, Dad. All right.' She moved away from him, staring hopelessly at the back of his head. She was going to break one of her own rules: talk about her brother. 'Look, what happened to Angus happened. You have to stop hating the world. It's okay to talk about him.' She could hear her voice rising; anger and frustration were taking hold. 'You ... *we* must face it. *Angus is gone, long gone. And you know it!*' Immediately she regretted her loss of control. But it was too late.

Painfully, he turned his entire body towards her. His face was no longer filled with fury; in its place was wide-eyed fear. 'You're wrong, girl,' he said, shaking his head, his white hair falling over his brow and into his dark eyes. 'Angus is back. His ghost must have escaped that grave you live by. I've seen him. And now he's coming for you!' His laugh was more a manic cackle. 'Ah-ha! And we both deserve it, don't we? To be haunted!'

She stood up and ran to the door, his words filling her ears before she could slam it shut behind her.

*'Believe me, Shelagh! He's coming to get his revenge!'*

# Twelve

Murray stood in the doorway of the head teacher's office.

'Hello, I'm Fiona Muir. Do come in.'

He accepted her firm handshake and sat in the chair offered. She was a tall, slender woman, well groomed, dressed in black trousers, jacket and white shirt, looking more like a lawyer than a teacher.

She moved back behind her desk and smiled at him. 'I'm really glad you called. Otherwise I was going to come and visit you after finishing here.'

'Really?' He was surprised.

'Yes, we were pupils here at the same time.'

Carefully, he took in all her facial features, but none sparked any memory. 'I'm sorry, I don't . . . we were too young . . .'

She tilted her head. 'I wouldn't have known you by sight now either, obviously, but when Denise, our secretary, mentioned your name, I recognized it immediately. How could I forget? You were Angus's best friend.' She paused but kept looking at him. 'And Lavinia Crombie was my aunt.'

He breathed in deeply. 'The teacher who died with Angus?'

She nodded.

'I knew that there was someone at the school related to her,' he went on, and then shrugged in apology. 'But I . . . in fact everybody seemed to be focused on Angus.'

Fiona Muir's smile had disappeared. 'Yes. Everyone except my family. She was my mother's sister. They were close. I was close to her. My aunt Lavinia spent a lot of time with me. Her death damaged our family.' She finished the sentence with an effort.

Murray began to feel real alarm, as he considered just how little he had thought about the reality of coming back here. Shelagh's presence was difficult enough. Now Fiona Muir. A feeling of claustrophobia gripped him, as if the event were closing in on him again.

'Are you okay?' She was leaning forward.

He sat up, trying to banish the unsettling feelings. 'Sorry. Yes, yes, I'm fine. I'm very sorry about your aunt. As I say, it . . . it passed me by.' He gestured towards the door. 'Would you mind if we had a walk around now?'

She stood up. 'Of course not. I can understand why you want to be here. I think often of Lavinia as I walk these corridors.' She pointed in the direction of the stairs. 'Let's start at the ground floor.'

They descended the steps in silence and stopped near the main school entrance. She turned to him. 'Left or right?' She had switched into a bustling, business-like mode.

Murray stood rooted to the spot, feeling temporarily marooned, looking from Fiona Muir's impatient face to the ground-floor corridor and then back again.

She made the decision for him. 'This way.'

Meekly, he followed her click-clacking heels. The corridor, though of the same narrow proportions he remembered from childhood, was now brightly lit, the walls painted and festooned with the pupils' colourful artwork. They reached one of the old classrooms.

She'd sensed his hesitation. 'It's okay. In you go.'

He entered and surveyed the room with approval. 'It's good they've kept the big windows. Do you remember how dingy that old corridor used to be? It was such a relief to get into the classroom and see some light.'

She gave a small laugh. 'That corridor definitely needed brightening up. It was a recipe for depression, if you ask me. I've been teaching here for years and thankfully the place was transformed by the time I'd arrived. It's all ultra-modern now.'

He scanned the layout of the room. Long gone were the heavy wooden desks with their hinged lids and grubby ink-holes. Now the room was filled with contemporary furniture and cheerful artwork. Behind him, he heard her feet shuffle. She was obviously impatient to be moving on. He wished he could roam the building on his own, but of course he knew that would be impossible.

Wordlessly, she led him back out into the corridor. As he walked along behind her he glanced quickly to his left and right, taking in other classrooms through their open doors, until they reached the dining hall. It had the same heavily varnished, dark wooden floor, but everything else had changed. There was no sign of the rows of long refectory benches and the cramped serving hatch he remembered from his school days. Instead, a number of generously spaced round tables and chairs were spread across the hall. A long counter and neat pile of trays replaced the meagre hatch. It was a very welcoming space now.

She turned to look at him. 'Some transformation, isn't it? And the best thing of all? Haven't you noticed?'

He shook his head, slightly bewildered.

She laughed more fully and genuinely this time. 'No smell of overcooked greens and fatty stew! We don't serve that sort of swill these days, and we have a state-of-the-art ventilation system.'

She spoke with a pride so personal that she might have been showing off her own home. She was clearly very attached to the school, and Murray had a strong suspicion that she saw it as her own highly protected fiefdom.

'Look, why don't we have a look upstairs and then grab a coffee in my office?' She was trying to make this easy for him and he appreciated that. Still, he hesitated.

She tilted her head back towards the upper floors. 'It's okay. Nothing's changed since they rebuilt the north wing. Where it happened's still a storeroom. Remember, they didn't use it as classroom after the fire. There's nothing to see. Trust me. Do you want to go up?'

The words came out before he'd consciously

thought them through. 'No, not today. Look, I'm sorry. Can we go *out* for that coffee, please. Now?'

They were seated in a small café near the school. Murray sipped at his espresso and watched as Fiona Muir slowly stirred the foam of her latte. The strong coffee was probably a mistake; he already felt light-headed and detached.

She stopped stirring and nudged her mug to one side. 'Look, I don't mean to pry, but all of a sudden you don't appear very happy. On the phone today you seemed keen to visit the school. Are you okay?'

He pushed his own coffee to one side, staring past her. Outside, the street was in darkness, broken only by the headlights of an occasional car sweeping down the road. 'I *did* want to see the school, but when I got in there it just felt a bit odd. It's funny, I don't remember much about the last year I spent there after Angus died. I think I just wanted to get through it and move on up to the big school.'

'I know what you mean. It was a weird time. I became really withdrawn.'

Murray studied her face. She had an almost tangible vibrancy about her, as if full of excited energy.

'But what does it feel like for you now? Teaching in the place?' he asked.

She cupped the mug in front of her and took a slow sip before answering. 'The truth is, I love it here. I had always promised myself to return one day. Aunt Lavinia's death was on my mind as a child a great deal

69

and then it faded when I hit my teens and twenties. I went away, too. Lived in Australia with my then husband, working as a teacher. I trained here originally, in Edinburgh, after university. I was a typical example of my generation, our generation, I suppose. I did an arts degree and bummed around for a bit. Then I needed to get a proper job.'

She shrugged in a surprisingly carefree manner. 'Teaching seemed a sensible option. My mother often said that Aunt Lavinia would have been so proud of me.' She broke off to smile at him. 'Actually, I took to teaching really well. You know what they say. Good teachers are born, not made. Maybe it's in my genes. But I *have* invested a lot of hard work and years into the school. Sadly, I hardly do any teaching now that I'm the head, and I miss it.' She took another sip. 'What about you? Job, career?'

He sat back, raking a hand through his hair. He felt emotionally tired, and this woman's energy and unguarded intimacy, though not without its charm, was draining. 'Me? Oh, I've had a career in academia. History. I was made redundant a while back, so we – me and my wife, Rowan – saw it as an opportunity to change our lives.'

'Change your lives?' Fiona smirked. 'That's quite an aspiration.'

The remark had a caustic edge, but he ignored it. 'It is, but we wanted a completely new lifestyle for us and Elliot, my teenage stepson. Rowan's packed in her career as a journalist and is taking up a senior media relations job at the Scottish Parliament. I hope to get another job here soon. I've not been looking too hard, what with the move. The best thing is that we've traded in a London flat for a six-bedroomed house with acres of space and a fabulous garden. It's a no-brainer, as they say.'

She cocked her head, regarding him quizzically. 'But? I sense there's a "but" somewhere in all this. Are you changing your mind about the move?' She looked sheepish. 'Sorry, that's none of my business. We're strangers. The school connection, you know ... made me a bit nosy. Listen, when you and your family have settled in, why not call me? I'll have you all over for dinner. I'd like to talk more to you.' She was getting to her feet.

He scraped his chair back and hesitated. 'Please, wait. I want to ask you something.'

Gently, she lowered herself back into her seat. 'Okay.'

His sense of detachment was leaking away. It was time to be more focused. He finished the cold espresso in one mouthful, grimacing at its bitterness. 'What do you think of me buying Angus's old family home?'

She looked at him pleasantly, seemingly unsurprised by the question. 'Well, the first thing I'd say is congratulations. It's a beautiful place.' She laughed. 'God, your redundancy payoff must have been of lottery proportions!'

'Not quite. My late father's estate helped.'

She offered a mock cringe. 'I'm sorry, that was crass of me.'

He shook his head. 'No, no. It's fine really. But you don't think there's anything wrong with me buying *that* house?'

She squinted as if weighing up the question seriously. 'All old houses have their histories. The older the property, the higher the chance its walls contain some past tragedy. I'm not sure if I could live in that house if I'd been Angus's best friend but, on the other hand, maybe you're the best person to do so. Lay its ghosts, *his* ghost, to rest.' She gave him a congratulatory wave. 'But hey, you were lucky the house came on the market just when you were looking to move. Great timing.'

He looked away from her and out towards the darkened street again, twisting the tiny coffee cup round and round in its saucer. 'I don't believe in ghosts. But I do believe in living people. Did you know Shelagh Gillan, or rather Shelagh *Kerr*, is back here? She came to pay me a neighbourly visit last night. We both just about collapsed when we worked out who each other was. I never in a million years expected her to be here.'

Fiona sat back, letting out an exaggeratedly loud sigh. 'Oh dear. Yes, I know. The school has some dealings with the church – that's how I ran into her. If you hadn't met her already, I would have told you about her. She came back about a year ago.'

'Did she know who you were?' Murray asked.

Fiona flashed him a sardonic look. 'Oh yes indeed. She came to see me at the school. She knew who I was all right. She had obviously done her research on the community before taking up her position.'

'And did *you* know who Shelagh was?'

'Not immediately. It's known in the community now, of course, but it was at our first meeting that she told me. She said that she'd come late to the cloth and had been working in prison chaplaincy for a while. But when the vacancy at St Margaret's came up, she wanted to return. To be near Angus and her ageing father.' Fiona laughed. 'She had the cheek to ask me if I'd returned because of Lavinia. I said I'd hoped to come back one day anyway, though Lavinia was often in my thoughts.' She shook her head. 'I left it like that. I couldn't believe she was here. In fact, I was astonished – and even more so that she was an ordained minister of the Church of Scotland, with a doctorate in theology, no less.'

'It's a pretty unusual career choice for anyone to make, and quite hard for a woman, I imagine.'

Half smiling, she met his eye. 'Oh, I don't know about that. I was more astonished at . . . well, it's either the ultimate in hair-shirt atonement or the ultimate in hypocrisy.'

'Hypocrisy?' He held his breath, wondering what was coming next.

She hesitated for a moment. 'I did want to talk to you about this at some point. I guess sooner's better than later.'

'What do you mean?'

Her face was grave as she met his eyes. 'I *mean*, I think she killed Angus and Lavinia.'

# Thirteen

Fiona Muir had insisted on buying two more coffees, and Murray accepted his with a nod. She seemed to be enjoying keeping him waiting before she carried on with her explanation.

'I'm sorry.' His patience was nearing its end. 'It just seems absurd. In fact, my distinct recollection is of how well Angus and Shelagh got on, despite their age difference. They seemed to love each other. Angus worshipped his sister, looked up to her.'

She stirred her coffee, not looking at him. 'I know it sounds ridiculous, but hear me out. Do you remember much about Angus's father?'

Murray didn't really want to get into this territory. Of course he remembered the father. Still, he did want to hear what she had to say. 'Not really. I hardly ever saw him. He was always working. I remember the mother though. She was a nice woman. Kind, gentle, very pretty.'

'Yes. Well, I can assure you the father was far from gentle and kind. He was extremely strict with his daughter. I know because my sister was in the same year as Shelagh at secondary school. The father was a bullying bastard. Ruled the house with the proverbial rod of iron.' She looked puzzled. 'I'm surprised you didn't know about this. Did Angus not say anything? Wasn't there an atmosphere in the house?'

Murray raised an eyebrow. 'No, not at all. I didn't pick up on any of that. Though grant you, I saw little of Robert Gillan since he was always working.' He delivered the lie easily. 'What was his job? I can't remember.' Murray waited, keen to hear what else this woman had to say about a family that she could never have known as well as he had.

She sipped at her coffee. 'He was an accountant. Worked, ironically, for the Church of Scotland.'

'Ah, yes. He was very chummy with the then minister at St Margaret's. We all had to go to Sunday service. I used to see him there. Did you?'

'No.' She shook her head. 'My parents weren't churchgoers. Anyway, Robert Gillan was a very senior bureaucrat in the Church. Would spend a lot of time away on trips to various parishes all over Scotland, checking the books and suchlike. The Church had a lot of money and he was well paid for his responsibilities. And well thought of.'

She shuffled her chair closer, until Murray felt they were in a near conspiratorial huddle, and lowered her voice. 'Robert Gillan was extremely controlling of Shelagh and her mother. Shelagh wasn't allowed to wear make-up, modern clothes, none of that. Her mother would secretly buy them for her, and Shelagh would put them on now and again when her father was away. But her mother warned her never to let him know.'

Murray looked at her. She seemed passionate about

the subject. The last thing he'd expected when they'd gone for coffee were these revelations. But he wanted, *needed*, to find out what was behind Fiona Muir's assertions. 'Robert Gillan sounds like he was a real bastard,' he said. 'But so what? It's still a huge leap from that to what you're suggesting.'

She turned to look around her as if suddenly unsure of going on. Satisfied that no one was paying them any attention, she spoke even more softly. 'Shelagh got herself a boyfriend. How, who, I don't know. But she told one or two friends at school and my sister got to know about it. It was quite a choice piece of gossip, believe me. Shelagh was seen as a bit square by the trendier elements in the school, my sister included. Some thought Shelagh had made it all up to make herself seem more interesting.'

Fiona shook her head. 'You know how nasty adolescent girls can be. Shelagh was pretty though, like her mother. Just hid it well. Anyway, apparently it was true about the boyfriend. And you know what? Angus knew about him. Not who the boyfriend was, but the fact that Shelagh had one. *And* his father got it out of him.'

Murray looked doubtfully at her. 'But I don't remember any of this. Angus never told me, and even if it *were* the case, there is no way he'd betray his sister.' This, at least, was true. He waited for her to go on.

Fiona sat back again. 'His father got it out of him by trickery. Basically, Angus let it slip. There was a big scene. Gillan dragged Shelagh up to the school to see the headmistress. No one ever got the name of the boyfriend out of her. Her father kept her out of school and grounded at home for a month. They told everyone that she had glandular fever. This was all just before that sports day.'

What Fiona Muir had just said was sparking a distant memory. 'You're right. There was a period before the sports day when Angus never took me back to his house. He always called for me at my house. Said something about Shelagh not being well and that I wasn't to come by.'

'Well then, at least something of what I've said rings a bell. I'll tell you something else. Do you know why Angus got detention? He'd never been in trouble before, had he?'

'No. That was odd,' Murray agreed. 'But I do know why it was. Angus had skived off school. He could at least have asked me. I would have talked him out if it. I was a good boy. So was he, usually. '

She exhaled loudly. 'I think it was a protest.'

'Protest?'

'Yes, I think Angus was annoyed, furious with his father about tricking him into betraying his sister. But he didn't know what to do about it – other than be disobedient and bunk off school. The school got in touch with his mother. Luckily, Robert Gillan was away on business that day. Angus's mother took the flak and told him to take his detention and let that be an end to it.' Fiona Muir stopped, realizing what she had just said. 'And yes, that *was* the end.'

Murray kept his face impassive as he asked the crucial question. 'But you've not explained why you think Shelagh set the fire.'

Fiona reached for her forgotten coffee, sipped once and slid the mug aside. 'Shelagh didn't have a best friend and wasn't part of a gang. She was a bit of a loner in some ways. But she did hang out with my older sister and her friends from time to time after the fire. I think my sister and her crowd felt sorry for her. The fact that they tolerated her says as much.'

'And her father let her go out as she wished?'

'Oh, by then he didn't care about anything. The word was that he was beginning to lose the plot. And the mother was taking sleeping tablets, according to Shelagh. Anyway, one day late that summer we all went up Corstorphine Hill for a picnic – me, my sister and her friends, and Shelagh. My mother had made my sister take me along.' She stopped and looked past him, as if picturing the scene in her mind. 'I knew when I wasn't wanted and was pretty cross about it. The thing is, my sister and her friends were drinking. They'd got hold of some sweet Martini and were swigging it back with lemonade. I was sworn to secrecy of course. I think it was a mixture of boredom and annoyance that made me do it.'

'Do what?' Murray asked. He wondered where this was going.

'I was off picking some flowers for Mum and I saw Shelagh. She'd been having a pee in the copse nearby. I trotted up to her and asked her if she was still seeing her boyfriend. Shelagh suddenly got really angry. She ripped the bunch of flowers from my hand and bent over me, hissing in my ear. I could smell the booze on her breath.'

Murray was beginning to feel uneasy. 'What did she say?'

Fiona shut her eyes for a moment and then stared back at him. 'She told me never, *ever* to say anything like that again. I stupidly said something like, "Or what you gonna do about it?" And she grasped my shoulder really tightly and said, "You'll end up like Angus. That's what happens to little bastards who can't keep their mouths shut." She stormed off, and later on I could see her having a row with my sister. It was about me. My sister gave me what for later.'

Murray studied her. She was looking upset now. Gone was the almost childish enthusiasm of earlier. 'Did you tell anyone what she'd said?'

'No, because I didn't really see it then the way I do now. My parents thought the janitor was guilty. That's what all the talk was about. But there was something about that episode with Shelagh that stuck with me. It was her expression of absolute ... fury. I've thought this through over the years and ... ' She faded away. Murray waited, leaving her to her thoughts. She seemed tired but she wasn't finished yet. 'I'm not surprised the mother killed herself. You know about that?'

He looked away from her, pretending to be preoccupied with his drink. 'Yes. I read about what happened. What do you know about it?'

'Not a lot. I wonder whether Ruth Gillan had guessed, or got an admission out of Shelagh, and wasn't going to turn her in but never wanted to let her forget what she'd done.'

He remained silent, wanting to let her talk, to discover what else she thought she knew.

She touched his arm lightly, forcing him to look up. 'And do you know what else?' He shook his head and she went on. 'I'm not alone in what I think about Shelagh, but maybe I'll tell you about that another time. Just think on what I've said.' She sat back, seeming satisfied. 'Your return here is a great boost to me. I assume you believe in justice?' She didn't wait for him to reply. 'If so, then maybe the ghosts of Angus and Lavinia can be laid to rest properly. Whatever drove Shelagh to do what she did that day, she shouldn't be allowed to get away with it.'

## The Fury

I thought I always hid it well.
The anger inside.
It's nearly impossible to describe the Fury.
It made me ill.
Lurking there, ready to erupt.
I remember how it felt.
When it really did erupt,
There was no stopping its burning heat.
It was too late.
Too late to raise the dead.

# Fourteen

Elliot shut down his computer and looked out of the window at the rain-soaked street below. Absent-mindedly, he reached for a slice of cold pizza from the massive cardboard box lying to the side of his desk. Chewing slowly and staring into space, the slam of a car door roused him. He peered down and saw, with relief, the harassed-looking figure of his mother, unloading her car, clutching newspapers, files and shopping bags in both hands, while trying to close the driver's door with her foot. In less than a minute he heard her key in the lock.

He swivelled round in his chair, anticipating her greeting. Silence. That was odd. He rose and moved to the door. Then he heard her voice, unusually low and mumbling. The mobile must have rung as she came up the stairs. Straining to make out what was being said, he opened the bedroom door a bit wider and listened.

Rowan cursed to herself as the second bag of shopping fell from her grasp just inside the living room. She grabbed the phone from where it was jammed between her chin and shoulder, and flung herself on to the sofa.

'I've been trying to get you all day, Murray. Where have you been?'

'I'm really sorry, the mobile went down. I don't have a spare battery with me.'

She sighed. He sounded genuinely contrite but she was still annoyed with him. 'Well, you'd better buy one then. So, what have you been doing? What was that you said last night about a neighbour?'

'Oh, just a woman from across the road. I'll tell you about it later. Anyway, how are you?'

She glanced at the opened bank statement sitting on the sideboard, and thought for a moment. Why shouldn't she tell him what a worrying day she'd had? 'Actually, I'm not good, Murray.'

'What's happened?' His tone was peevish, as if this was the last response he'd expected.

She rested her head against the sofa and closed her eyes. 'I'm sorry, Murray, but I opened a piece of mail for you by mistake. Your savings account statement. I began reading before I realized it wasn't mine. An awful lot of cash has been taken out of it recently. Have we not been able to cover everything from our joint account? Or has your account just been defrauded of a small fortune?'

She waited, eyes still closed. *It's okay. You were going to have to tell him sometime, so why not now?*

'Is there any other mail for me?'

She opened her eyes and sat forward. What kind of response was that?

'Rowan, is there any other mail for me?'

'No, but wh–'

'Fine, I'm not expecting anything important. Oh, and don't worry about the savings account. It's complicated, I'll explain later. Absolutely nothing to worry about. Listen, you sound tired. Have a bath and a nice glass of wine. I love you. Night, night. Sleep tight.'

'But, Mur–' Too late, he'd gone.

What the hell was wrong with him? He'd been patronizing – the don't-worry-your-pretty-little-head type of patronizing – and evasive. But she could tell that behind the devil-may-care tone, something was troubling him. Maybe she should go up there. Perhaps there was something seriously wrong with the house? If so, he'd feel terrible about that. Maybe that was why he didn't want her or Elliot there just now. Was that what the money was for? To do expensive repairs without her knowing?

She smiled to herself. It was sometimes easy to forget how insecure he could be. He *did* love her, and he obviously wanted everything to be perfect. The pain of his first marriage had left him so emotionally scarred; his wife's infidelity had almost finished him off. He'd been absolutely open about that from the start. She shook her head, still smiling. *Remember that sometimes he can be delicate. Give him a bit of slack.*

'Mum?'

She twisted round. 'Elliot, darling. I'm sorry. I thought you must be out. You okay? Have you eaten?'

'Yeah, had pizza. That was Murray, wasn't it? You sounded worried about something. What's up?'

He looked tired and was too thin. She moved over and threw her arms around his long, slim torso, hugging him tight. 'I'm fine, really.' Then she stood back, worried that she'd been too cloying. 'It's you I'm worried about. You look tired. Why don't you shut the computer off and have an early night, eh?'

He half turned to go. 'Maybe.' Then he stopped. 'Mum? Are you going to be happy in Scotland?'

'Of course, darling.' She tried to keep her tone as light as possible. 'We're all going to be happy.'

At that, he turned to go, raising a hand as he walked away. 'G'night, Mum.'

Back in his room, Elliot sat at the open window and lit a cigarette. The rain spattered his face as he leaned out, blowing smoke into the night. He looked out across the city, one persistent question running back and forth in his mind:

Did his mother know – *really know* – the man she had married?

# Fifteen

The hammering at the front door had Murray sitting bolt upright. Momentarily disorientated, he blinked at the glowing display of the digital clock on his bedside table: 3.54. Dragging on jeans, he stumbled barefoot down the stairs. Through the stained-glass door he could see blurred silhouettes and, behind them, flashing blue lights.

'It's the fire service! We need to get in.'

Once unlocked, the door was pushed opened with a force that sent him staggering backwards.

'Sir, we've had a report of a fire in the grounds of your property. May we have access to the back?' Without waiting for an answer, the first man, clad in full firefighter's protective clothing and helmet, strode past.

Murray, trying to wake himself up properly, stammered out, 'Y-y-yes, of course, access is through the kitchen back there and then through the patio doors. Or . . . er . . . or you can go down the side of the house through the gate. It's unlocked.'

He was aware of a flurry of activity, and then, as it fully dawned on him what was happening, he ran through the house, out into the garden. The ice-cold stone of the patio hit his bare feet before he leapt on to the soft turf and raced towards the glow of the fire.

Within seconds, the bulky firefighter was standing in front of him, hand raised. Reluctantly, Murray slowed down and came to a halt, ignoring the chill taking hold of him.

'No further, sir. Please, it isn't safe.' The firefighter made Murray look into his eyes and concentrate, asking, 'What *is* that structure, sir? Is there likely to be anyone in it?'

Murray felt himself trembling. It was more than shivering. He shook his head dumbly, trying to find the words. 'No, no one's in there. It's just a summerhouse.'

The firefighter mumbled something into his radio and then looked back at Murray. 'The wooden structure's very flammable. I'm afraid you'll lose the building.'

Murray stared past the man to the raging fire beyond, its fierce heat cutting through the freezing air to warm his face. He felt a heavy hand on his shoulder. 'Please, sir, why don't you wait in the kitchen? We'll let you know when we've got this under control.'

The two plain-clothes police officers had arrived after the fire had been extinguished and most of the firefighters had left. The remaining senior fire officer and the police had huddled together in the hallway, talking *sotto voce*, nodding occasionally to one another. Finally, the police officers returned and sat opposite Murray. The older one spoke first.

'It seems this was deliberate. Petrol was the accelerant. They could have got in through your side gate, although that's a bit risky – someone from the manse or the other houses in the lane might have spotted that. It's more likely that they got in over your wall at the back. It's very secluded down there.' The officer paused to look at his younger, female colleague, who now took over.

'Mr Shaw, I believe that you're new to the area. It may be that some prankster didn't know about this house being occupied again – someone who fancied a bit of wanton vandalism.'

Murray frowned. 'And they were carrying round a handy supply of petrol just in case? I doubt it.'

The older officer replied, 'We may have an arsonist on our hands. Or perhaps someone around here doesn't welcome newcomers. Who knows why? This is a low-crime area. Big on neighbourhood watch and liaison with local police. We certainly don't get much vandalism.' He stopped to close his notebook, and looked around the room. 'It's certainly a strange one. I don't expect you've been here long enough to make enemies. I can see you've barely moved in. But keep your eyes open and let us know if you notice anything out of the ordinary.'

Murray escorted the officers to the door. On the front step the older officer paused, glanced up at the exterior of the house and looked back at him. 'This place has seen its fair share of tragedy. Do you know that?'

'Yes, I know.'

The man shrugged. 'Before my time, but very sad. I think that summerhouse must have a jinx on it.'

Murray caught the fleeting look of puzzlement on the female officer's face, and noticed her colleague giving her a nod to indicate that he'd tell her about it later.

With a final, faint smile, she turned to go. 'Goodbye, sir, and please do watch out.'

Murray shut the door, checked the locks and then grabbed a torch from the hallway cupboard. Slipping on his boots over bare feet, he let himself out the back and into the cold night air. Shivering in only a T-shirt and jeans, he marched to the bottom of the garden, the acrid reek of smoke increasing with every step.

He switched on the torch and allowed its powerful beam to flicker over the blackened ruins of the summerhouse. Oddly, one corner of the structure had remained nearly intact. A bit of window frame still clung to the lower left-hand side, its green paint still visible, though blistered and peeling.

He moved past and walked briskly down to the bottom of the garden. Behind a thicket of bushes and a tall, ancient beech tree was the perimeter wall: of solid, stone construction, it stood over six feet high. Murray scanned its length with the torch. Tomorrow he'd arrange for razor wire to be put on top.

As he walked back up the garden past the ruined summerhouse and then into the warmth of the kitchen, a wave of anxiety flooded over him. He stopped to peer into the darkness of the garden once more, an image of Ruth Gillan's inert body forcing its way into his thoughts. He shivered again. Whatever he thought he was doing by coming back here was disintegrating in front of his eyes.

Dragging on some warm clothing, he shuffled up to the top of the house. His makeshift office was far roomier than the one in Rowan's London flat. He looked out the window towards the church; it and the manse lay in darkness. The arrival of the fire service had disturbed no one there.

The much-handled letter lay beside a mess of paperwork. His eye caught sight of the house plans. He placed them to one side as he switched on the desk lamp and then leafed through the letter's pages. His eyes ran across the passage he wanted to reread yet again.

*Ruth was going to leave the suicide note by her body, but she changed her mind. She called me from the house. They never checked the phones, otherwise the police would have been all over me, asking questions. She left the note somewhere in the house. She was going to destroy it, but how? There was nothing to burn it with. She was near to death. She didn't want me to come over there. She was adamant. So, she ended up hiding it.*

*I remember exactly what she said: 'I cannot do anything with what I know now. It would destroy too much. If it's found, so be it. If not, it wasn't meant to be. Or maybe it will be found too far into the future for it to matter. I'm leaving it to Fate, or rather to God. Yes, despite all that has happened, I believe in*

*Him, more than ever.' Her words have stayed with me for so long. And I have done nothing. Maybe you can achieve what I have not. Think about that. And about what I told you.*

Murray switched off the lamp. Plunged into darkness, he slumped back into the chair, staring across at the churchyard, imagining himself wandering through the gravestones and stopping at where Angus lay. Closing his eyes, Murray heard his own trembling voice whisper into the darkness, 'If I'd known then what I know now . . . if I had been able to change things, I would have. Oh, God. Please forgive me.'

# Sixteen

'Hello? Murray?'

The muffled voice broke through his thoughts. He looked up from his uneaten breakfast. Staring into the kitchen through the patio doors was Fiona Muir, her face inches from the glass. As Murray unlocked the doors to let her in, he felt a gust of cold air.

'I've been knocking at the front door for ages. Didn't you hear me?'

He moved swiftly towards the radio, instantly silencing the morning newsreader's crisp tones. 'Sorry, no.' He glanced back into the garden. 'How did you get round here?'

She'd dumped her bag on to the kitchen table and was unbuttoning her coat. 'Your side gate. It's unlocked.'

Murray grabbed at his coffee cup, which she'd almost knocked over in her bustling entry to his home. She seemed glowing with energy again. Just the opposite of how he felt. He cursed himself. How had he gone to bed with the house and grounds *still* unsecured after all that had happened?

She was standing, arms outstretched. 'What's been going on here? I heard there was a fire.'

'You did?'

'Yes, Denise – you know, our secretary? She's married to a local firefighter. She phoned me. What happened?'

The last thing he wanted was for her to be here. He needed to be alone with his thoughts. But what could he do? He couldn't exactly order her off the premises. Besides, he had to make a show of normality. He motioned for her to sit down, and poured her a mug of coffee. She seemed to be studying his face.

He remained standing and turned to look out of the window, shaking his head. 'It was about four this morning. The fire brigade were hammering at the door.' He pointed towards the garden. 'It was the summerhouse. Someone doused it in petrol. It was an inferno by the time the fire engines got here. Practically burnt to the bloody ground.'

'No.' She looked genuinely shocked.

'Come and have a look.'

She followed him down the garden in silence. It was his second visit since sunrise, and the charred ruin looked worse than ever in the harsh sunlight. He watched Fiona skirt round the blackened structure.

Her face was crumpled into a scowl. 'What a shame. This was a genuine Victorian summerhouse, wasn't it?'

'It was.'

She circled the remains once more and then stopped. 'And very odd. Especially since Ruth Gillan died he–'

'Yes, I know,' he cut in. 'I've thought about that. An unfortunate coincidence.'

She stepped back from the ruins. 'Coincidence? But who the hell would do this? What did the fire people say?'

He picked at the remaining blistered paint, the stench of smoke still pungent. 'Actually, it was the police who talked to me. You could see that they didn't have a clue. They tried to make out it had been carried out by some opportunist at first. But whoever did it came prepared with enough petrol to raze the place.'

He stopped picking at the paint and stepped back. 'Basically, the possibilities are limited. This was either a deliberate act of arson by someone who went out last night determined to torch something, and to that extent it was random. Or it was aimed at this house. Or at me personally.' He paused to look at her. 'Take your pick. Any one of them's a pretty rotten option.'

They began strolling back up to the house. Fiona glanced behind her, a worried look on her face. 'Which theory do you go for? I mean, the summerhouse of all places and Ruth Gillan. I th–'

He cut her off a second time. 'No. It's a coincidence. And as for thinking that this was a deliberate attack against me, I'm definitely not going for that.' He sighed. 'No one knows me here.'

She paused in her stride. 'Except me and Shelagh.'

He shook his head. 'No, despite what you think of her, I cannot believe Shelagh Kerr would be running around at night in her cassock with cans of petrol. It's

95

too ludicrous. It's much more probable that there's a budding arsonist around. Maybe they thought this house was still empty.'

He looked at Fiona as they reached the kitchen, but she kept silent, staring at the ground, obviously deep in thought. Murray closed the patio doors. The urge to be on his own was overwhelming. He needed time to think through what had happened. Despite what he had said to her, the idea that the fire was a coincidence seemed unlikely. But who . . .

Suddenly he heard the familiar rat-a-tat of the front door. 'That'll be the plumber. He's doing some work here today.'

Fiona gulped down her coffee and simultaneously reached for her bag. 'Right, I need to get on too.'

Murray hurried towards the front door, a polite, welcoming smile at the ready. But as he opened the door and flung it wide, his smile vanished. Positioned uncertainly on the bottom step, looking up at him, was Shelagh Kerr.

'Hello, Murray. I . . . I hope you don't mind me coming back. I . . . just wanted to say tha–'

'Murray, I really must be on my wa–' Fiona's voice broke in; she clearly hadn't seen who the visitor was. Her clacking heels stopped abruptly as Murray moved aside, allowing the women to view each other.

The silence seemed to last an age. Shelagh Kerr was the first to break it.

'Oh, Fiona? Hello.' Shelagh appeared momentarily puzzled. 'Ah . . . of course, you would have known each other at school, silly me. How nice that you've met up. How are you, Fiona?'

Murray fought the urge to turn around and see Fiona's reaction. He heard the scrape of her heels as, slowly, she approached the open door. 'I'm fine, Shelagh, just fine.'

He noticed that Shelagh had backed away and was now standing in the driveway. 'Murray, I was just popping by to say that we'd like to invite you over for dinner. Gordon's back. I was going to leave you a note if you weren't in. Here.' Tentatively, she took a step up towards him, handed over a small white envelope and then quickly withdrew. 'I hope you can come. Let me know. Bye. Goodbye, Fiona.'

Without waiting for a reply, she began trotting down the path, almost leaping into the passenger seat of a large car with its engine running. At the wheel was a middle-aged man. Her husband? In a moment the lane was filled by the revving of the car as it sped off.

Fiona brushed past Murray and stood on a lower step, staring after it. 'Will you go to dinner?'

He tore his gaze from the end of the lane to look at her. 'What? Oh . . . I don't know.'

Fiona moved on to the bottom step. 'She's pretty good at it.'

'Good at what?'

Apparently unruffled by Shelagh's arrival, Fiona began strolling down the driveway and then stopped to glance back at him. 'Hiding what she feels. Shelagh's pretending to be friendly. But I think it's obvious. I'm sure Shelagh would love it if *I* wasn't here. And, despite her friendly appearance, I think she most definitely doesn't want *you* here.' She turned away and resumed her leisurely pace down the driveway, the final words barely audible.

'Watch out.'

# Seventeen

Murray stood in the hallway, checking his watch: two minutes to eight. He fingered the handwritten note, glancing for the umpteenth time at the elegantly formed lettering.

> Dear Murray
>
> Do forgive my behaviour the other evening. I was just a bit taken aback. I hope you and your family will be very happy in your new home. It's just what the place needs. I'm anxious that you feel no discomfort over the matter. My husband, Gordon, is back and we would very much like you to come to dinner tonight at the manse, if you're free, at 8 p.m. Don't bring anything. Gordon keeps a rather fine wine cellar.
>
> Best wishes
> Shelagh Kerr

Murray refolded the letter and placed it in his jacket pocket. Then he checked his mobile phone to see if Rowan had replied to his earlier message. Nothing. Should he take the phone with him? No, it was going to be an awkward enough encounter without having to explain to Rowan where he was and who he was with.

He combed his hair again and straightened his

shirt. He'd thought long and hard all day as the plumber clattered about the house and the security contractors fixed vicious-looking coils of razor wire to his back wall. The invitation had been an unexpected move from Shelagh Kerr. Or had it? Perhaps it was just Fiona Muir's highly clouded view of her that had made him suspicious. If Shelagh Kerr wanted to be friendly with him, then that suited him perfectly. For his part, as with Fiona Muir, he would go along with things. Just for now. But the women's presence had left him with an additional worry: how to explain to Rowan why he'd bought this house. And how to explain the cash withdrawals. He was still furious at her for opening his mail.

'*Shit!*' He threw the comb down on the hallway table. Worry upon worry.

Opening the front door, he was met by silence. The thickening haar that had crept in from the coast during the afternoon had deadened all sound. The grey blanket glowed almost luminous in parts as first the streetlamps and then the more distant outer light of the manse tried to penetrate it. Securing the door, he padded down the steps and then hesitated. Moving to his right, he peered at the dark silhouette of the side gate. He inched forward and immediately the newly installed security light was ablaze. He checked the latch. Secure.

Taking a deep breath, he turned and made his way across the lane. The church and graveyard lay in darkness; only the outside lamp of the manse offered any illumination. The mist seemed to shift every few seconds, momentarily exposing the occasional out-line of an ancient tombstone. The silence remained unbroken. Reaching the front door he looked around, searching for a knocker or bell. Then, to his left, he saw the old-fashioned Victorian bell pull and gave it a sharp tug. He could hear its faint echo ring out from somewhere deep inside the house. The sound of an inner door opening was followed by the unlocking of the front one. Moments later a smiling man greeted him with a firm handshake.

'Hello, welcome. I'm Gordon Kerr.'

He was dressed in a perfectly ironed pale blue shirt, unbuttoned at the neck, and navy chinos, with a near knife-edge crease. His soft black loafers looked new. He looked fit – as tall as himself but more muscular. Murray immediately recognized him as a regular gym-user. Clearly balding, Shelagh's husband had opted to keep what hair he had closely shorn, making it diffi-cult to guess his age.

Murray returned the greeting, anxious to appear friendly and open. It was the best tactic. 'Good to meet you. Thanks for the invitation.' He wondered if Gor-don had ever been in the military. He had the bearing of an officer: confident and competent. Murray released himself from the firm handshake. He knew he was sounding stiff. Trying a smile, he spread his arms, indicating that they were empty. 'Shelagh said in her note not to bring anything. I hope that's still okay?'

'Oh, yes.' Gordon ushered him into the wide hall-way. 'We're not short of wine here. You like the stuff?'

'Yes, I do.'

'Well, you're in for a treat. Wine is one of my hobbies. I keep a cellar of it.' The accent was public-school Scottish, anglicized but definitely not English.

Murray followed his host along the hallway, admiring the few choice woodcuts hanging to his left, which depicted various scenes of the old village of Corstorphine. To his right, the rather grand, heavily carpeted staircase, flanked by an ornate wooden banister, seemed to lead up into endless darkness. The air of the place was of another era, the atmosphere bordering on the oppressive.

'This way please, Murray.'

Gordon had turned left, and Murray found himself in a huge, well-lit, modern-furnished room. The brooding feeling of the house had vanished. An original fireplace with a roaring real fire was the room's centrepiece. Like his own living room, it had been knocked through, and the equally large open-plan kitchen made the place seem vast. Shelagh approached. Murray struggled to stay calm, unruffled. He couldn't help scrutinizing her features, searching for any similarity between the adult Shelagh and the teenage girl he had known. But only her dark eyes sparked any memory in him.

Covered with a full apron in a dark green tartan and looking slightly flushed, she was brushing a stray hair from her eyes. 'Hello, Murray, so glad you could come. Excuse me for not shaking hands, but they're covered in butter. I'm making a rather wholesome dessert: apple crumble. Made with our own home-grown apples.' She wiped her hands on the apron. 'I've gone for cosy, comfort food tonight, given the rotten weather. Organic homemade chilli with jacket potatoes or rice. And the pud. Hope it appeals.'

As she outlined the food on offer, Murray felt suddenly ravenous, scenting the appetizing air like a hungry animal. 'It sounds wonderful. I'm not doing much ... well, I'm not doing *any* cooking at the moment. I just don't seem to have the time. So your cooking will be a most welcome change to takeaways.'

He caught an almost imperceptible communication between husband and wife. Gordon placed a hand lightly on Murray's shoulder. 'We heard you had the fire brigade out last night. We both slept through it, so we missed all the action. What was going on?'

Murray looked from husband to wife. 'Someone took it upon themselves to burn down my summer-house.' He continued observing Shelagh, watching for a reaction to the news about the place where her mother had died, but her face was unreadable. He went on. 'The police were round. They think it's vandalism. I've beefed up the security on my back wall and at the side of the house. I don't expect a repetition.'

Shelagh seemed concerned. 'Well, if there are vandals on the loose, I'd better have the security around the churchyard looked at. I suppose we're an obvious target.'

She flicked a quick glance at her husband and Murray felt Gordon's grip on his shoulder tighten slightly. 'Why don't we let Shelagh get on and we'll have a snifter by the fire, eh?'

It was clear to Murray that they were going to ignore the episode. That suited him perfectly for now. Gordon ushered him gently to one of the two large leather sofas placed at right angles to the fire. 'Whisky, G and T?'

Murray sat down in the enveloping leather. 'Oh, gin and tonic – Slimline, if you have it, please.'

'Coming up.'

He was aware of low-level mumbling in the kitchen and the clinking of glassware. He stared at the fire, the flickering flames having an almost hypnotic effect, its roaring warmth stinging his cheeks. He felt weary and slightly stupefied. On and off this past day or two he'd felt a sense of detachment, periodically entering a near dreamlike state. Perhaps it was because he was sleeping so badly, tormented by nightmares whose details seemed to elude him when he woke up.

'. . . Murray?'

'Wha– Oh, I'm sorry. Have you been there for long?'

Standing by his left shoulder, Gordon was smiling down at him, offering him the drink he'd asked for. 'You were in a little trance of your own. Open fires encourage that, I always think.' He took a generous mouthful of what looked to be a single malt whisky.

'Cheers, Murray.'

Murray lifted his own glass. 'Cheers.' He watched as his host moved to the mantelpiece. From the top of a cigar box he selected one of two polished chrome

Zippo lighters, both intricately tooled with a leaf pattern, and lit the three thick church candles evenly spaced atop the mantelpiece.

'Wait for me, you two. I'm not staying chained to the cooker all night!' Shelagh appeared, glass in hand. She had removed the tartan apron and brushed her short but expertly cut grey hair. She was wearing a flattering jersey dress in chocolate brown. Murray noticed that she'd changed her leather pumps for stylish court shoes. She was too thin but it was a highly fashionable emaciation, and her clothes clearly looked good on her. Her elegance contrasted vividly with the equally well-groomed but more obvious good looks of Fiona Muir.

Murray felt a sudden discomfort on recognizing her undeniable sexual attractiveness. She was very aware of it, he thought, and took steps – albeit subtle ones – to show it off.

Both husband and wife selected what Murray took to be their regular chairs either side of the hearth, leaving him set back a little from them. Balancing her whisky in one hand, Shelagh kicked off the elegant shoes, tucked both feet underneath her body and then sipped slowly at her drink. She looked directly at Murray as Gordon sank back into his chair, turning his face away towards the glowing fire. Light from the flames flickered across Shelagh's handsome features as she spoke in a low but clear voice. 'Gordon and I have been talking at some length about your arrival and I want, if you'll let me, to do some plain speaking.'

Without waiting for his assent, she went on. 'We

don't know, nor want to know, why you moved back here to St Margaret's House, but we *do* want you to know that you're very welcome. The past is the past. Forty years is a lifetime ago and a lot has happened to us all in that time, I'm sure.' She paused to sip at her drink, still gazing directly at him. Gordon hadn't moved; he remained facing the fire. It was almost as if he wasn't there. Murray felt the intensity of Shelagh's stare drawing him in as her low tones rose above the hiss of the fire.

'The truth is, Murray, I'm over Angus's death. I have dealt with it. Yes, he lies in a grave out there and I tend that grave from time to time. It's important to be near him. That's why we moved back here. And to be near my father.' She furrowed her brow as if trying to form her next words. 'But I don't think about Angus so much any more, I don't have to. He is near and he is at peace. That is enough for me.'

There was the slightest movement from Gordon's foot, but his face was still turned towards the fire. Looking at them both, Murray gave a nervous preparatory cough before leaning forward. Her carefully modulated voice was highly seductive. Part of him wanted to leap up and tell all, to explain why he was back here. But he fought against the urge. 'Thank you for being so . . . welcoming and . . . well, honest. Let me be equally frank.' He swallowed the gin, welcoming its biting, invigorating flavour. 'It was really a matter of blind luck, St Margaret's coming on to the market just when we were looking to move to Edinburgh.'

'It certainly was,' Shelagh said.

Murray continued. 'But when I was first sent the details, the house name didn't register. I mean, Corstorphine was ideal for us. I liked the idea of moving back to where I was brought up. I'd never managed to show Rowan round the area when we visited Edinburgh. We usually managed just a quick dash up and down from London for the festival. Anyway, it was only when my estate agent friend said that the house had sad connections that things registered.'

He sighed and smiled apologetically. 'But, with so much time having gone by, I thought it would be okay to try and buy it. I really didn't think in a million years that you would be here. I'm truly sorry.'

At last Gordon turned to face him. 'Look, don't be sorry. Listen to what Shelagh has said. The past is the past.' Murray caught another silent communication between the couple as, simultaneously, they both rose. Shelagh was smiling. 'Why don't you let Gordon show off his wine cellar? I'll get on with dinner.'

Gordon patted him on the shoulder again. 'Come on, let's go and choose some wine.'

Murray allowed himself to be propelled gently out into the hall and towards the cellar door.

Shelagh Kerr listened as the mumbling voices and scraping footsteps faded into the cavern below her. Reaching for the single malt bottle standing on the worktop, she poured herself another generous measure, her unsteady hand causing the bottle to clink against the side of the glass. The noise sounded thunderous in the huge, silent kitchen. She took two burning gulps and leaned against one of the store cupboards. The sudden ring of the phone had the glass almost toppling from her grasp. She grabbed for the cordless handset mounted on the kitchen wall.

'Hello?'

Silence.

'Hello, this is St Margaret's manse. Can I help you?'

Nothing.

'*Hello?*' She could hear the rising tension in her voice and felt her stomach muscles tighten as the line stayed open but silent. 'Is that you? Is it? Stop phoning, stop writing. Do you understand? *Stop it!*'

She slammed the handset back into its cradle and moved to one of the breakfast stools, resting against it for support as she threw back the rest of the whisky. Momentarily hesitating, she marched across the room. Trembling fingers switched the phone to silent. Within a few minutes she had padded around the rest of the house turning all the handsets to silent and, finally, switching off the answering machine.

Stopping in the hallway, she put an ear to the cellar door. The faintest clinking of glass and the occasional mumbling voice could be heard. Reluctantly she moved back to the kitchen to prepare a dinner she felt unable to eat.

# Eighteen

Murray watched as Gordon opened the fourth bottle of red.

'Come on, try this one. It doesn't matter how many I open, they'll all get drunk over the next few days. I think this is the one for Shelagh's fabulous chilli. It's a gold-medal-winning Australian Shiraz. Perfect for a spicy dish.'

Murray shivered. He was getting cold down in the vast cellar, despite the copious amounts of warming red wine that Gordon was encouraging him to taste. They were sitting at a rough wooden sampling table, the paraphernalia of wine tasting surrounding them: glasses, corkscrews, even a sawdust-filled spittoon. To his surprise, Murray realized that they must have put away over half a bottle each already, along with the gin, which had deadened his palate anyway. He was feeling the effects and wished they could go upstairs to eat.

But his host, swirling the latest offering and holding the liquid up to the light, showed no signs of being ready to go. He spoke with the glass held at forehead height.

'Shelagh's an amazing woman, you know. Overcoming personal tragedy and then giving herself to the

Church. She's such a devout, generous person. Lesser mortals would have buckled under what happened.'

Murray found the sudden change in conversation unexpected. 'Yes, it . . . it must have been so hard for her to come to terms with what happened to Angus and her mother.'

Gordon had stopped swirling the wine, but still held the glass aloft, staring through it. 'Oh, it wasn't just the loss of Angus.' He turned his head to look at Murray, his eyes squinting from the bright overhead light. 'Shelagh's had other hurts. She understands suffering. That's what makes her so gifted at pastoral work.' He lowered the glass and took a long draught of the wine, licking his lips in obvious satisfaction. 'She should have been a mother.'

Murray stayed silent. The intimate atmosphere, drawing him in as an unwilling confidant, had left him wrong-footed. What did this man want? Had he – and Shelagh – somehow fathomed that he had much deeper motives for returning here? No, he disregarded that for now; there was no evidence. More likely Gordon was more intoxicated than he seemed and it had loosened his tongue. Not wishing to be pulled in further, Murray turned to safer ground. 'How did you two meet? Through the Church?'

To his surprise, Gordon laughed, refilling both their glasses. 'Yes and no. I'm a firm non-believer, so we didn't bump into each other in the pews, as it were. But the Church *did* play a part.' He paused, clearly remembering the event as if it had happened yesterday. 'I was a military archivist for a while. I'd spent some time in the Army but it wasn't for me. Anyway, I was working on a paper about forces' chaplaincy. I had a friend who was an army chaplain, and he introduced me to Shelagh, who was considering forces' chaplaincy. As it happens, she eventually did a stint as a prison chaplain. That's a hard and thankless job, believe me, working with the scum of humanity. But another example of her devotion to people.'

Without warning, he jumped up, slapping a hand on the wooden table. 'Right, dinner. Let's take a couple of bottles of the Shiraz up. Shelagh will be glad. She loves this one.' He moved agilely to the wine racks, plucked two bottles out and held them in one hand. With the other, he picked up his glass and the opened bottle, motioning for Murray to follow him upstairs.

The evening had been tiring. Shelagh sat naked on the edge of her bed listening to the low boom of male voices below, loud with the cheer from too much wine and postprandial cognac. At least she knew Gordon wouldn't dare light up any cigars in the house, even though she'd gone to bed. If that's what they wanted to do, they could freeze out in the garden. She'd absented herself twenty minutes earlier to shower, get ready for bed and, she hoped, slip into some badly needed sleep. The meal had been a success in her view, and presumably in Gordon's too. He'd got all he wanted to drink and a male companion to join him. Most of all, he had suppressed his anger well. The power of his eruption when she'd told him who was living across the road had frightened her. But he'd quickly realized that her tactic of friendliness and inclusion was the only way forward if they wanted to stay here. Observing their guest, she could see nothing in the man to remind her of that small boy who had spent so much time with Angus.

She reached for her silk pyjamas and stood up, pulling the buttoned jacket over her head and then slipping into the trousers. The truth was, other than his obvious attractiveness, she had found Murray Shaw surprisingly dull. In fact, he seemed very different from the charming man who had welcomed her into his new home so recently. She wondered why. Maybe Gordon had been too garrulous, had dominated the conversation too much, and Murray had felt inhibited. Gordon certainly loved to show off about his archival work and knowledge of wine.

Still, Murray had seemed happy to sit back, drink the fine wines and let Gordon get on with it. Perhaps his passivity was a deliberate tactic. After all, the dinner could have been a potentially tricky and embarrassing situation for him. What better way than to bide your time and watch? But if that had been the case – and she thought it unlikely – then she was sure that her own performance had been equally persuasive. She saw no sign that their guest hadn't believed her when she'd claimed, 'The past is the past.' If she could fool Gordon into believing that, then she could easily persuade a stranger.

The voices below seemed to be getting louder. Gordon must be seeing their guest out. She extinguished the bedside lamp and stood up to peer out of the windows. Their new neighbour was striding slightly unsteadily across the lane, carrying an unopened bottle: a gift from Gordon. Moments later, the ground floor of St Margaret's House was ablaze and then just as quickly back into darkness. The hall light went on and, through the landing window, she caught sight of Murray's figure climbing the stairs and going into a front bedroom. Another light was switched on. There was no attempt to close any curtains or blinds. Her new neighbour was either too drunk or didn't think he would be under observation.

She watched as he pulled off his jacket, followed quickly by his shirt and jeans. He walked away and then, minutes later, his naked body appeared at the window. He must have had a shower. Arms held high, he dried his black hair with a pristine white towel. She almost pulled back, convinced that he could see her, but the view held her attention. It was a remarkably vulnerable, yet erotic, pose. He flicked the towel across his left shoulder and held it there. She almost gasped out loud. Standing contrapposto and uplit by the lamp into a striking chiaroscuro image, his contoured body looked like Michelangelo's *David*.

She heard a shuffle of feet on the landing and swung round, taking a few swift steps over to the door. But Gordon's footsteps, coupled with the clinking of bottle and glass, passed her by as he made his slow way up to the top floor. The creaking of the floorboards told her which room he was heading for: the one directly above. Moving back to the window, she wondered if he would see the same sight, across the lane. Carefully, she pulled the curtain back and felt her heart beat a little more quickly. But the Michelangelo beauty had gone, replaced by a darkened window. Disappointed, she lay down in bed, closed her eyes and conjured up the image one more time before sleep.

## Desire

I have felt all sorts of desire.
For old, for young.
Violent desire.
Gentle desire.
Aching desire.
With you, I didn't mean what happened to happen.
Though I did nothing to stop it.
But neither did you.
So, you deserve your pain, your suffering.

# Nineteen

*Edinburgh, one week later*

Murray looked at his watch. Twelve-thirty. He'd calculated that Rowan and Elliot would take at least seven and a half hours to drive, including rest breaks. The motorways would be busy, given that it was a Saturday, and the removal van might take considerably longer, but the packing had all been done the day before, so it was just a matter of driving. Rowan had told him to look out for her and Elliot from around lunchtime.

Sipping at his coffee, he slid the patio doors open and wandered out into the cold air, then sat on one of the outdoor chairs, the wrought iron icy beneath his thighs. He tried to identify the unsettling mixture of emotions flowing through him. Although there was undoubted excitement at the thought of Rowan's arrival, his overriding feelings were clear. Fear and the sense of failure stood head and shoulders above any others. Over the past few days, worry about how he was going to explain why he'd kept silent about this house and his connection to it had been subsumed by the creeping realization that the events of forty years ago were much nearer than he could ever have imagined. And *far* from being under his control. Fiona? Shelagh and Gordon? And perhaps there were other, unseen forces.

More urgently, he had searched the house from top to bottom and still hadn't found what he was looking for. Only one part of the attic remained unexplored. It was an awkward space, unmodernized, and he wanted to go over it thoroughly, inch by inch. But he'd worked out his cover story: the space was unsafe and awaiting expert assessment. That would keep Elliot out of the way.

He made his way back into the house, through the living room to the front windows. Opposite, the church seemed quiet. He'd tried to keep out of Shelagh and Gordon's sight this past week, ensuring that he was visible at the front of the house only when overseeing tradespeople, and greeting the couple with exaggerated cheerfulness when he couldn't avoid them. He'd noticed that she had been absent – her car missing from its parking space – for much of the time. An apparently lonely Gordon, clearly at a loose end, had invited him over one night but Murray had declined, stating truthfully that he had some decorators turning up at the crack of dawn. The thought of meeting them with a hangover had made resisting the offer easy.

However, what had made it even easier was the simple truth that, without Shelagh, the evening would have been tedious. He'd been thinking a great deal about that dinner over the past few days. Gordon obviously knew about wine and had a fair bit to say about working for the National Archives – some of it interesting – but there seemed to be little else to him, and he seemed quite insecure. It had been Shelagh who had been the more animated and engaging conversationalist, exhibiting a wide general knowledge and various cultural interests. In addition, she had an unusual job and that, whether you were a believer or an atheist, made her intriguing.

Murray sighed. The more he thought about that evening, the more he kept changing his mind about its outcome. Sometimes he felt as if he had been expertly handled by Shelagh – by both of them perhaps. And that thought had made him feel exposed. Their hospitality had been impressive, her plain speaking straightforward and reassuring – seductively so. Had it all been carefully planned and choreographed? Had Gordon been instructed to take him down to the cellar to get him well oiled before the evening began? Had her domestic-goddess presentation – superb but unfussy cuisine, sensual dress and manner – been another attempt at seducing him into liking them?

But at other times he chastised himself for such thoughts. That would have been Fiona Muir's interpretation. Maybe the Kerrs were just as they seemed: pleasant and perfectly willing to let the past be. At least they appeared to readily accept his claim that he had stumbled upon St Margaret's House by accident.

As for Fiona? He had met her just once recently: the day after his dinner with the Kerrs. She clearly couldn't wait to hear how it had gone, and seemed overly disappointed at his positive comments on the evening. His instincts were telling him to distance himself from her. Yet he wanted to know more of what she knew about Shelagh.

He wandered back into the kitchen and checked the fridge. He had two bottles of chilled champagne ready so that they could toast the new house. Elliot would be allowed a glass and that, Murray hoped, would keep him reasonably happy. As he slammed the fridge door, there was the crunch of tyres on gravel. They were here. Jogging down the hall towards the front door, his mobile rang. Fumbling in his jeans pocket to reach his phone and open the door at the same time, he answered breathlessly.

'Yes, hello?'

'It's Fiona.'

'Oh . . . right. Look, can you call later? Rowan and Elliot have just arrived and I nee–'

'Okay, that's fine,' she said, cutting in, 'but I just wanted to let you know.' Her voice sounded shaky and uncertain.

He stopped, the door half open. 'Know what?'

'That someone tried to burn down my school last night.'

# Twenty

They were on to their second glass of champagne. Elliot had gone out into the garden, football thrust under his arm. Murray smiled as Rowan spun around joyfully, spilling champagne on to the kitchen floor. He had tried to appear thrilled at her arrival and it had taken all he had to hide his shock at Fiona's news.

As he suppressed another wave of panic, Rowan turned around again, brushing his cheek at the same time. 'There's so much space! I forgot how big this place is. God, the London flat seems like a rabbit hutch compared to this. You're a bloody star finding this treasure!' She cocked her head at him. 'You okay?'

'Of course I am.' He grabbed her by the waist and drew her to him, trying to hide his expression as he attempted to keep his voice light. 'But remember, we've a removal van's worth of stuff to fill it.'

She threw her head back, laughing. 'And we'll still be rattling around. It's great.'

The patio doors slid open and Elliot stood there, football still under one arm, his face sour. His glance took in their embrace and he retreated two steps into the garden, bobbing his head towards the far end. 'What's with the razor wire? It's lethal. What happens when I kick my ball over the wall? I'll be torn to shreds trying to get it back.' He shook his head, turned on his heel and marched back down the garden.

Rowan pulled away from Murray's embrace. 'What's he talking about?'

The spell had been broken. Murray silently cursed Elliot. Determined not to lose the physical connection with her, which suddenly seemed so important, he took Rowan's hand, placing her champagne glass carefully on the worktop.

'Come with me.'

He led her down the garden. Immediately she noticed what was missing. 'Where's the summerhouse? Why have you taken it away?' She sounded annoyed, cheated, and pulled her hand from his.

Murray shook his head. 'I didn't take it down; it burnt down. The police think it was vandalism.'

Rowan looked at him. 'For God's sake. I thought we'd left all that in London.'

Elliot had appeared from between the trees at the end of the garden, nudging the football in front of him with his foot. 'Vandalism? Why?'

Murray tried to sound unworried. 'Vandals are vandals. I don't think they need a reason.'

'No, I don't mean that.' Elliot had stopped, his foot now resting on the top of the football. 'I mean, why *you*, why target you?'

Murray immediately felt defensive. 'Well, I don't think the target was *me* as such. In fact, the police said that those who did it might have thought the property was empty.' He kept silent on their other theories.

Elliot looked unconvinced, and Rowan caught his eye. 'Look, darling, of course it wasn't aimed at Murray. Why would it be?' She glanced back at the house. 'It's just . . . just a bit of a bad start to our life here. But these things happen.'

It was then that she noticed the razor wire and slowly walked towards the back wall. Murray looked at Elliot, who booted the ball back up to the patio area before walking over to join his mother.

She was standing at the wall, staring in disbelief. 'Murray, this is ghastly. It's like living in a prison compound! For goodness sake, this is a ludicrously excessive reaction. It's ugly and dangerous. I want it taken down, please.'

She brushed past him, reaching out a hand to Elliot. 'Come on. Let's unpack those couple of boxes from the car. The removal van will be here any minute and we'll have more than enough to do then.'

Murray watched mother and son, arm in arm, as they walked slowly up to the house, talking quietly between themselves. He could feel the irritation and anger rise in him. Not only that, but something far worse was making its presence felt.

The bitter, lonely sense of exclusion.

# Twenty-one

They were still surrounded by boxes, but the furniture was all in place now. Murray was slumped on the couch, exhausted and tense. At least the atmosphere had warmed up again. They had all worked well as a team. Elliot, in particular, seemed impressed with his new room and with the attic room that they had given him to use as a second space. Both he and his mother had appeared to accept the story about the other part of the attic being out of bounds. Murray was relieved at that. He was glad too that Elliot had now gone out for a wander and Rowan was upstairs in the bath. It gave him time to think.

He was going to have to tell her something about why he'd bought this house. But it wouldn't, *couldn't* be the truth. With every hour that passed, he dreaded a knock on the door, imagining Shelagh Kerr's smiling face as she breezed in to welcome Rowan and Elliot. Surreptitiously, he had made regular checks across the road. Thankfully, her car had been away all day; she wouldn't even know that they had arrived. He had seen no sign of Gordon, but tomorrow was Sunday, so Shelagh would be back and on duty. Murray bit his bottom lip. He had to get this sorted now.

\*

Rowan looked at her reflection in the condensation-clouded mirror. She rubbed a finger under her eyes. Now the make-up had been removed, the dark smudges told her what she already knew. She was tired, physically and emotionally. Her send-off from the paper had been anti-climactic: a swanky meal, followed by a visit to a West End club, where the usual hedonistic set got hopelessly drunk, while the others, including herself, looked furtively at their watches, craving to go home. She had slipped off as early as was respectable, given that it was her party, and accepted Ben's offer of a lift home. He'd seemed worried about her. Was she *really* ready now that the time to move was upon her? Yes, had been her half-truthful answer.

Shaking off the recent memories, she brushed her wet hair. Back in the bedroom and keeping the light turned off, she moved over to the windows. Across the lane the church lay in darkness. The nearby manse showed a faint light coming from somewhere on the ground floor. It was reassuring having a church and graveyard opposite; she found it peaceful, and there was no chance of developers turning up to ruin the view. Murray had done a great job buying this place. She wanted to get out and explore the area as soon as possible, to see where Murray had been brought up – perhaps give her a bit more insight into the man she loved but couldn't always understand.

Rowan felt tearful, but not from sadness. This was a great chance for her. She so wanted to be happy here, for them all to be happy together. Maybe Murray losing his job was a blessing in disguise. It was a chance for her to really settle down. With her fortieth birthday a couple of years away, the notion of her settling down for the first time in her life seemed incredible. But it was true. She'd pretty much let her career dictate where and how she lived. This move was a fresh start, and she was determined to embrace it.

She closed the curtains, switched the light on and changed into comfortable clothes. Putting on the lightest of make-up, just enough to hide her exhaustion, she prepared to go back downstairs, relishing a bit of quiet time with Murray and another glass of champagne to seal their move. He'd seemed tired too this afternoon, a little quieter than usual. But he'd picked up after their takeaway dinner and was happy to give Elliot a quick rundown of the area, telling him that a huge shopping complex, open seven days a week, was only a short bus ride away, and that if he fancied going to the cinema, a longer bus ride into Edinburgh city centre would take him there. The news seemed to lighten Elliot's mood. Knowing him, he'd probably make straight for the movies tonight.

At the bottom of the stairs she paused. Murray had put on some blues – not her favourite music, but they had to have their differences. He'd lit a few candles. She approved of that. The fire was glowing hot now with smokeless coal and logs. He was lounging on the sofa, champagne glass in hand, staring into the fire, his features looking more finely etched than usual. Sometimes she forgot just how attractive he was, and – this was the best part – he seemed un-aware of it.

Rowan felt a flicker of concern. Was Murray going to flourish here, find a new job, be truly happy? There was no doubt that he'd not been himself. She thought back to their early encounters. He'd been very honest about the period immediately after the break-up of his marriage, when he had gone off the rails, and about the extreme anger he'd felt towards his wife. He had been deeply ashamed that an injunction had been taken out against him. Rowan had been disturbed by that admission but had given him huge credit for tell-ing her. He could, after all, have hidden the fact, since it had occurred a long time before they met. But there was another, more important consequence of that marriage break-up: the collapse in his self-confidence, which still remained. She was sure that his doubts over finding another job were seeded somewhere in that marital failure.

And then there was his devastation at the death of his father. She was still hurting from being shut out of that period. Murray had gone on lone visits to his father during his short illness, coming back brooding and silent. She could do nothing for him but be there.

Rowan studied his serious face. No, the scars hadn't healed yet. Occasionally he'd still go quiet and even she found it difficult to figure out what was going on in his head. His determination to be strong just left her feeling frozen out or irritated. The razor-wire issue was a classic example. What better symbol was

there of an attempt to overcome his feelings of vulnerability than that? She might have been a bit sharp
with him about it, but he knew he had overreacted.
They might even talk about it tonight. She felt the
need to get close again after their time apart and his
overwhelming preoccupation in recent months with
finding a house.

'Rowan? Ah, there you are.' Murray was pouring
out a glass of champagne for her. 'Elliot rang when
you were in the bath. He's gone to see a film. Finishes
about ten. I've told him which buses will bring him
back here, but said that if he's unsure, he's to get a cab
and I'll sort out the fare when he gets home. He
sounded fine.'

She sat down on the floor, one elbow resting against
the sofa, and looked up at him. 'Of course he's fine. I
think it's great that he wants to explore the area and
go into town so soon after arriving. He's starting
school in a week and I want him to find his feet here
before then. I'm starting my new job the same day,
which isn't perfect, but you'll be here for him when he
comes home. Oh, and I'm taking him to see the head
teacher later in the week. Just to . . . well, you know.
To make sure everything's okay.'

She hated having to remind him of what the next
few days held. She had explained all this before,
more than once, but so often recently she had wondered if he'd been listening to her. All his attention,
it seemed, had been focused on buying a house, this
house. A great prize indeed, but now she wanted them

to be together, back on the same wavelength, as a couple and, ideally, as a family. Rowan waited for a response. Yet again, she wondered if he had been listening. After holding out the glass to her, his eyes had strayed towards the fire and remained there.

'Murray, did you hear what I said?'

'Yes, of course. I'll be here for him.' He reached out his hand and she felt its warmth on her cheek. 'You feeling okay about work?'

She sipped at her drink, and felt herself beginning to relax. 'Ah, it'll be fine. The initial week or two will probably feel strange, but I don't care. I just want to get settled in. But look.' She moved up beside him on the sofa. 'Forget work. I wanted to say that I've missed you and that you've done a wonderful job getting this place. I know I'm going to love it. How could I not?' She kissed him and brushed a hand through his hair.

Rowan watched as he shut his eyes, obviously wallowing in her caress. She touched his hand. 'Does Elliot have his own house keys?'

He opened his eyes. 'Yeah, I gave him the spare set before he went out. Why?'

She laughed. 'You're a bit slow on the uptake, Mr Shaw. There's no need to stay up. Let's go to bed.' With that, she took his hand and led him slowly towards the stairs, feeling happier than she'd been in weeks.

# Twenty-two

It was after ten in the morning. Rowan paused once more at Elliot's bedroom door. Like Murray, he was still fast asleep, but they'd all been working so hard, she could forgive their laziness. Unlocking the front door, she paused: the keys. Were the ones in the door Murray's or the spare set? She'd heard Elliot come in about half past ten and Murray had gone downstairs to check if he was comfortable for his first night in the new house. That was all she could remember. Murray had exhausted her. It had been a good evening, an important re-bonding.

She looked back at the coat rack. She needed a set of keys, just in case Murray and Elliot decided to go out. Quietly, she padded back down the hall and pulled Murray's jacket off the hook. Shaking it, she thought she heard the jangle of keys. Or was it coins? She rifled through one pocket, then another. The keys were there, so she could take the ones in the door. As she lifted the jacket to the coat hook, a piece of folded paper fell to the ground.

Allowing curiosity to win through, Rowan scanned the brief note. The handwriting was unfamiliar, as was the signature: *Shelagh Kerr.*

*Do forgive my behaviour the other evening. I was just a bit taken aback . . . I'm anxious that you feel no discomfort over the matter . . . we would very much like you to come to dinner tonight at the manse . . .*

Rowan stood in the hallway, blinking down at the words, reading and rereading them. Suddenly she looked up, thinking that she could hear stirring upstairs. No, all was silent. Hesitantly, she placed the note back carefully into the jacket pocket, tiptoed back down the hallway and eased open the front door, closing it carefully behind her. As an afterthought, she scrabbled about in her bag, found pen and paper, and jotted down a few lines explaining that she had gone for a walk. With cold, trembling fingers she slid the piece of paper through the letter box and turned to go.

But her progress stalled on the first step. Directly across the lane, a straggle of worshippers was trickling through the church door. Greeting them was their minister: a slim woman in late middle age, clothed in dark cassock and white clerical collar. Rowan thought the woman seemed to sense her presence, since she looked up immediately, smiled pleasantly and nodded her head in greeting before bending down to speak to an elderly man in a wheelchair. Slowly, Rowan descended the steps from the front door and watched as the minister grasped the handles of the wheelchair and propelled the worshipper into the church. As the pair moved into the darkness of the vestibule, a tall, extremely thin but attractive young man, also clad in a dark cassock, appeared and began to close the inner church doors. On impulse, Rowan ran across the road.

He looked up, his bony face anxious. 'Oh, do you want to join the service? It's okay, you're not too late.' He spoke with a gentle, Highland lilt.

'No, I . . . I wanted to see your minister some time today. Her name *is* Shelagh Kerr, isn't it?'

'Yes. The Reverend Doctor Shelagh Kerr.'

The young man enunciated her full title with great care and pride, Rowan thought. So, she was an ordained minister and with a doctorate in theology, perhaps? But what else? Was it this woman that Murray had referred to on the phone when he'd said a neighbour was visiting? It had to be.

She was aware that the young clergyman was waiting for some kind of response. 'Oh, good. You see, I'm a new neighbour. I've moved into St Margaret's House and I just wanted to say hello. Perhaps you've met my husband already?'

He shook his head. 'Sorry, no. Look, I have to go in now. If you want to see Reverend Kerr, why not come by later?'

She could hear the strains of the first hymn seeping out through the church doorway. 'Of course, thank you.'

Minutes later she found herself on a main road and made for an appealing-looking coffee shop. Her brain felt locked, almost paralysed. She had woken up feeling warm, secure and happy. Now where was she? What on earth was that note about, and why hadn't

Murray told her about having had dinner with Shelagh Kerr? The letter didn't make sense. Why was she asking him to 'forgive' her behaviour? And why had she been 'taken aback'? It wasn't the usual note you'd expect from a new neighbour.

Rowan shivered at the outside table, warmed not very successfully by a tall gas heater. Still, she needed the fresh air. The main road was quiet; the Sunday traffic was light. Stirring the steaming black coffee and enjoying its rich aroma, she reached for her mobile phone. Thumbing through the address book, she paused now and again, before moving on. Already she felt homesick. If this had been London, she could have arranged to meet with various people, and if in dire emotional need, one or both of her best friends would have joined her. Except both were overseas at the moment and had been for months, pursuing their journalistic careers to even greater heights. Unlike her. Time differences meant email was her sole method of communication with them, and even that had tailed off in recent weeks. It was only now the hubbub of finding a new job and moving was over that she realized how much she missed the security of having good friends on her doorstep.

Rowan picked at a croissant, forcing herself to eat a few morsels, and then dropped the pastry. The sense of isolation and confusion caught at her throat. Why was she reacting like this? There was undoubtedly a rational explanation for the neighbour's note – and for the cash withdrawals from Murray's account – so why did she suddenly rush to doubt him? She sat back, looking at nothing.

After two cups of coffee she retraced her steps, more slowly this time, getting to know the geography of the area, and found herself in the park. It was surprisingly quiet, except for a lone mother who was pushing her toddler on a swing, the child giggling with delight. Rowan couldn't help but smile at the laughter. It seemed such a short while ago that she had done the very same thing with Elliot; now he was almost a man. She turned away and began walking down the long path.

The wind had picked up by the time she reached the churchyard. She had identified a side gate, invisible from the windows of St Margaret's House and wandered towards it. Then a movement on the left stopped her. Shelagh Kerr, still dressed in her Sunday service robes, was in a far corner, kneeling at a grave. Rowan made her way over, watching the older woman, who seemed lost in thought, tracing a hand across the weather-worn lettering of a tombstone. Moving closer, Rowan could see that it was the grave of a child and suddenly felt like an intruder. Just as she was considering backing away, Shelagh Kerr turned her head. For a moment the woman remained lost in thought and then her eyes focused on Rowan.

Feeling even more like an intruder, Rowan took the initiative. 'Ah . . . hello. I'm sorry, hope I'm not disturbing you. It's just that I was crossing the churchyard and saw you and thought I'd introduce myself. I'm Rowan, Rowan Shaw. Your new neighbour at St Margaret's House.'

Disconcertingly, Shelagh Kerr remained kneeling and unsmiling. Then she seemed to rouse herself and stood up, holding out a slim, well-manicured hand. 'Of course. I saw you outside the house this morning. Welcome. I've met your husband and heard a fair bit about you. Are you and your son settling in now?'

Rowan released the cool hand and accepted the woman's invitation to sit on a nearby bench. 'Well, we've just arrived, so the house is still full of boxes, but we'll get there. I just wanted to get a better sense of the area, so I've been walking around for a while. It's even lovelier than I remember. It's wonderful living opposite your church and graveyard – such a beautiful view each morning.'

To her surprise, the minister stood up. 'It's a bit chilly, the wind's getting the better of us even in this sheltered corner. Would you like to see inside the church?'

'Please.' Rowan fell into step beside the other woman. They walked in silence until they reached the vestibule, where Shelagh Kerr paused to make a minor rearrangement of the vase of fresh flowers. Inside, the church was silent and Rowan allowed herself to be led slowly around its perimeter.

'Do you enjoy churches?'

The question took Rowan by surprise. 'Er . . . yes, yes I do. I'll often visit one when I'm on holiday, admiring the art, feeling their atmosphere.' She laughed.

'Murray's not such a fan, nor Elliot. But I like to wander around them on my own. I enjoy the stillness.'

The minister seemed to think about this. 'Yes, stillness. Though during and after a service I often feel anything but stillness in here. I feel people's woes, their railing, a disruption in the firmament.'

Rowan's heart sank. She hoped that the woman wasn't going to start some sort of informal sermonizing. But as she watched, it became clear that the minister seemed to have been talking more to herself. For the second time in their encounter she appeared to rouse herself out of other thoughts. 'But . . . yes, churches are places to be visited, enjoyed. Please feel free to come over here whenever you want. Murray should too. Especially if he wants to visit Angus's grave.'

Rowan dropped back behind the minister and moved into the shadows, listening with increasing puzzlement and anxiety. She was relieved that the woman couldn't see her expression.

'Funnily enough, since meeting Murray again, I have a memory of him visiting Angus's grave, as a child, and talking to it. I think it's a real memory, not imagined.' The woman's voice sounded hushed, but still it echoed eerily through the empty church. 'After all, I don't think it would have been a morbid thing to do. Surely it's natural to want to visit the grave of the best friend you've just lost, and so tragically.' She turned suddenly. 'Don't you agree?'

Rowan was thankful for both the shadows and the

cool, stone wall of the church as she propped herself against it for support. She feigned a cough, as the strangled words struggled to get out. 'Y-yes . . . I completely agree.'

Shelagh Kerr appeared satisfied by the stock response and turned away again, lost in thought once more. 'I do hope that Murray has got over the way I reacted the other night. It was just such a shock, but I think we made up over dinner. You think he's okay?'

Forcing herself to find something approaching a normal voice, Rowan managed another dull reply. 'Oh, he's fine, just fine.' She took a chance. 'It was kind of you to have him over.'

The minister had turned again, smiling into the shadows at Rowan. 'Not at all. We must do it again. With all of you.' She began walking back up the church, towards the light creeping through the front door. 'You know, I've been thinking about things so much these past few days. I should be thanking Murray. And I will.' She stopped to look around again, clearly anxious not to lose her visitor's attention.

Rowan felt a shaft of treacherous sunlight hit her face. 'Thank him, really?' Could she get away with it? This woman *must* be able to read her thoughts.

'Yes, indeed. I owe him for being such a good friend to my little brother right up to the end.' They had reached the cold, bright, unforgiving outdoors. The minister bobbed her head in the direction of St Margaret's House. 'And for bringing happy family life back to our old home.'

As Rowan feigned another cough, wanting desperately to flee, one persistent question rang round her head: what other secrets about her husband were waiting to be uncovered?

# Twenty-three

Elliot hefted another box marked 'DVDs' and cursed. There had to be more than his movie collection in this one. He felt the sweat prickling on his forehead, and paused to scan the attic space. This was going to make a great recreation room: movies, snooker table, music collection. Perfect. If – no, *when* – he had made new friends they could all come up here and have some privacy. The thought raised a smile. Maybe things weren't so bad after all. His gaze strayed out through the dormer window. Suddenly his smile faded. His mother was hurrying across the churchyard opposite, but something was wrong. Her face. It looked strange, contorted, as if she was about to cry. There was a woman behind her: a female minister, standing at the church door, waving her hand in farewell. But she was smiling broadly, as if they had just parted on the best of terms. He watched his mother veer off the path and disappear behind the church. She wasn't coming home.

A stack of boxes tripped him up on his dash out of the room. Viciously, he kicked them out of his way and began leaping down each flight of stairs as fast as he could. Jumping the last four steps into the hallway on the ground floor, he heard Murray sliding the patio doors open. He'd said he wanted to work in the garden this morning. Fine. Let him get on with it.

Once outside, Elliot couldn't see any sign of the minister – presumably she'd gone back inside the church. He raced full pelt across the lane and down the right-hand side of the church, where he'd last seen his mother. He jumped over a couple of low tombstones and kept running until he found himself at the back of the churchyard. Frantically, he looked in all directions, spinning on his heel. She wasn't there. A nearby path led to a residential street, which connected to the main road. It was where he'd caught the bus last night. Although it was Sunday lunchtime and the afternoon was cold, there were plenty of people about on the street. But no sign of Rowan.

Murray leaned heavily against the beech tree and counted the bags of leaves he'd collected. Raking them up had been a back-breaking job, but the garden looked better. He checked his watch, wondering when Rowan was coming back. Maybe they could all go out for lunch somewhere. He'd prefer it to be just the two of them since he *had* to talk to her today about the house, offer her a plausible explanation. But Elliot had been doing his fair share of slaving away up in the attic and would want his reward. The nagging worry that Rowan might bump into Shelagh Kerr kept interrupting his thoughts. But he felt sure that it was unlikely. Sunday was presumably a minister's busiest day – no time for seeking out the new neighbours –

and Rowan had left early. As he lifted one of the bags, his mobile rang. Expecting it to be Rowan, he answered quickly.

'About time. Where are you?'

'Murray? It's Fiona.'

'Oh, right. Hi.'

'I need to see you.' Her voice sounded oddly high-pitched and breathless. 'Can you make it tonight? I . . . I'm glad your family's here and it would be great to meet them, but I want to talk to you – alone. It's about the fire at my school.'

It was the last thing Murray wanted to deal with. He dropped the rubbish sack at his feet and sighed. 'Look, I'm really busy here. Up to my eyes. I ju–'

'There are similarities.' She seemed on edge.

'What?'

'Between your fire and the one at the school. The police and fire people have said so. I'm surprised they've not been to see you again.' Her voice was regaining its assertive tone. 'Please. Just half an hour? For Angus's sake?'

He leaned back against the beech again, feeling momentarily disorientated, and stared at the charred plot where the summerhouse had stood. 'Okay. Where?'

'The Trinity Hotel bar at seven-thirty. You know it?'

'Yes. Okay.'

She'd rung off without as much as a goodbye.

His eyes blurred as he stared at the burnt ground

and absent-mindedly put his mobile back in his pocket. He sensed Rowan's arrival before he saw her. Slowly, lifting his head, his eyes took in her winter boots, then her coat and, finally, her pale face. She looked ill.

He began running up the garden towards her. 'Rowan, what's wrong?'

She backed away, clutching her coat tightly around her body. 'Everything. *Everything's wrong.*'

# Twenty-four

Rowan shivered. The cold had seeped deep into her. 'Stay where you are. Where's Elliot?'

Murray stopped a few feet from her. 'What? He's up in the attic unpacking. Why? Look, what *is* this?'

Her anxiety dropped a fraction. Elliot wouldn't be hurrying downstairs any time soon. She shook her head disbelievingly at Murray. 'What *is* this? You tell me. I don't know what the hell's going on. I've just been talking to Shelagh Kerr.'

He was looking in her direction, but his eyes seemed unfocused. She could see a deep furrow between them, as if he was nursing a headache.

She tried again. 'I know about Angus.' She threw her hands up. 'And about this house. *Speak to me!*'

He continued to stare ahead, his face drawn and pinched by the freezing air.

'Let's go inside, Rowan. Please.'

She began shaking her head and placed a wrought-iron garden chair in front of her as a barrier. She didn't want him to try to touch or embrace her.

He tried again. 'Okay. Then please, just sit down.'

Dumbly, she kept shaking her head.

'*Sit down. Please!* I can't talk to you like this.'

Slowly, she lowered herself on to the edge of

another chair. The first one was still positioned defensively between them. Murray remained standing. She felt even more chilled, trying and failing to quell the shivering that was running in waves through her body. She followed his every move as he raised both hands in surrender.

'Believe me, this is the last thing I wanted. I tried to talk to you last night.' His eyes kept slewing away from her as he spoke, and he took a step backwards.

She banged the iron table with the palm of her hand, ignoring the stinging pain. 'Well, you didn't try very fucking hard, did you? You *bastard*! Other things on your mind?' The sudden loss of control, partly fuelled by anger at herself, frightened her. After all, it was she who had initiated sex the night before. She swept the memory aside. *Keep control. Force yourself into some form of detachment. If you can do it at work, you can do it here.*

Breathing slowly and deeply, she looked directly at him. 'Right. Try telling me now.' She gestured towards the house. 'Firstly, I want to know about this place.'

Again his eyes flicked back and forth. The rising wind kept blowing his hair into his eyes and he raked a hand through it, holding his fingers there in a gesture of utter despair, pulling the flesh of his face so taut that his cheekbones shone through. 'It's . . . it's like I explained to Shelagh Kerr. When I was looking for a place up here, this house caught my eye. Its details were sent with scores of others, you know that. You saw all the shit I was being sent by estate agents.

Loads of rubbish or unsuitable stuff. It didn't even register as a place I knew. Its plus points were obvious. It was a great size, affordable *and*, yes, it was in a part of Edinburgh I knew from childhood. But so were some other properties.'

He let his hand drop for a moment and the wind blew his hair back into his eyes. His features had slackened, but the furrow on his forehead remained. He seemed in pain. 'Look, the place wasn't even called St Margaret's House in those days. The place I used to visit I knew just as Angus's home.'

She kept her stinging palm placed downwards on the cold table. 'Who was Angus? What happened to him?'

He sat on the bottom step that led down from the patio to the lawn. He was turned away from her, elbows on knees, hands hanging loosely in front of him, head down. But his voice was surprisingly clear.

'It happened at primary school. It was the annual summer sports day. In the local park. Angus was my best friend, but he had detention that day. He and a teacher died in a fire in the school. They . . . they thought a janitor did it. He'd had a row with the teacher. But nothing could be proved.'

He coughed nervously and looked down the garden before continuing. 'Angus's family moved away.' He shook his head. 'I never, *ever* would have believed she'd be here today.'

Rowan remained silent for a minute. The unimaginable pain of the little boy's family gripped her. But when she spoke, her voice was cold. 'You must have known, once you'd seen the details – the house's exact location, the address – what you were going to view. Why on earth did you go through with it? And why not tell me the truth about the house? When I came up here and you showed me round the area, an area you knew so well, I never dreamed you'd been so . . . so intimate with the house. Why not tell me?'

His shoulders hunched in a frozen shrug. 'I . . . I don't know, Rowan.' He dropped his head again. 'I had always loved this place. I was forever round here as a child. At first I was scared you'd wouldn't move here if you knew. I so wanted the house.' He began raking his hand through his hair again. Suddenly, he stood up and turned to face her. 'When it looked as if I could really own this place, then I . . . I just couldn't stop. The whole thing took on a life of its own. I know I should have told you then. I wanted to tell you, I did.' He slumped into a nearby chair.

She was trying to process all the information, but all she knew was that she felt sick, angry and cheated. One way or another, Murray had lied to her. She felt he was still lying to her. There was something else going on. As far as she knew, he had never lied to her before. Or had he? A flood of doubts began to wash through her. Maybe it was worse. Maybe he had never intended to tell her about the house's history. As it had all happened so long ago, maybe he thought he'd get away with it.

She stood up, her stiff limbs aching with cold and

tension. 'I don't know what to believe. All I do know is that you lied to me. Okay, lied by omission, but it's still lying. I don't understand it. Right at this moment, I don't know who you are.'

He got to his feet, a hand reaching out to her. 'Please, Row—'

'Don't, Murray. Just don't. I need to speak to Elliot. We gave up everything to be here with you. I don't know what to tell him.'

There was the shuffle of footsteps from inside the kitchen. 'You don't need to tell me anything, Mum. I've heard it all.'

She thought Elliot was going to give her a reassuring hug and held out a hand to him. But instead he brushed past her, marched briskly towards Murray and thumped him in the chest, leaving him teetering on the patio steps until he lost his footing.

'No, Elliot, no!' But she was too late. The dull thud as his foot hit Murray's stomach had her running forwards.

Elliot was crouching down, his face inches from Murray's. 'You are a complete shit! A liar and a shit! I know more about you than you think, you fucker!' He turned to face his mother. 'He had it planned, Mum. I'm telling you. I heard him *before* we left London, *before* he bought the house.'

She looked frantically from her son's angry face to that of her dumbstruck husband. 'Planned – what do you mean, "planned"?'

Elliot sat back on his heels, holding out his long,

thin arm, and pointed an accusing finger at Murray. 'I heard him on the phone. He was offered an interview at the LSE long before we moved. And you know what he said?'

Rowan shook her head once as Elliot continued pointing. 'He said, "I think our plans are changing. Looks like Rowan and I may be in for a big move."'

She tried to pull Elliot back, but suddenly he stood up. 'And you know what else I'm wondering about? I'm wondering if his redundancy *was* compulsory!' He aimed a final vicious kick at Murray's leg. 'Well, *was* it?'

Elliot moved behind her, but she could hear his heavy breathing. She stood on the patio, watching Murray get to his feet. She knew from his face that her son's wild accusation had hit home.

She stared coldly at him. 'Tell me about the redundancy.'

Murray tried to move towards her, but she held up a hand and stepped backwards towards the patio doors, hearing the scuffing of Elliot's feet behind her. She tried again. 'I'll find out, you know. There are people I can ask.' She could hear her voice rising and knew she was at the limits of her control. 'Is it true? Just tell me. Yes or no? *Tell me!*'

Her shout sounded unnaturally loud in the still air of the garden.

'Yes.' Murray's reply was so quiet that she barely heard it. He stood unsteadily, both hands clutching his stomach. He wouldn't look at her. 'It wasn't compulsory.'

'What?'

He looked at her now. 'It was voluntary. I took voluntary redundancy.'

She felt herself sway slightly, and Elliot put a hand on her shoulder. 'You okay, Mum?'

In answer, she placed her hand on top of his and squeezed it gently. *Keep control. For Elliot's sake. Keep control.* She released her son's hand and glared at her husband. 'What are you doing to us? *What?*'

'I . . . I . . . needed a change . . . I was going to discuss it with you but you were so busy with your work, your career.'

Rowan felt the anger burn. In a second, Elliot had moved around her and was standing between them. Now it was her son who was looking from face to face.

She held up a hand to him. 'It's okay, darling.' She turned to her husband. 'You have exactly five minutes to pack a bag and leave here.'

'I'm not leaving the house. Don't be so bloody ridiculous. We can sort this out.'

'*Listen.*' She tried to keep her voice quiet and steady. 'I want you to give me space, a bit of distance. I wan–'

'No, I'm not leaving the house!'

She shut her eyes tight, trying to hold back her tears. 'If you don't do this for me now, you'll be forcing me to consider putting some *permanent* distance between us. I mean it.'

'Yes!' Elliot punched the air. 'Get the fuck out of here! For good!' With that, he ran into the kitchen and through to the hallway, slamming the door behind him.

As she turned back to look at Murray, his face crumpled, she felt the dizzying sensation of her world imploding.

# Twenty-five

It was his third whisky in an hour, but they were having no effect.

'Murray?'

Fiona Muir was walking towards him, into the darkened corner of the quiet bar. She stopped and looked at the empty glasses. 'You must have been here a while. I thought you might find it hard to get away.'

He stood up. 'What you drinking?'

'Same as you. No ice, no water.'

As he returned with their drinks, he could see that she was preoccupied. He would hear what she had to say about the fire, although right now he didn't care one whit. All he could think about was how to get back into the house.

Fiona slung her coat across a spare chair and then snatched up her glass. 'Cheers.' Hesitating, she placed it back on the table. 'Something's wrong.'

He rubbed his temple, trying to chase away the headache that was settling in. Maybe he'd had enough whisky for now. 'It's complicated. But the long and short of it is that Rowan has asked me to leave the house. I've checked in here.'

'*What?*' She looked astonished. 'Why? For how long?'

He threw his head back and rolled his shoulders, trying to reduce some of the tension in them and make a show of being unworried. 'It's all my stupid fault.' He sat up straight again and let out a bitter laugh. 'She bumped into bloody Shelagh Kerr. That's what.'

'So? Wh—'

He spoke across her. 'Listen. I never told Rowan. About the house, who'd lived there, or about Angus and the fire. Nothing.' He held up a hand to stop her interrupting. 'Don't ask me to explain why I didn't. I was going to. But I'd sort of let it drift . . . I was going to tell her last night. I mean, I had no choice, what with Shelagh Kerr living on our doorstep.' Tentatively, he sipped at his drink. 'And what happens this morning? Rowan goes out and meets Shelagh, who assumes she knows everything. It's a fucking disaster.'

He waited for her response.

'Look,' she said, frowning, 'this isn't my business, but since you've mentioned it, I have to say it seems strange. I don't have a problem with you wanting to live in the house.' She paused to look up at him, a half smile twisting her lips. 'Some people might say it was odd — a bit morbid perhaps. Not me. But why on earth wouldn't you tell your own wife?' She looked down into her glass. 'I mean, why didn't you tell her as soon as you realized whose house it was, when the estate agent sent you the full details? What was there to hide?'

He sat up straight, pushing his drink away from

him. 'Nothing. There's nothing to hide. It was just a complication at a time when there were a lot of complications. For example, the little matter of asking her and Elliot to uproot themselves from all they knew. I kept leaving it and leaving it. I *knew* I should have dealt with it, but I never expected anyone from Angus's family to be here.'

He stopped talking, hoping that this woman wouldn't try to scrape below the surface of the story he'd given her. While he tried to work out a way to get back into the house, he might as well keep her close. She was hell-bent on unearthing the truth from all those years ago, as was he.

Fiona shifted uneasily in her seat. She had looked preoccupied when she arrived; now she seemed troubled. 'Did your wife say what she thought of Shelagh Kerr?'

'No. But I suspect she's the sort of person Rowan would like. A strong woman.'

Fiona grimaced. 'Aha. Another one about to come under her spell.'

'What d'you mean?'

'Come on, Murray. Shelagh and her husband did the same thing to you. At that dinner. Made you like her, like them both.'

He began fiddling with a beer mat, sliding it to and fro. 'I don't know about that. But she does seem perfectly likeable to me. I don't think she's upset that I've bought St Margaret's House. She said as much. "The past is the past" is how she put it.'

Fiona shook her head. 'Well, I don't think it is. History would seem to be repeating itself.'

Murray looked at her quizzically. She was waiting for him to work out what she was getting at. Then he gave a small laugh. 'Ah yes, you mean this fire at your school. Of course, I forgot all about it. What happened? More vandalism?'

She reached for her glass and, to his surprise, downed the whisky in one. 'It's a bit more than that. I meant it when I said history was repeating itself.' She leaned towards him, so close that he caught the subtle scent of her perfume.

'They've found a body.'

# Twenty-six

She watched as he tried to absorb the news. His eyes showed a flicker of – what? Pain? Fear? He leaned away from her.

'Not . . . not a child?'

'It's an adult. That's all they can say at the moment. The blaze was fierce. It's going to take some time to work out what they've got.' She gestured to the barman to set up more drinks and turned back to Murray. He looked as if he needed another.

'Is it someone from the school?'

'No, that was my main worry. I checked as soon as I knew. No one's missing.'

'But how did they get in? You said they thought there were similarities to the fire at my place. That means it was definitely deliberate, surely?' He looked anxious.

She stood up. 'Just a minute, let me get these drinks.' At the bar, she watched him lift his shoulders, still trying to ease the tension in them.

She made her way back to the corner table. 'There you go.' She handed Murray his drink and sat down. 'I'll tell you what I know. The fire has pretty much destroyed an old part of the east wing. We can still run the school though, thank God. They've just cordoned off part of the playground where the school backs on to the park. A police patrol raised the alarm in the early hours of yesterday morning. That area's so quiet at night. No one's ever around. The fire started in the basement, apparently. It had probably been going for a while – since late Friday night, they think – before the alarm went up.'

'No smoke detectors or sprinklers?'

She shook her head firmly. 'Nope. That wing isn't used for teaching. Children don't go in there. Cutbacks meant that when the electrics were being done, it was decided to give that wing only the bare minimum.'

'Where was the body found?'

'At the seat of the fire, in the basement.'

'What caused it?'

She shrugged. 'Oh, they don't know that yet. But they're looking into all recent fires. That's why I was surprised that the police hadn't talked to you yet.'

'But that . . . that's silly.' He felt worried but tried to keep his voice level. 'Some tearaways torching my summerhouse is a world away from destroying part of a school and killing a man.'

'A man?'

'Sorry, figure of speech. Killing a *person*. Intentionally or unintentionally, someone's still dead. How can it be connected to the fire in my garden?'

She crossed and recrossed her legs, trying to get comfortable. 'No one's said they're connected. But it would seem logical for the police to look into all arson attempts in the area. In my book they should be looking *very* close to home.' She sighed. 'Like across the road from you.'

'Oh, come on.' He held both hands up in protest. 'Do *not* try to tell me you think Shelagh Kerr has anything to do with all this. That is plain ridiculous.'

She sighed. Why did he seem determined to play devil's advocate? She tapped the table once to emphasize her point. 'Not so ridiculous when you know that she was seen. Late on Friday night.'

'What? Where? Who saw her?'

'I told you before that I'm not the only one around here who has worries about Shelagh. They saw her and that's all I'm going to say right now.' She tapped the table once more. 'Shelagh was spotted near the park. Coming out of the narrow path that runs down the side of it to the high street. The path used to be used as a shortcut when the park was locked up.'

He looked sceptical. 'So what? This is a small community. She is a parish minister. She has *pastoral* duties. That means she may have been out on a visit.'

She sighed again. He was really exasperating her. 'Look, that path is overgrown and unlit. No one uses it these days. *Especially* not a woman on her own. You'd only use it at night if you were in a hurry, a very big hurry, and wanted to keep under cover. Unfortunately for Shelagh, she was seen.'

'Well, if you're so suspicious, why don't you ask her what she was doing? Or tell the police?'

'Hardly. She's protected. Don't you see?'

He shook his head. 'Protected by whom?'

She lifted her drink in a mock toast.

'Not by *whom*. By *what*.' She took a generous gulp, enjoying the warming sensation as the liquid made its way into her system. 'Shelagh Kerr is protected by her position. She's in camouflage.'

'Camouflage?'

She looked at him until he averted his gaze. 'Shelagh Kerr is the devil in God's clothing.'

# Twenty-seven

Rowan opened her eyes at the creak of the living-room door.

'Elliot?'

She stretched across the sofa and switched on a table lamp. He was standing in the doorway, looking thinner than ever in baggy hoody and trousers.

'Hi, Mum.' He squinted at the rug she was pulling from her body. 'You been sleeping in here?'

She leapt up and embraced him. 'Not sleeping really. Just waiting here till you came home. Darling, you're freezing. Where did you go after Murray left?'

'Just out and about.' He moved from her grasp to sit on the sofa and switched on the television with the remote control, first muting the sound and then flicking through the array of channels as he spoke. 'I suppose you're furious at me. For not telling you about him.'

She made to sit beside him and then hesitated, instead lowering herself into a nearby armchair. 'I'm not furious.' Rowan knew she had to tread carefully. She needed to keep him close. The last thing she wanted was for him to go off the rails again. 'I was worried. You've been gone for hours. You didn't answer your phone.'

He nodded, his fingers still working the remote as he surfed his way back and forth before settling on a music channel. The volume remained mute.

'I know. I'm sorry.' He flashed a look at her. 'Murray's definitely gone?'

Rowan sighed. 'He's gone. For now. There's a lot to think about.' She willed him to look at her. 'He said to tell you that he was sorry.'

She watched as Elliot began flicking through the channels again, his face stony. 'Oh, really? It's *you* he should be saying sorry to. He's a bloody liar!'

At last he looked at her properly, tossing the remote control on to the table. He was near to tears. She was trying to keep her composure. 'Darling, it isn't as black and white as that.' She held up her hand to halt any interruption. 'Yes, he *should* have told me about this house and his job. But he must have had his reasons for not doing so. I believe he was going to tell us sometime. I just don't know why he left it so late. It's not so much about the house, and . . . well, with his job . . . if he wanted a change, he should have said. It's his not being honest and open about things that's so bad.'

Elliot looked away from her, his eyes to the floor. 'I'm sorry, Mum, you're wrong. I've been thinking about this. Why would *anyone* want to buy a house with such creepy connections? It's weird. And then to lie about his job so that he'd have an excuse to move in here. It's worse than weird. Why can't you see that?'

'Of course, darling. But Murray's my husband and

he's had his share of troubles in the past. Murray's a good man. Just . . . complicated. And I think he's still suffering from the loss of his father.'

'Oh yeah, and what about *my* father? He's dumped me!'

Elliot's voice was beginning to sound peevish. The last thing Rowan wanted was for him to have one of his outbursts. She kept her voice deliberately low, the tone soothing without being patronizing. 'I know, Elliot. I'm sorry. All I can say is that I'm here for you. Always.'

He seemed to relax a bit.

'Look, darling, let's leave it for now. Until I know *exactly* what's been going through Murray's mind, I'm going to reserve judgement. Of course it seems odd. Remember, I've just asked him to move out.'

He lifted his head and flung her a sarcastic smile. 'For now.'

'Yes, for now. I need to think about things. I can't just turn my back on Murray. But I'm not going to turn my back on you either. I love you and I want you to be happy, but you need to give me some time to work out what to do. Please. I'm not going to make any major decisions without talking to you.'

Rowan paused, feeling the stranglehold of tears beginning to take a grip. Quickly, she stood up. 'Do you need anything to eat?'

'No, I grabbed something when I was out.'

'Okay. Well, look, I need to get to bed early. Have a clear head for the morning.'

Elliot waved a hand as she walked away. 'Sure. I'm going to stay up. Watch some TV down here.' He reached for the remote control and brought up the sound, raucous music blaring out before he had time to reduce the volume. 'Mum? Do you know where he's staying?'

Rowan paused at the door to the hallway. Elliot continued staring at the screen. She lifted her voice above the sound of the music. 'Yes, he called to let me know. He's at a local hotel. The Trinity. I've asked him not to come here unless invited.'

Elliot showed no sign of having heard. She turned for the stairs and then stopped. 'Darling?'

Slowly he twisted round to look at her. 'Yeah?'

'Promise you'll tell me if there's anything else about Murray that worries you?'

He brandished the remote control in one hand. 'Of course.' Then he went back to watching television. 'I promise, Mum.'

Rowan turned away, praying that he was telling her the truth.

Half an hour later, Elliot slipped quietly out of the front door. He paused on the front step. Opposite, the church and manse lay in darkness. He pulled the zip of his top up to his chin, flicked the hood over his head and made for the high street. A quick online check had told him that the Trinity Hotel was only a few minutes' walk away. The entrance was near a bus stop. He stood, pretending to study the timetable, and lit up a cigarette. Now and again he would look round, taking in the frontage of the hotel. There was a wide entrance that seemed to lead directly into a huge bar area and restaurant. At one side was the driveway to the hotel car park, which lay behind the building.

He sucked hard on the cigarette as he thought through his plan of action. It was possible that Murray was either eating late in the restaurant or having a drink. If so, he couldn't take the chance of barging in and being seen. Hiding further into his hood, he continued staring at the bus timetable. He wasn't sure why he was even here. He just wanted to know where Murray was, needed to know where to find him if he had to. As a bus pulled up and disgorged several passengers, he took advantage of the small crowd and stepped briskly round the side of the building into the car park. There was a back entrance to the hotel for car-park users, but as he drew close he could see that access was controlled by a swipe-card system. He cursed under his breath.

As he turned to go back round to the front, he heard a giggling group of girls – obviously in the final stages of a hen weekend. They bustled through the door and made for a waiting taxi. Elliot grabbed the closing door before it clicked to. Inside, there was a small entrance area with a wall-mounted payphone and a rack of brochures advertising local attractions, reminding him that Edinburgh, including this part of it, was a year-round tourist city. That no doubt explained why this place was so busy on a Sunday night. Quickly, he pulled his hood down, unzipped his top and smoothed his hair. Directly in front of him were stairs and signage directing residents to various room numbers. On the right was a door leading to the bar. It sounded busy. He thought for a moment. Grabbing the payphone handset and clutching it to his ear, he waited. The first suitable group turned up within a couple of minutes: a crowd of young men who, by the look of the dirty kit spilling out of their holdalls, had been playing football. Elliot tagged on to the end of the group as they pushed through into the heaving bar.

Immediately he made for the nearest fruit machine and started feeding it with coins. He breathed a sigh of relief. This was a good vantage point for a number of reasons. He could observe without being observed. Most people, except other gamblers, paid no heed to fruit machine users and, even better, he couldn't be seen by the bar staff, who might work out he was underage. There was a clattering of coins. Luck was with him tonight. He bent to retrieve his winnings and ploughed them back in again as he worked out the layout of the place.

It was a warren made more confusing by the array of huge mirrors on every wall. Elliot pushed in what was going to be his final coin, when he saw it. He peered into the mirror to his right. There was no doubt: it was Murray's profile. He was at a table in a darkened corner, sipping a short drink. To his right was an attractive woman.

Elliot could feel his heart pick up. He needed to get nearer. Scanning the area, he saw signs for the men's toilets. The journey there would take him closer. But suddenly both Murray and the well-groomed woman stood up. Hidden by the fruit machine, Elliot followed their progress into the main part of the bar, towards him. He tried to slow down his breathing. They were now just a few feet away. Surely Murray must sense his presence? But no, Elliot tracked the pair as they went through the door he himself had come through minutes before. Leaving the safety of the fruit machine, he used the crowd at the bar as cover and followed them.

Elliot expected them to go straight upstairs to a bedroom, but they had stopped near the payphone and tourist brochures. With his face turned away and still using the exiting crowd for cover, Elliot strained to hear as Murray bent towards the woman and talked in hushed tones.

'Have the police given any estimate about when the body will be identified?'

The woman shook her head. 'No. Nor when they'll be able to confirm if it's arson.' She paused. 'But I'm not going to wait for that.'

'What do you mean? What are you going to do?'

'I'll let you know later.'

Elliot strained again to hear. Suddenly he was swept aside as a flurry of arrivals poured through the outer door. The wave of drinkers brought in a gust of chilly wind with them. Elliot stood on tiptoe trying to keep

Murray and the woman in sight, but they'd gone. Upstairs or outside? Carefully, he opened the outer door and saw them disappear round the side of the hotel into the street. He ran after them but was brought up short; they had stopped again, this time at the front entrance. The woman was saying something and touching Murray's arm. Then they split up, Murray going back into the hotel, while the woman began walking briskly along the street. Keeping well back, Elliot followed her down a side road until he found himself in a quiet cul-de-sac of two-storey stone-built cottages. Five doors along – the last cottage – she took a left turn and disappeared through the front gate.

Elliot reached for his cigarette packet. He wasn't sure what he had just witnessed, but one thing was for sure. His mother must know nothing about it until he knew the truth.

# Twenty-eight

Shelagh locked the front door of the manse as her assistant looked over her shoulder, keen to get her attention.

'Is your father all right, Shelagh? Not an emergency or anything? I just thought if Gordon's going with you that maybe . . .'

'No, no, Sandy. Gordon's got some time off, so he's offered to take me in his car. I'm relieved. Look at the weather. I hate driving in the rain.' Shelagh skipped over a large puddle, settled herself in the passenger seat and spoke through the open window. 'If you need me, call the mobile.'

Minutes later, they were in busy afternoon traffic heading for the Forth Road Bridge. 'Gordon, will you please slow down. Why do you always have to be in the fast lane, especially in these conditions? You're practically up his backside. If he brakes then—'

'Oh, come on, Shelagh. How long have I been driving? And not one accident. You don't want to be late, do you?'

Saying nothing further, Shelagh turned up the volume on the soothing choral music and sank back into the soft leather upholstery. She closed her eyes. Though she'd snapped at him over his driving, she prayed that Gordon had not picked up on the level of her anxiety. The nursing home matron had been clear: her father's mental condition was deteriorating to such an extent that 'alternative facilities' might have to be considered. Worst-case scenario meant they might be looking at a permanent psychiatric hospital arrangement. The thought made her feel ill. His physical condition, though frail, was not fatal. He could live for years, but as what? A tortured, demented wreck? And what of her? She carried the dark thoughts with her as she slipped into sleep.

'. . . We're here. Wake up . . . Shelagh? At least the weather's a bit brighter this side of the Firth.'

She stretched her stiff limbs and saw the pale, honey-coloured stone of the nursing home loom into view. Peppered across the wide lawn and front gardens were small groups of people, each comprising a resident – either in a wheelchair or using a walking stick – and their visitors. She found the sight depressing.

Gordon pulled up at the main entrance, smiling. 'Okay. Good luck. Call me when you've had enough. I know you don't want this.' He laid a hand lightly on her cheek. 'Go on, and when you've finished I have a surprise for you.'

She got out the car and watched him drive away, feeling a mixture of guilt and gratitude. They'd grown apart so gradually. But he seemed content with that. She was not. What could have been . . . But she had been a fool, a dangerous fool, thinking that she could change her lot. Another, higher, power was in control of that.

A few minutes later she found herself in what looked like a conference room, sitting opposite the GP and nursing home matron. Something was wrong, very wrong. She stared across the divide, acutely aware of the doctor's sombre demeanour.

'I've taken a second opinion on this, Reverend Kerr, and –'

'Shelagh, please.'

'Thank you, Shelagh. Your father has been seen by a highly respected gerontologist. She is a physician and psychiatrist who specializes in the aged.'

Shelagh felt herself tense up, stomach muscles contracting. 'This sounds very serious. Listen, I want to see my father. I want to know *exactly* what's been going on.' She looked to the matron for support, but all she received was a weak smile.

The doctor took up the reins again. 'You father's rapid mental deterioration has us all baffled, hence the gerontologist's involvement. I needed some expert advice. You *will* see your father shortly and . . . I'm afraid it's going to be a shock. He has become practically catatonic, immobile and, most worryingly, refuses to eat. However, he has become animated – agitated, even – on a few occasions. These appear to have one thing in common.'

'And what is that?'

'They are at night. In the early hours. And there's something else.'

Shelagh dreaded what was coming. 'Go on.'

'Your father is convinced that he is being visited by the ghost of your dead brother.'

She said nothing but sat waiting. Again, the GP swallowed awkwardly, giving a short preparatory cough.

'I must ask this for clinical reasons. It was put to me by my gerontologist colleague and I have no answer.' He looked away from her momentarily, before resuming his steady but worried gaze. 'Your father seems to be suffering intolerable guilt and anxiety.'

'Guilt?' Involuntarily, she clasped her hands more tightly.

'All the signs are there. As I said, I have to ask. Was there any suggestion that your father may have been or have felt responsible for the death of your brother?'

She felt sick. Both matron and GP twisted in their seats. Shelagh sat up straighter, looking them in the eye. They had obviously dreaded asking the question. She had her response.

'Doctor, I don't know what clinical route your gerontologist colleague is going down – dabbling in forensic psychology, perhaps? – but she is utterly wasting her time.'

Shelagh stood up, carefully manoeuvring herself around the chair. 'My father was devastated by the loss of Angus. I'm surprised – no, *astonished* – that you can't see that *that* is at the root of his illness. I don't think I want to hear any more of this ludicrous theorizing by your expert. I suggest she sticks to what she knows.'

Walking slowly towards the door, Shelagh prayed that they couldn't detect the fear in her voice. 'As for ghosts – the only ghosts my father is seeing are those in his sick mind.'

# Twenty-nine

The doctor had not understated the situation: her father looked skeletal. Under his baggy pullover and corduroy trousers – both once a perfect fit – she could see the outline of skinny knees and elbows.

'Dad?'

'It's unlikely he'll respond.' The matron had accompanied her to his room and pointed to the opposite corner. 'We're taking him out and about in a wheelchair at the moment.'

Shelagh ignored her and moved forwards. Her father was sitting in his usual chair, staring blankly out of the window. He barely blinked.

'Dad? It's me.' She touched his arm.

The sinewy arm was like steel cord. Shelagh felt the choking sensation of both shock and tears. The matron approached and gently removed her hand. 'Let's wheel him down to the conservatory. Allow me.'

Shelagh stood back and let the other woman take over. In a few minutes they were in the home's vast conservatory overlooking the rear garden, with its well-tended lawn, tasteful water feature and distant sea view.

The matron touched her shoulder. 'Take as much time as you like. I'm closing off the conservatory. No one will disturb you. When you need me, ring that buzzer. The white one, mind. The red one's an alarm, and behind that mesh grill is a speaker. You can talk to me through it, if you need anything.'

Then at last Shelagh and her father were alone. So far he'd uttered not one word, nor had he spared her a single glance. His only eye contact had been with the floors, carpets, his lap, the middle distance. The matron had positioned him at a precise angle; he could watch the outdoors and Shelagh could read his face. But what was there to see except blankness?

She lowered herself on to a nearby chair. All the way to the conservatory, while she trailed behind the matron, Shelagh had been considering what tactics to use. It was clear that he wasn't going to respond to anything she said. So, perhaps she should just talk *at* him. She rummaged in her handbag and pulled out a bar of his favourite chocolate, laying it in his lap. No response.

'The journey up here was pretty tricky. The rain. Absolutely bucketing. And Gordon will persist in driving too fast, whatever the conditions.' She paused. Should she have mentioned Gordon? Her father had never approved of him. *'You can do better than some ex-Army boor. Thick as pigs, no finesse. Boors, all boors.'* Gordon had reciprocated the loathing in full.

With some relief she noticed that the heavens had opened; at least it offered her a talking point. Various residents and their visitors were scrabbling for cover. 'Gosh, looks like I've brought the bad weather with me. Still, we're okay in here.'

Shelagh looked above her through the glass roof. The skies were battleship grey and the rain was falling in stair-rod formation. The hammering on the glass structure surrounding them was momentarily unnerving. She had a sudden fantasy of the watery rods morphing into all-too-real spears, shattering through the glass, piercing them both through the heart.

She sat back, calming her breathing, and tried again to bring some sense of normality to the room. 'The church has got a busy time ahead of it. Christmas is getting closer and closer, so I'll be thinking about my services. Oh, and we have two weddings coming up. St Margaret's is such a perfect church for weddings. Beautiful.' She paused, aware that she was talking too fast, nerves turning her monologue into an incoherent babble. 'And we've started up a toddlers' group in the church hall. And then we have one for older children, up to ten years old, during holidays. It's going really we—'

'He's not ten any more.'

The rain continued battering at the glass, almost drowning out what her father had just muttered. 'What, Dad?' She noticed a slight movement of his shoulder before he spoke.

'I'm telling you, he's not ten any more.'

She stood up and pulled the handle of the wheelchair roughly, juddering her father round to face her fully. 'Dad? What did you say?'

He wouldn't look at her. Instead, painfully, he craned his neck and gawped at the rain bouncing off the conservatory roof. '*Are you a fool? I am telling you, he is not a child any more! His ghost is huge. Angus is an adult now. He's grown up at last! Hah!*'

She found herself shaking his thin frame. 'Dad? What are you talking about? Stop this!'

Once more, his speed astonished her. In one movement he had shoved her away, thrust himself out of the wheelchair and was standing inches from her, his face a twisted sneer. 'You don't believe me, girl. But you'd better believe me because he's coming for you. He told me so! *And your God won't be able to help you!*'

With his final words he had lifted a coffee table and held it above his head, arms and knees trembling with the effort. Then he hurled it towards one side of the conservatory. As the glass shattered with an ear-splitting crash, a flying shard bit into his cheek, opening up a vicious-looking gash. Instinctively Shelagh ducked, hearing the crunch as her heel trod on a broken pane. She ran towards him, holding out her left hand as she did so and punching it into the red alarm button, immediately setting off a deafening siren.

She was too late to catch her father as he toppled. She knelt by him, trying to prop his head up with a cushion snatched from the nearest chair. He was lying supine, staring up at the sheeting rain still attacking the glass roof. Above the cacophony of the rain and shrilling siren, she tried to make herself heard.

'Dad, please. Tell me what's wrong. Angus is gone. *Gone*. He can't be visiting you. He's *dead*! *He was a little*

175

*boy and he's dead! He ca–'* The choking panic cut off her words.

As if in slow motion his bloodied face turned to her, a wide grimace showing brown stained teeth. 'If he's so dead, then you tell me something.' Her father's voice was reedy and she watched his eyes close, the lids trembling.

She shouted above the noise. 'Tell you what, Dad? Tell you what?'

His eyes flickered opened, his stare piercing.

*'Tell me how he's managed to torch the school and burn someone alive!'*

# Thirty

Locked in the welcome seclusion of a small cloak-room, staring back at her bedraggled reflection in the mirror, Shelagh tried to breathe more deeply. *Slow it down, slow it down.* She longed to be in clerical collar and cassock. Somehow, that would have offered her some security, made her feel more in control. For the fifth time she sloshed freezing cold water over her face. The past twenty minutes had been spent weeping and retching over the small white basin in front of her. She turned and drank greedily from the water fountain. Why couldn't she wash the taste of vomit from her mouth?

Wiping her face with a rough paper towel, she stepped backwards and slumped down on a nearby plastic chair. The soft rap on the door made her jump.

'Shelagh?' It was the matron. 'Are you ready for some tea?'

'Er . . . yes, thank you. Be with you in a couple of minutes.' Quickly, she pulled a hairbrush and make-up from her bag to effect what repairs she could, finishing off with a generous spray of perfume. Arm round her shoulders, the matron led her into her office. The GP was finishing a phone call and then joined them.

He cleared his throat, bent his head briefly to the notes in front of him and then began. 'Your father is comfortable upstairs. His wounds have been dressed and he is sleeping under sedation now. I have just arranged to have him transferred tomorrow morning to a ward in the Royal Edinburgh. We can't look after him here any more, I'm afraid. He needs specialist psychiatric care.'

Shelagh accepted the cup of tea offered by the matron and turned to the GP. She had decided to adopt a pose of calm detachment. It was the only way to get through the meeting. 'Doctor, there are a number of things that I simply don't understand about my father's sudden deterioration. And there is something in particular that is baffling me.'

'Yes?'

'How could an old man, who is severely arthritic and isn't eating properly, summon up the energy to throw a heavy table through plate glass?'

The doctor shrugged. 'We can't say. It's really more about what's driving him inside, what's going on in his mind. It's the same with dementia patients who are also physically frail. They can be found wandering miles away from home, having got on a train or bus, going wherever their mind wants to take them. Whatever is driving them won't let physical weakness impede them. It's a very strange and disturbing phenomenon.'

The doctor paused, his look now challenging. 'But I and my psychiatric colleague believe that your father is involved in self-persecutory behaviour.'

Shelagh met his eye without wavering. 'What do you mean?'

The doctor replied firmly, 'I mean that if your father feels overwhelming *guilt*' – the word was given slow, deliberate emphasis – '*and* if he thinks he is being haunted, then that fear will drive him to superhuman efforts to escape.' He shook his head pityingly. 'Sadly, he is trying to run away from the inescapable. Himself.'

It was dark by the time Shelagh saw the headlights of Gordon's car cutting through the rain as he pulled up to the nursing home entrance. She offered a weary farewell wave to the grim-faced matron, who was standing at her office window, and climbed into the car.

Gordon greeted her with a peck on the cheek. 'You really should have let me come earlier. With all that going on, I could have helped. I rang the matron's office you know, after you phoned. She said you were okay.'

They set off, and Shelagh gazed at the shiny black snake of road ahead, the swish of the windscreen wipers offering a soothing rhythm. 'They're putting my father into the Royal Edinburgh. It doesn't get more definitive than that. A mental hospital. That's it then.' She dropped her head into both hands. 'I can't stand it, Gordon. What am I going to do?'

Eyes fixed on the wet road, he placed his hand on hers. 'What are *we* going to do. We're in this together, Shelagh. You can't deal with this on your own. They are not going to keep him in a hospital ward for ever. We'll find another facility.'

'I'm scared, Gordon.'

'Scared?'

She lifted her head, regretting her admission. 'Oh, never mind.' The last thing she was going to do was share with Gordon the close questioning she'd just undergone about her father and Angus. It was all too late; Gordon couldn't help her now. She peered ahead. 'Where are we going? We're on the wrong road.'

'No, we're not. Remember this morning I said I had a surprise for you? I've booked us a couple of rooms at your favourite hotel in St Andrews. And don't worry. I called Sandy. Said that we'd be back after lunch tomorrow. He can hold the fort until then, he's a big boy. An evening and morning of luxury is what you need. You are very, very tired, and after this thing with your father, you really need some pampering.'

She didn't reply, just nodded, hiding her relief that Gordon had booked separate rooms. This 'surprise' clearly wasn't going to be an attempt at reducing the distance that had grown between them. Perhaps he had given up completely on that. He loved her. Slavishly. And like a faithful old dog, loyal to the last, she felt he would always stand by her. Perhaps their companionship would satisfy him long-term. After all, some couples managed to live out their lives quite successfully after the magic had gone.

But would Gordon really be content to see out the rest of his life with no sexual contact between them?

Or with others? In truth, she wouldn't care if he found some pleasure elsewhere. It might be preferable to his drinking, which was getting worse. And what of her needs? Gazing at the hypnotic waves of the wind-screen wipers, she blocked that line of thought. Did she never learn? After all, her own desires had led her only one way.

Into unforgivable transgressions.

# Thirty-one

The day had dragged for Fiona Muir. She'd lost count of the number of times she had checked her watch or glanced at the clock on her office wall. Now it was night. Now it was time. She owned many black clothes, but they were all too smart. So she'd had to do a bit of last-minute shopping. She grinned at her reflection in the full-length bedroom mirror. If the assistant at the local sports shop had known why she was buying a black tracksuit, backpack and balaclava . . .

Strangely, she felt no nervousness. Instead, she experienced a frisson of excitement that was almost sexual, savouring the feeling of anticipation. As she padded down the stairs to the front door of her cottage, she hesitated. Checklist: she had gloves, Maglite, even spare batteries. She grinned again. *You have a natural talent for this, girl. Maybe you should think about a career change.*

But in a moment her excitement had faded. She sat down on the bottom stair, breathing deeply. She suddenly had the overwhelming feeling that events were taking control of her. A year ago she could never have imagined she would be here, contemplating an illegal act. Still, perhaps fate was taking a hand. She shook her head disbelievingly. She had moved back here for a quieter life; it had turned out to be anything but that. She had found and lost love. That had been a bitter blow. Now, worse: the distant past was slapping her in the face. Shelagh Kerr's presence here had awoken dark thoughts in her. And she wasn't alone. Someone else had been similarly affected: the anonymous helper who had guided her here. An ally, or a puppet master pulling her strings? Whoever he was, Murray Shaw's arrival was surely going to be the final catalyst. She took two deep calming breaths. It was funny. She harboured no religious or even spiritual beliefs that she could properly describe. But she had always believed that there had to be a reckoning for bad deeds. *So be it.* Part willingly, part reluctant, she stood up; it was time to let the momentum carry her on.

Before stepping out of the front door and into the cul-de-sac, she poked her covered head out. No one was about. Once on the street she began a slow jogging. *Keep it realistic. You're just another exercise nut who won't let a bit of cold weather stop you.* As she jogged, she thought over the previous night's encounter with Murray. He was proving to be a bit of an enigma. Initially he'd seemed charming, almost flirtatious; now he had changed. More importantly, his early interest in the school, its past, Angus, all of that, seemed to be less of a priority to him now. Strangest, though, was to move his family way up here to *that* house without explaining its significance to them. There must be something else going on with him. What that was, she couldn't be sure.

She slowed down as her destination came into view: the manse. Her safest approach would be via the path at the back of the church. She entered the graveyard slowly, keeping to the shadows. To her left lay the rear entrance of the house. Edging her way to the kitchen door, she reached for the handle and noticed, to her surprise, that her gloved fingers were trembling. *Yes, the adrenaline's pumping now, girl. Stay alert.*

As expected, the door opened easily and she entered quickly, closing it silently behind her. The place was in darkness except for the faint orange glow from the streetlamps out front. At the foot of the stairs she paused, holding her breath. No one should be here. She exhaled loudly. No one was. As she made her way up each flight, guided by the tiniest spot of torchlight, the temptation to stop and look around was almost irresistible. What was their bedroom like? Did Shelagh have sexy lingerie secreted away, to wear beneath those severe cassocks? Hadn't that always been her way – from schoolgirlhood to now – appearing to be demure and respectable while underneath she was something quite other?

On the top landing, Fiona halted. She was at the attic door, just as the written instructions had described. As she reached out for the door's brass handle, which glinted invitingly in the torchlight, she noticed that her fingers were no longer trembling. The door swung open and she climbed the few creaking steps, flicking the Maglite beam from left to right. Nearby she saw a light switch and turned it on. It was safe. There were no windows in here that light could escape from. The bare bulb overhead, swaying slightly from the movement of air, gave out the weakest of glows, so she decided to keep the torch on. The wooden trunk was where she expected it to be: in the far left-hand corner. She made her way across the attic floor. She knelt down to examine the metal hasp. It was hanging loose and she lifted the heavy lid until it was leaning safely against the wall.

The contents were less dusty than she'd expected. The piles of bright blue jotters lay in two neat rows. A quick shuffle through, looking at the covers, told her that they were catalogued by month and year. She pulled out the pile for 1969 and found the jotter for June. Holding the end of the Maglite in her mouth, she used both hands to thumb through the notebook. Stopping at one entry, she nodded and then moved on to the next, and the next.

'*Jesus!*' It was more than she'd expected or even dared to hope for, but exactly what she needed.

Quickly she slammed the notebook shut, shrugged off her empty backpack and began placing all that year's jotters carefully inside. Then she left the trunk as she found it, switched off the attic light and slung the backpack over her shoulders. It was time to go.

Back on the second-floor landing, she froze. She could hear a car – the sound of this one much louder than those she'd heard passing down the lane in the past few minutes. Peering over the banister, she could see the flash of headlights shining through the fanlight above the front door. A car was pulling up outside! In a split second she ran through her options, and then heard a key rattling in the lock. Too late. She was trapped. Two floors up, she crouched and watched. First the hall light was ablaze, followed by an exhausted-looking Shelagh, who was unbuttoning her coat. Next she spied Gordon, carrying a holdall, which he dumped with a loud thump by the coat stand. She struggled to hear what he was saying.

'. . . I know what you mean, Shelagh. It *is* good to be home, and don't worry about the hotel. They'll forgive us for cancelling at such short notice. Do you want a drink?'

'Maybe a nightcap. I'm going straight to bed.'

She heard the reply floating out from the kitchen and was gripped by fear. What if one of them noticed that the back door was unlocked? Would they immediately search the house? Of course not. They would just think that one or other of them had forgotten to lock up properly. She turned to the main problem that faced her: how to get out unnoticed? She'd already discounted trying to climb out of windows or making for the front door as too risky. There was only one thing to do: wait until they were asleep.

As quietly as possible, she stood up. There was no question of going back up to the attic. For one thing the stairs were too creaky. She scanned along the top landing. There were four doors: one at each end and two in the middle. She tried the nearest one, pushing the door open slowly. It was a bedroom with no sign of current occupancy; clearly a guest room. There was a large walk-in wardrobe, en-suite bathroom and a double bed. She moved over to the windows; they looked out over the graveyard and the back of the church lay to her left. For a moment her heart leapt. Maybe she could get out this way. But one glance down showed her the sickening drop below. She'd have to wait.

One advantage of this room was that it overlooked the kitchen windows, and the lights down there had just gone out. Were they on their way up? Rushing to the door, she listened: she could hear one set of footsteps on the stairs and then walking along the landing below. She risked moving out on to her own landing and, peering down to the next floor, saw Shelagh Kerr disappearing into a room at the front of the house. *Surely her husband wouldn't be long now? Come on, come on.* Moments later, she heard heavier footsteps and the sound of glass clinking. She spied over the banister. Gordon Kerr was walking along the hallway, clutching a whisky bottle and tumbler. She pulled back and listened as he approached the first landing. *That's it, hurry up, give your wife that nightcap.* She waited for the sound of the bedroom door opening and closing but nothing happened. Then she heard a shuffle of feet.

'Goodnight, Shelagh. Sleep well.'

The footsteps resumed. *He's coming up to the second landing!* She scurried back into her refuge and left the door slightly ajar, her pulse racing. *Don't come in here! Don't!* She watched the door for a few heart-stopping seconds and then breathed a sigh of relief. He had gone into the room at the far end of the landing; the one directly above his wife's. *That must be his room. They don't sleep together.*

Slowly, she shut the door, moved across the room and sat down on the edge of the bed, prepared to wait patiently until she could escape. Pulling off her backpack, she cradled it on her lap. *So, Shelagh, after all these years, we get to see the real you. A sham marriage. Why? What are you hiding? What would your parishioners say about that?* She patted the bag one last time and then allowed herself to lie back across the end of the bed. *What will they say about who you really are? What you really are?*

Half an hour later the house was silent. Clutching her trainers in one hand, and with her bag of treasures on her back, Fiona began to tiptoe down two flights of stairs. As she crept back along the hallway and into the kitchen, she prayed that the door was still unlocked.

She was in luck. The door opened with ease and she stepped out into the night. Slipping her trainers back on, she checked to see if all was clear before setting off at a gentle jog, unaware of the watching eyes that had been waiting patiently to catch a glimpse of her: the puppet.

# Thirty-two

Rowan stood at the entrance to her driveway and stared over at the church. She was grateful for the biting wind. It would keep her alert. Sleep had come to her only intermittently. She had woken up countless times, on each occasion the realization of what had been happening hitting her afresh, setting off a panic response. Just after six o'clock she'd given up. For the past three hours she had drunk tea, taken the longest of cleansing baths and argued with herself about who to call. Thankfully, Elliot hadn't stirred, nor would he for a while yet.

Eventually, she had texted her best friends – one in South Africa, the other in Thailand – asking them to call when they had time. But she had deliberately kept any sense of urgency out of the brief messages. Knowing how busy they both were, pursuing their careers, it could be days, possibly weeks before they called back. Anyway, she needed to speak to someone she trusted, over a drink, and see their reaction, face to face. Ben had been at his desk by seven, as usual. She didn't have to say much. His response had been immediate. 'I'll fly up on Saturday evening.' Of course he couldn't just drop everything. Saturday would be fine. In fact, she might have more to tell him by then.

She was hesitating. Should she go over to the church and talk with Shelagh Kerr? But what would she say? *'My husband is lying to me and behaving strangely and I think it's to do with your brother.'* Ridiculous. No, for now she should keep away. When she'd had more time to think, perhaps then she could talk to her. After all, she seemed decent. In fact, Shelagh Kerr was a woman she thought she could like quite easily.

It took only a minute to walk around the back of the church and over to the corner of the graveyard where she'd first met Shelagh Kerr. Rowan crouched down to read the tombstone's inscription. Then she stood up and walked the short journey to the library.

Rowan's enquiry was dealt with promptly, the young librarian guiding her to a corner of the main reading area. 'The local press archives for 1969 aren't online yet. You'll have to use a microfilm reader and print off what you want.' She paused to look at Rowan. 'It's funny. This is the second request for that year I've had in the last couple of weeks. I had a guy ask for exactly the same thing. Quite a coincidence, eh?'

'Oh, really?'

'Yes, I haven't seen him around before. He spent a good while here. Don't know exactly what he was looking into. He didn't say. What's your area of interest?'

'Oh . . . I'm a journalist. Just looking into local history, local events. It's for a series on the sixties.'

The librarian's interest faded as she looked over her

shoulder and saw that a queue was forming at the issue desk. 'We're understaffed today. I'll need to get back. Do you know how to use this machine?'

'Yes, I've used many over the years. Thanks very much for your help.'

Rowan settled into the quiet corner, loaded the film and began.

She avoided going to the café on the main road that she'd visited before. It was too close to Murray's hotel. On reflection, perhaps it wasn't such a good idea for him to stay in the area. Maybe she should call him and ask him to find somewhere in the city centre.

She sat on a bench in the park looking across the wide expanse of grass to the distant Pentland Hills. The cold day had kept the place deserted and, grateful for the peaceful surroundings, once more she looked over the news reports she'd found. She'd missed the significance of the quote from the family friend on initial reading. But looking at it again, she now realized what it meant.

'They had to move on. In particular, St Margaret's House, once the home of a fine and decent family, has become tainted by tragedy.'

St Margaret's House. Murray had lied to her. He'd said that the place wasn't called that in those days. But there was more.

## CHILD WITNESS

The search continues for a child, thought to be a boy, who was seen running from the back of the school on the afternoon of the fire. The child was wearing shorts and was carrying what may have been a cricket bat. Police are concerned that this child could be a vital witness, possibly a school pupil, who is afraid to come forward. Teachers and parents are being invited to encourage their children to admit if they were in the school that day.

Could it be? Could that child witness have been Murray? Had he been there, seen something or, heaven forbid, been involved? *No, don't be ridiculous. There must be another explanation for his strange behaviour. There has to be.* She leafed through the articles but there were no more mentions of the child. All the subsequent coverage had concentrated on the janitor, the main suspect, and his eventual release. She crumpled the article in her lap. The world around her, her new life, was beginning to seem unreal. Suddenly she had the sensation of being stranded on that bench, unable to move or control where she went.

'Do you mind?'

She twisted round. An elderly man, holding a newspaper in one gloved hand and unclipping the leash of a Jack Russell terrier with the other, was smiling down at her. 'May I sit?'

She waved a hand in welcome. 'Of course, please.'

The old man lowered himself slowly on to the bench. 'On you go, Fudge, have a good runaround.'

He tracked the small dog as it bounded away. 'Looks like we've got the park all to ourselves, eh? The cold's keeping the regulars away, I suppose. Not hardy enough.' He turned to look at her. 'What brings you out here?'

'I just fancied some fresh air. It's a lovely spot.'

He turned his attention back to his dog; the animal was racing away at breakneck speed to the far side of the park, yapping exuberantly. 'She does love being off the leash, the old girl. Aye, it is a lovely spot. I've not seen you here before. You visiting?'

She smiled as the little dog began running in circles, its shrill barking more manic than ever. 'No, I've moved here. From London.'

'London, eh? You'll find it a bit of a change here, then. Much quieter. It's busier in the city centre, mind. Good shops and all that. But this place, it's slower, not much happens round h–' He broke off to shout at his dog and then stood up. 'I'm sorry, I'll need to go and get Fudge. She's spoiling for a fight with that big brute of a mongrel over there. She can't resist it. Jack Russells, I tell you. Napoleon complex, every last one of them.'

Only half listening, Rowan watched as he hobbled off. Turning to her right, she noticed that he had left his newspaper. Grabbing it, she stood up. 'Excuse m–' She bit off the last word and dropped back on to the bench, staring disbelievingly at the front page, the banner headline screaming out at her: BODY FOUND IN LOCAL SCHOOL BLAZE. Rowan could feel the panic rising. She skim-read the piece rapidly and then stood up. Keeping her pace moderate until she reached the park gates, she then broke into a run, heading for the house.

All was quiet. Elliot was obviously still in bed. She stepped quietly over to the corner of the living room where her laptop was set up. Moments later she was calling up as many online stories about the fire as she could. She checked the chronology of events. It had happened on Friday night, just before she and Elliot had arrived.

Rowan sat back, frowning at the screen. Didn't she have trouble getting hold of Murray on the phone that night? He'd said he'd passed out in front of the TV. *Alibi.* She tried to block the word from her mind but it stuck there. *Why can't you think of this as a coincidence? Why did you automatically link Murray's name to this as soon as you saw the headline?*

She lifted the phone and called his mobile.

'Hello?' He sounded tired.

'It's me.' She kept her voice steady, determined to maintain a neutral tone. 'Did you know there had been a fire at the school? Someone's dead.'

There was a pause. 'Yes, why?' He seemed unruffled by the question.

'When did you find out?'

Another pause. 'Can't remember. Must have seen it on the local news or read it in the paper.'

She found that hard to believe. The weekend had been a round of non-stop unpacking and she didn't recall the radio or TV being on; certainly no newspapers had been bought. No one would have had time to read them.

'Rowan?' His tone had softened. 'Are you all right? I'm missing you ... It's such a mess. Sorry. I'm so sorry.'

Her own voice took on an icier edge. 'I don't know how I am. I need to think. Have some space.' She sighed, unsure how to phrase what she wanted to say. 'Look, Murray. I don't feel comfortable with you staying so close. I'd like you to get a room in town. Just for a few days. With you just up the road ... well, Elliot could bump into you. And so could I.'

She waited, half expecting him to explode at the suggestion, accuse her of overreacting, which she may well have been. Nevertheless, she wanted him completely out of the way while she thought things over.

Silence. Had he hung up? No. She heard his breathing. 'Fine. I won't contact you. I'll leave that up to you. By the way, you can keep hold of our car. Public transport will do me just fine.'

'Murray ... Murray?' This time he had hung up.

She slumped back in her seat, glancing around the room. *This beautiful room in this beautiful house. A house I don't think I can live in.* The feeling from the park was back. Again, she had the sensation of floating, alone, stranded, unable to get a hold on reality. *But this is reality and you need to find a way of getting through it. Look at it logically. As a set of problems, something to investigate. Like work.*

Sitting up straight, she began tapping away at the

keyboard, a sense of purpose beginning to take her over. Her aim? To search for any and all references to that dreadful event in 1969 until she finally found out the truth.

Even if that truth destroyed her family.

# Thirty-three

Murray threw his mobile on to the unmade bed and stood at the window, feeling utterly drained. Below, the main road was busy with traffic and shoppers. One thing he wasn't going to do was move out of Corstorphine. He needed to be near the house, to get back in there soon. But how? A yawning chasm was developing between him and Rowan. Only one thing gave him hope. If she *had* wanted to end it all, she would have said so already. No, she was obviously thinking things through. But what decision was she likely to reach? *Prepare yourself for the end. It may come. But don't be afraid. And if you lose everything else, make sure that you keep the house.*

As he watched the queue of cars, nose to tail, he caught sight of a figure weaving in and out of them. Fiona Muir was making a final dash to his side of the road, clutching a dark backpack. He raced down the hotel stairs to the lobby, just as the receptionist was calling his room.

'Hello, Murray.' She looked different from the last time he'd seen her: flushed, excited. 'Can we talk somewhere private? Your room?'

Caught off-guard, he looked around guiltily, half expecting Rowan to come rushing in, checking that he was moving out. 'Yes ... okay. The room's not been done, so it's a bit untidy.'

'That doesn't matter, come on.'

Upstairs, he showed her to the two armchairs at the far side of the room. Immediately she began pulling what looked like old school jotters from her backpack.

'Before I explain these, I have a lot to tell you. Things have ... well, moved far more quickly than I expected.'

He couldn't fathom her expression. Triumphant? Challenging? 'What are you talking about, Fiona?'

Carefully, she placed the pile of notebooks on the coffee table between them and then sat back, taking a few seconds to make herself comfortable. 'Soon after Shelagh and her husband came to live here last year there was a Christmas event at the village hall, near the church. She and her husband had organized the whole thing. It was a sort of "get to know the new minister" community do and was better fun than I expected. There was a live band, booze, all that.'

He watched as she stood up and, clearly restless, moved towards the window. Staring down at the bustling street, she went on. 'It's funny. I remember the evening so well. The atmosphere, the deep snow. Anyway, I'd had a few drinks and was in the toilets, when I overheard a bit of chit-chat from the older locals, saying how amazing it was that she had the strength to come back, to be near Angus. They were obviously impressed by Gordon too.' She paused for a moment. 'In fact they couldn't get over what a lovely couple they were, and were revelling in the fact that Shelagh had been a prison chaplain working among "dreadful murderers and rapists", as they called them. She had a ready-made fan club.' Fiona glanced over her shoulder to check that he was still listening to her.

He felt emotionally exhausted, but was worried too. *Where the hell is all this going? Will it help or hinder me?*

She seemed oblivious of his growing unease and rattled on. 'At one point there was some carol singing. Then, during "In the Bleak Midwinter", I noticed something.'

'What did you see?' Murray followed her progress as she moved from the window and made a circuit of the room. She seemed like a caged animal, wired and ready for escape. Finally, she ended up back at the window.

'It was Shelagh. She had turned away and seemed to be near to tears. I watched her slip out the hall by a side exit. I followed her but she was nowhere to be seen, so I decided to take a walk around the churchyard. It looked incredibly pretty, blanketed in snow, shimmering in the moonlight. It really was like a Christmas-card scene, and the snow had made everything so quiet.'

She paused, turning to face him. 'I wonder about life sometimes. About fate.' She waved her hand towards the pile of jotters. 'That brought me – brought us – here.'

He breathed in deeply. 'Go on. Tell me what happened.'

She turned away again. 'I was shuffling through the

snow like a child, my boots kicking at the drifts. I even thought, drunkenly, about building a snowman! Then I heard it.'

'Heard what?'

She kept him waiting a moment longer. 'Two things. Talking and sobbing. I thought I was imagining it at first, but I followed the sound anyway. It was so quiet, no one could have heard me. I found Shelagh in the corner. She was talking to Angus's grave, obviously tearful. Maybe she'd had as much to drink as me, who knows?'

Murray swallowed hard. 'What was she saying?'

There was no reply from Fiona at first. Then she walked slowly back to the armchair. 'I remember it well. She said, "I'm sorry. Dad is still alive but ill, dead inside. Mother is gone, of course. I'm sorry, so sorry. Forgive me. I'm here now, Angus. To be good. To make up for everything."'

# Thirty-four

Fiona was wide-eyed as she carried on with her tale. 'I think she was more shocked to see me standing there in the snow than I was to see her crouching down at the grave. I knew whose grave it was. When I first came back here I went to look at it. Lavinia is buried in Aberdeenshire, where she was born, so Angus's grave is the only physical reminder of what happened.'

'What did she do?' Murray asked.

'Nothing at first. There was, I suppose, a moment of mutual awkwardness, embarrassment. Suddenly she seemed anxious to get away, to get back to the hall. For days afterwards I thought and thought about what I had seen, what I had heard. I didn't mention it to anyone. And then, about a week later, she invited me over to the church, ostensibly to discuss some school business.'

'Ostensibly?'

'Oh, yes. That wasn't her real reason to get me over there. She had quite a frosty air about her. I asked her why she had come back, said that I had overheard her talking about making up for something when I saw her at Angus's grave. Shelagh said that she was on her final "spiritual journey of healing" in getting over the loss of her brother. When I asked her how she felt about no one ever being caught for the fire, she became colder than ever and didn't answer. She could see it in my eyes and I could see it in hers. There was no getting away from that time she'd threatened me when we were kids.'

Murray leaned forward, suddenly uncomfortable in the constricting chair. 'I don't understand.' He gestured to the pile of jotters. 'What have these got to do with all this?'

Fiona raised a hand. 'Just bear with me. As she showed me out, dear Reverend Shelagh had a parting shot. She said that she had no doubt that I'd respect her feelings about Angus as she'd respect mine about my aunt, and would leave the matter to rest. After all, we both had something we wished to keep private. In life and love. She stressed the word *love*, made it sound like the threat that it was.'

'Threat?'

'I think – no, I'm *certain* – that it was a reference to a relationship I had had before she arrived. It was with the previous head teacher. He was married and left the school because of it. It was very messy. I thought it had been our secret; I wouldn't have got his job if it was public knowledge. But I guess someone knew and that someone told Shelagh Kerr.'

Murray studied the woman before him. He was beginning to become familiar with her gestures and body language. She was driven. But not in the way he was, not with the fears he had. She was waiting for some sort of response.

He began talking slowly. 'I'm not sure about your idea of a "threat". But look. Perhaps she simply wanted to return to where she was brought up, have a quiet life. I've done that, you've done the same. It's perfectly possible that she wanted to be near Angus's grave or closer to her sick father.'

'Oh, yeah?' Fiona smirked.

He ignored the interruption. 'And anyway, what business is it of yours or mine or anyone else's? And look, why are you telling *me* all this?'

'I'll tell you why it's our business. I want you to have a look at something.' She handed him one of the jotters. 'Now, please.'

It was a command more than a request. She pointed to the left-hand page. The writing was that of a young person's, though joined up and surprisingly neat.

*7 June 1969*
*The deed is done. Two of them have gone. That was a mistake.*
*It was only meant for one.*

### Revenge

*No one will ever know my true pain,*
*What hell I now live in.*
*I was an innocent,*
*Love was killed.*
*So, a life for a life it is,*
*A sister's life avenged.*
*A wretched brother's life gone,*
*And so deserved!*

Murray looked up at her. 'What the hell is this?' He quickly flicked through the thin jotter and then closed it to look at the cover. The same handwriting appeared on the front.

DATE: *June 1969*
NAME: *Shelagh Gillan*

# Thirty-five

Fiona broke the silence. 'Yes, that's right. It's hers.'

Murray looked up at her again. He knew what he'd read, but it wasn't sinking in. She leaned over and took the jotter away from him, adding it to the pile on the table. 'These are a gift. Literally. They were given to me.'

He had to keep his breathing even, his face impassive. 'Where did you get them?'

She remained leaning towards him, her eyes fixed on the jotter. 'When we first met I know you didn't believe a word I said about Shelagh Kerr. Don't deny it. It's perfectly understandable. The thing is, soon after she moved here, I began to get letters . . . no, rather they were notes. Notes about *her*.'

She looked at him, triumphantly. 'I told you there was someone else around here who knows things about Shelagh. And the notes have escalated since you arrived. They're more detailed, more . . . helpful.' She paused for a moment. 'They are anonymous, and initially were sent to my home. All must have been hand delivered – a bit risky since I live in a small cul-de-sac. Then they started being sent to the school – always sealed in two envelopes, so that if my secretary ignores the private headings and opens the first envelope, she will come across another envelope similarly marked.'

Murray began to feel cold. He stayed silent for a while, his mouth dry. Finally he asked, 'So what were they like, what did they say?'

He watched, fascinated, as she reached into her bag and handed him a well-worn envelope. 'This was the first one.'

Carefully he removed the single sheet of notepaper. The handwriting was in small capital letters, picked out in black ink.

DEAR MISS MUIR

I BELIEVE THAT YOU HAVE HAD SOME RATHER NEGATIVE CONTACT WITH OUR NEW REVEREND. I HAVE HAD A SIMILAR EXPERIENCE. I BELIEVE SHE WILL DO WHAT SHE CAN TO KEEP HER DREADFUL SECRET UNTOLD. UNTIL THERE IS PROOF OF WHAT SHE DID TO LITTLE ANGUS AND YOUR AUNT, I WOULD URGE YOU TO REMAIN QUIET. I WILL CONTACT YOU WHEN I CAN. IT MAY NOT BE OFTEN. IT IS DIFFICULT FOR ME.

He handed back the note, shaking his head. 'What do the other ones say? Have you any idea who they're from?'

She reached for the piece of paper and laid it on top of the pile of jotters. 'Since Shelagh moved back at the end of last year, I've had five notes including the one that said she was seen near the school the night of the fire. They have been much in the same vein as the one you've just read. Until the last one. It was very specific. It said that if I went to the manse yesterday evening, the Kerrs would be away all night. I was to go up to the top floor and, in the attic, I would find a trunk with old school jotters in it. There, I would read something very interesting. What you've seen is only a tiny part. There's loads of very disturbing stuff.'

She laid a hand back on the pile. 'As to who is doing this? I think they've overheard conversations between me and Shelagh. I also think it's an older person, hence the rather formal 'Miss Muir'. Maybe they're connected to the church in some way – that place has hordes of volunteers: doing flowers, cleaning, you name it. Same with the office, especially if they're preparing for a church or charity event. And I've seen people coming in and out of the manse many a time. Or perhaps it's someone at the school.' She patted the pile of jotters. 'I do think your moving back here has been an extra catalyst. Most of all, that's why I'm telling you this. It's no coincidence. Whoever's helping me knows that you're back, knows who you are.'

The thought disturbed him and he stood up. 'There's no proof that this person knows anything about me. That's *your* supposition. And I don't know what to make of these jotters, but I'm not sure you should have taken them.'

'Why not?' She got to her feet to face him. 'They're proof.'

He shook his head. 'Perhaps. But they're just as likely to be the adolescent outpourings of a very hurt and grieving girl.'

'And my note writer?'

He walked over to the window. 'I don't know.'

'And the fire. The body? My note writer seeing her near there that night?'

He turned to face her, his head throbbing. The room's stuffiness was becoming unbearable. 'All right, *all right*! What do you want me to do? You have your proof. *Take it to the police!*'

She walked over to join him at the window. 'If you care about Angus and what happened' – her tone softened – 'at least try to support me.'

He took a step away from her. 'What are you going to do?'

'I'm not sure. My note writer asked me to hold back. They said there would be something better soon. But I'm inclined not to go to the police at the moment, anyway. Like you've implied, they'd laugh at me. I've got *my* position to think of. I feel stuck, but perhaps I can scare the horses a bit.'

'What do you mean?'

He watched as she turned away and began stuffing the jotters into her backpack. Weighed down, she stood at the door, her expression solemn.

'I think I'll pay Reverend Shelagh a visit. Very soon.'

# Thirty-six

Rowan pushed her way through the arrivals hall. Gatwick airport was busier than she'd ever remembered it. Hurrying down to the train station, she was relieved to see the Brighton service waiting at the platform. Soon she would be seeing someone who might just be able to give her some straight answers about her new home and what had happened there.

She settled herself into a quiet corner seat, closed her eyes as the train pulled slowly away and thought over the past few hours. The early morning flight from Edinburgh had been a torment of guilt and doubt. Elliot had been fine about her having to make the trip at very short notice. Yes, he could kill half a day in Brighton, no problem. But then she had hesitated. What if her visit took longer? If something went wrong and she was delayed? She couldn't, or rather she *wouldn't*, consider leaving him on his own for any length of time at the moment. Yes, she had to admit that part of her didn't trust him, but mainly she didn't trust the situation. By now, she hoped Murray was well away, staying in Edinburgh city centre, but she wanted to play it absolutely safe. There was no way of knowing what might happen if he and Elliot met accidentally. With emotions between them running so high, it was better by far to keep them apart.

The solution had presented itself quite unexpectedly. Elliot had already made contact with an old school friend who had moved to Glasgow a year ago. She knew the mother and the boy. He'd broken his collarbone at rugby and was having a couple of weeks' recuperation at home and was bored. Both boy and mother said they'd welcome Elliot spending the day with them.

Rowan thought back to the morning and how he had seemed perfectly happy as she loaded him on to the Glasgow-bound train. He'd asked surprisingly few questions about what she was doing. She had tried to reassure him, saying that it was something she had to do concerning Murray, but his expression had hardened. With a sinking heart, she began to face the real possibility that he would never again accept Murray. If that was the case then she would have no choice. But there was a way to go yet, she hoped.

She paid the taxi driver and took a step back, looking upwards. The building was an imposing seafront Regency mansion block. Checking the scrap of paper in her hand, she selected the numbered buzzer she wanted. A male voice answered and asked her to look in the camera and state who she was. He then told her to make her way to the fifth floor. As the lift doors parted, a corresponding door directly in front of her was opened.

'Ms Shaw? Please come in.'

She shook the offered hand. 'Hello, Mr Baxter.

Thanks so much for agreeing to see me and at such short notice.'

Her host led the way into a vast, high-ceilinged room which had a breathtaking view of the sea. Rowan stood in wonder for a moment, gazing through the huge windows.

'Rather spectacular, isn't it?'

She turned to him. 'Completely. A view like that must brighten up every waking moment.'

'What a lovely way to put it. It's true. Now, let me have your coat and, please, take a seat. I have tea with lemon at this time of day. Will you join me?'

She sank into the comfortable leather wing-backed chair. 'Thank you, Mr Baxter.'

'Please, call me Viv. I hate unnecessary formality.' His voice still held a trace of a Scottish accent, but was heavily anglicized. She wondered how long he had been living down here. Probably many years, if not decades.

She studied him as he prepared the drinks. By her calculation, he had to be about seventy or more, but he looked considerably younger. Exceptionally tall, he was lean, fit and tanned. The depth of his tan made her think that either he regularly spent time abroad or he kept a boat. His dark hair had precious little grey showing, and the rimless designer glasses accentuated the strong bone structure of his face. Dressed in a smart fitted shirt, faded jeans and brown ankle boots, exhibiting a younger man's taste, he carried off the ensemble with ease. She took in her surroundings.

Apart from the period furniture and fireplace, the walls were hung with a few select pieces of artwork. On the baby grand piano in the corner stood an array of photographs of a deeply tanned white-haired man aged about sixty, both individual portraits and shots of him with her host. The men were clearly partners.

Eventually he settled himself in front of her. 'You've come a long way at short notice. I'm perfectly happy to see you. I covered that fire in some detail, and it was a very big story for me. I haven't forgotten it. But I just wondered. Why the hurry?'

Rowan thought back to their telephone conversation the day before. She had eventually made contact with him after a few well-placed calls to fellow journalists. He had seemed open and willing to share his knowledge of the story. Now, having met the man, she felt even more uncomfortable about having to spin any further the lie she'd started over the phone. 'Like I said, I've moved up to Edinburgh from London to live in Corstorphine. I found out about the fire recently and wanted to know more. I have a journalistic background in the national dailies. But I'm taking a career break. My husband's starting a new job. I've time on my hands – too much time – and I don't want to be idle. I'm not sure what I have in mind exactly. A lengthy article, a book? I don't know what interest there may still be. But it's still an unsolved case.'

She offered her final explanation. 'As a chief reporter who covered the story over the years, I thought you'd be the prime person to start with.'

The man was obviously thinking through what she'd said. 'I think the only interest would be if you could solve the case. Is that what you're trying to do?'

'Well, what journalist wouldn't?'

He sipped at his tea. 'I sense there's something else that's driving you. Am I right?'

She'd been waiting for this, having deliberately, albeit guiltily, kept it out of their initial telephone conversation. 'You *are* right. I have . . . well, a personal, *almost* personal, reason. I'm living in the house where Angus lived.'

His eyes opened wide. 'Wow. Not intentionally, I assume? No. Well, I can understand your interest. It's important to know the history of one's home. It's funny. I remember St Margaret's House rather well. A lovely bit of architecture.'

'You've been there?' Rowan was surprised.

'Oh, yes. I struck up a useful relationship with the investigating officer, Jimmy McCabe. Poor bloke. I think the case just about did for him. Jimmy was convinced that it was the janitor, absolutely convinced.' Her host stopped to squeeze more lemon into his tea. 'Anyway, he arranged for me to see the grieving family. As you'll have seen from the coverage, they never gave any on-the-record interviews, but I got to see them a few times, for background use only.'

'Really?' This was better than Rowan had expected. 'And what were your impressions?'

He got up suddenly and stepped over to a bureau, returning with a battered box file. 'I've been going through my notes and cuttings since you called.' He laughed. 'I've never thrown anything out from my old journalistic days. Can't bear to. Looking through this brought the whole thing back of course, and it brought back one element in particular.'

Rowan waited.

The old man offered her a piercing look, his features taut. 'The atmosphere – of the house, of the case. I'd like to visit that house now, see if it has changed. I'm sure it has if you're living there. Back then I thought it had a rather dark feel to it, and I don't mean the decor. In fact, physically it was light and airy, a lovely house. I think the atmosphere came from the people who lived there. Something was clearly wrong, and it wasn't just to do with the little boy's death.'

'How do you mean?' Rowan felt a tingle of apprehension.

'There was something off about that family. I think it had to do with the father.' He raised a hand to deflect the obvious reaction. 'I don't mean sexual abuse. No, it wasn't that. It was tricky because Robert Gillan worked for the Church, and in those days that was ultra respectable. No one was going to say anything about him other than that he was an upstanding member of the community, model husband and father. Still, I heard little bits here and there about the family, most of it after they had moved away.'

He tapped the box file with his finger. 'I continued to keep a watching brief on things, you see. My journalistic nose getting the better of me. Anyway, I did hear some *very* intriguing things from a long-time friend of Ruth Gillan. The friend's dead now. Apparently Robert Gillan was a manic depressive and paranoiac. He could get very nasty at times. The friend said that Ruth Gillan managed to put up with it mainly because her husband was away on business so much.'

'Right. And I suppose things were worse in those days. I mean, mental illness having a really bad stigma then?'

'Absolutely,' Viv agreed. 'But there's more. This friend said that she thought Ruth Gillan was having an affair. Had been having an affair for years, and that – get this.'

'What?'

'That Robert Gillan might not have been Angus's father.'

'Good grief.' Rowan was astonished. 'Really?'

He nodded vigorously. 'This friend said that Ruth was a very private woman, but she'd asked her out-right. The woman said Ruth denied it, but the *way* she denied it left the friend believing she was right.'

# Thirty-seven

Viv exhaled loudly. 'But whether that was true, whether Robert Gillan knew, whether it was a factor, I just don't know. Though if Gillan did kill Angus and that teacher, he got his just deserts up to a point.'

'How do you mean?'

He took a deep breath. 'The irony is that Gillan really lost the plot mentally after Angus's death. Whatever mental illness existed before the tragedy took hold of him completely afterwards.' He looked at her. 'Crippling depression, anxiety, paranoia, the whole shooting match. Symptoms of guilt? Anyway, the Church kept his job open, but he ceased to function. I understand they pensioned him off generously, but he was in and out of psychiatric facilities after that. I don't know if he's still alive.'

'Neither do I.'

Her host shook his head. 'I doubt it. I wouldn't be surprised if he'd done himself in by now. Anyway, the family moved away pretty quickly. I managed to find out where to via Jimmy McCabe, who was still plugging away at the case, five years on. I did a follow-up piece for one of the Sunday supplements. Robert Gillan, his wife and . . . what was the daughter's name?'

'Shelagh.' Rowan was tempted to tell him what

Angus's sister was doing now and where she was living, but held back. *Golden rule: let your interviewee talk. Let them fill the silences.*

'Shelagh. Yes. Pretty – rather beautiful in fact, though it was kept well hidden. Father's instructions, no doubt. And she was very quiet, timid. Anyway, I managed to get to see them. Robert Gillan was too incapacitated by then to object. They were living in a remote loch-side house up towards Inverness. Well, I tell you. If I thought St Margaret's House had a creepy atmosphere, this place was twenty times worse.'

'Did you meet all three of them?'

'Oh, yes. It was awful. Robert Gillan sat in a corner, staring out at the loch and saying not one word. Shelagh made the tea and was extraordinarily polite but didn't add much. And the mother said the expected things. The family was destroyed by grief and, yes, they were pleased that the police were still investigating. She didn't sound or look very pleased though. They managed to go outside so that my photographer could shoot some pictures of them by the water, and that was that. I felt very sad for the mother and daughter.' He sighed. 'And a few months later, she was dead.'

'Dead? What happened?'

'You mean you don't know?' Viv looked surprised.

Rowan shook her head, anxiety rising.

'Well.' Viv sat forwards. 'Nearly six years after Angus died, Ruth Gillan travelled to Edinburgh, to Corstorphine. St Margaret's House was owned by a small charity then. Ironically, a mental health one. In fact, I found out later that Ruth Gillan was being helped by them. Anyway, the place was unoccupied at the time. Being refurbished.'

He paused. 'She was found by workmen, dead from an overdose. In the summerhouse.'

Rowan felt chilled to the bone.

Viv reached across and touched her hand gently. 'Are you okay? I'm sorry, I didn't mean to upset you.'

The soft touch of his hand roused her. 'Oh . . . I . . . it's okay. I'm just . . . well, a bit . . . ' Momentarily she tailed off, but she was determined not to make any mention of the arson attack on the summerhouse. 'Did Ruth Gillan leave a note or anything?'

Vic shook his head. 'It seems not. But it's odd. The police said there was evidence of her having been looking around the house.'

'Looking around?'

'Yes. Very odd.'

'And what happened to Shelagh and Robert Gillan?' Rowan asked.

'Last I heard, she went off to university and her father became a recluse in that godforsaken Highlands house.'

Rowan tried to recover herself. She knew it was time. 'Viv, there is something else that's driven me to look back into all of this.'

'What's that then?'

'This will be an enormous surprise, I'm sure. But Shelagh Gillan is back living in Corstorphine. Believe it or not, she is the minister of St Margaret's Church.'

She watched as his features turned from puzzle-ment to astonishment. 'My God, you *are* joking!'

They'd spent the past half-hour walking along the seafront. Rowan had done her best to gather what she could from the retired journalist. Now they were sitting on a bench, drinking takeaway coffees and watching seagulls swooping down to the shore.

Rowan had allowed the conversation to drift, let-ting the old man talk about his life, how he'd given up journalism and trained as a clinical psychologist, finally retiring happily with his partner to the coast. But she was getting anxious about the time and she still hadn't raised her chief concern. 'Tell me, what's your overall feeling about what happened that day?'

He blew at the steaming coffee while following the swooping gulls with his eyes. 'I think you can gather from what I've said that I believe the reason for Angus's death lies in the family. This wasn't about some aggrieved janitor. I think Robert Gillan is where the answer's to be found. I believe it was done with the intention of incriminating the janitor, by using his petrol supplies. Gillan would have been up to the school for parents' days, would have known the set-up, where the janitor's shed was.'

Rowan looked at him. 'But why? Even if he knew Angus wasn't his son, it's an awful thing to even con-template.'

'I know. But this was an act of fury, and I believe that Robert Gillan was a very, very angry man. Angry with life. Remember, both victims were knocked unconscious *before* the fire was set and then left to be burnt alive. That's an act of fury.'

As they began strolling back towards the flat, she slowed her pace. 'In the early coverage, there was talk of a child witness, maybe a boy who might have been at the school. What became of that?'

'Ah yes.' He nodded. 'A local sweetshop owner thought she'd seen someone she assumed was a pupil, a boy, running from the school that day. But she seemed to be less sure the more she was asked. Besides, once the main focus was on the poor bloody janitor, that line of enquiry wasn't pursued.'

'Did you talk to the sweetshop owner?'

'Oh, yes. I interviewed her twice. Why? What's your interest?'

Rowan felt that she had to be on her guard once again. 'Oh, I just wondered.'

He squinted, as if trying to recall something. 'I remember there was a very short period when Jimmy McCabe was looking into the possibility that the whole thing might have been carried out by a child or a group. The product of bullying.' He turned to her, smiling. 'Police methods and indeed ways of chasing lines of enquiry were more limited in those days. No 24-hour TV news or World Wide Web to keep hammering away at theories, either.' He looked away again. 'Anyway, that notion went away very quickly when Jimmy decided that the case against the janitor was the one to go for. The child seen by the sweetshop owner was dismissed as a potential witness who couldn't be identified.'

'Did you ever interview the janitor? I mean, after he was released?'

He shook his head. 'No, wish I had, poor sod. He seemed to disappear into the ether. Not surprising. Mud sticks.'

She let the silence lie as they walked, knowing that she had to choose her next words carefully. 'I know what you've said about Robert Gillan, but do you think there could be any credence in the child-bullying theory? The boy was seen with a cricket bat, after all. A weapon to beat the victims with? Kids can do terrible things sometimes, can't they?'

They had reached the mansion block's front door. Pausing, he looked at her. 'I agree. It *is* possible, I suppose. A pupil would have known about the janitor's shed, the petrol, all of that. But beating them both? Including an adult?' He paused again, thinking it through. 'If they were well-aimed hits and the victims were sitting down, unsuspecting, it's possible, I suppose.'

He ushered her into the smart lobby and stopped at the lift. 'If it *did* involve a young boy, then he must have been very ill. And I'll tell you something else.'

Rowan looked up at him. 'What's that?'

'I'd be terrified to come across him today.'

# Thirty-eight

Elliot was pleased with himself. Having hopped off the Glasgow-bound train at the first stop after Edinburgh, he'd delivered the lie to his friend's mother with ease. She had sounded rushed and readily accepted the story that his own mother's business trip had been cancelled. Even if she rang his mother's mobile to check, it would be okay. He had taken the phone from her bag before they'd left the house. He hated all the deception, but it was necessary. In fact it was essential if he was to help her, to save her even.

He stood at the bus stop near the Trinity Hotel and finished his cigarette. On his way through Corstorphine, he'd seen the woman Murray had been with at the hotel. She was going into the local school. He'd assumed she must be a teacher, and then another woman had called to her, addressing her as 'Ms Muir'. The school's welcome board completed the picture. *Head teacher: Ms Fiona Muir.* The other thing that hadn't escaped his notice was the fire-blackened ruin of one entire wing of the school, cordoned off by police tape.

He ground the cigarette butt out under his trainer, straightened his clothes, and went into the hotel, heading for reception. As expected, Murray Shaw was still registered as a guest there. Three minutes later, he appeared.

'What are you doing here, Elliot?'

Elliot struggled to control his voice, the bored-looking receptionist clearly determined to eavesdrop. He turned his back to her and hissed at Murray. 'Let's go to your room. *Now*. I mean it, unless you want me to make a scene.'

He watched as Murray looked over his shoulder, quickly assessed the situation and, without a word, began leading him towards the stairs.

Before the door was shut, Elliot held up his hand, jabbing a finger at his stepfather. 'Why are you still here? Mum said you were moving into town.' He slammed the door shut and stood, arms crossed, legs apart, waiting for an answer.

Murray seemed momentarily taken aback. 'I . . . I am going to move. Soon.'

Elliot stood his ground. 'Mum thinks you've moved already. What's the big delay? There's not exactly a shortage of hotel rooms in central Edinburgh.' He wondered what tactic Murray would use. His step-father had to be furious with him, but that approach would be futile. Elliot waited.

Murray moved towards him as he spoke. 'Look, Elliot, can we calm down and talk about this properly? Believe me, I didn't want things to turn out like this.'

Elliot stepped away. 'Then how did you want them to turn out, *exactly*?'

'I just wanted us to be happy, living in a lovely place,

as a family. It was just a coincidence. The house coming up when I was looking. The redundancy . . . well, that's complicated.'

'I don't believe you. I think you planned all this. I just don't know why. I think all that money that's missing from your account has something to do with it.' Elliot could see that he'd hit home. 'Yes, I know all about that. Mum's worried about it and I think you owe her an explanation.' He tracked Murray's movement across the room until he sat down on the edge of the bed.

'There is nothing to worry about. The money was needed for work on the house. I paid cash to get a significant discount. Look, Elliot, it's clear that you can't stand the sight of me at the moment, but that's no reason to see demons where none exist. I made a mistake in not telling your mother about the house, about my job. That's it.' He sighed, shaking his head. 'I loved that house as a child. Angus was my friend. Why shouldn't I live in his old home, forty years on?'

'What happened the day Angus died?' Elliot uncrossed his arms and took a step forward. 'What did you do?'

'What do you mean, what did *I* do?'

'Oh, come on! First the fire in the back garden, then the fire at the school. Someone's dead because of that. I don't believe in coincidences. You know what I *do* believe? Either you had something to do with those or someone's sending you a pretty powerful message. A message from the past.'

He waited for the denial. Instead, Murray just kept staring at him, blankly. Then he stood up.

Elliot inched backwards, anxious to be near the door. 'Well?'

'Elliot, I know you've been troubled this past year or two, and moving away from all that you know isn't easy. I understand that. But this . . . this rubbish you're coming out with is simply delusional.' He stepped forwards. 'Why don't you go home. I won't tell your mother that you were here or what you're alleging. Let's forget about it. Just go home.'

'It's not my fucking home! And you're damn right you won't tell Mum. Unless you want me to tell her about Fiona Muir! I saw you with her at this hotel. I heard you.'

Murray stopped in his tracks. Again he said nothing immediately. The tactic, if that's what it was, Elliot thought, was proving unnerving. He wanted nothing more than to be out of the room, down those stairs and into the open street.

Murray gave a short, forced laugh. 'So. Is that what all this is about? For your information, Fiona Muir is an old friend. We were at the local school together. You can check up on that if you want. Ask her, for God's sake! She's nothing more than that.'

Elliot flung the door open. 'She better fucking not be or I'll sort you both out!' He paused, shaking his head. 'You know, Mum's still trying to "understand" you, fuck knows why. Not me. And I'll tell you this. Whatever you're up to, I'm going to get to the bottom of it, I swear. Then heaven help you!'

# Thirty-nine

Fiona Muir shifted the weight of the backpack, slinging it from one shoulder to the other as she approached the church office door. Pausing at the threshold, she checked her watch: nearly 6 p.m. She looked upwards; the evening was clear but chilly and the wind was rising. Peering through the darkness, she could see a faint light coming from the ground floor of the manse. Shelagh's car sat in the darkened driveway; Gordon's vehicle was nowhere to be seen. To Fiona's left lay the church, doors closed; the porch light was out, but she could detect a dim glow coming from the rear.

She pushed open the office door, recognizing Shelagh's assistant, who was reaching for a heavy overcoat from a stand in the corner.

'Hi, Sandy. I'm looking for Shelagh. I thought she worked in the office on Wednesday evenings.'

Sandy unhooked his coat. 'Oh, hello, Fiona. Yes . . . Shelagh's here, but she's in the vestry tonight.' He began dragging on his coat and gestured towards the outside. 'Go down to the rear door of the church. It leads into the vestry. There's a light on above the door, so you should be able to find your way from here.' He fumbled about with a bunch of keys as he walked her out of the office. 'Sorry, but I must lock up.'

Outside the office building they parted company. Fiona waited until Sandy was well up the lane and almost out of sight. Carefully she made her way across the graveyard and down the side of the church until she reached the rear door. Standing in a pool of yellow light, the wind picking at her hair, she was about to knock and then changed her mind. Slowly she tried the handle. There was a faint creak but she kept easing the door open until she could slip inside.

Shelagh stood a few metres away, her tall slim figure robed in a dark cassock, a look of surprise rooting her to the spot. Fiona noticed that her right fist was clenched; ready for fight rather than flight?

In a second, Shelagh had recovered her composure. 'Fiona? What are you doing here? We don't have an appointment, do we?'

'You know very well we don't.' Fiona slung the backpack on to a nearby chair. 'We need to talk.' She hauled a second chair towards her, the noise of its scraping on the ancient flagging echoing through the space. 'Or rather, you need to see what I have to show you.'

Shelagh's eyes flicked from the backpack to Fiona's unwavering stare. 'That sounds rather like a threat. What's in the bag?' She half smiled. 'It's not your usual style of accessory. You want to talk? Fine, take a seat.'

As Shelagh moved behind the desk to take her own seat, Fiona sensed that the other woman was making an effort to seem unruffled. But she could see the lines of tension creasing Shelagh's brow and that she couldn't stop clenching and unclenching her right fist. Now

Shelagh was refusing to look directly at her, instead fiddling with some papers on the desk between them. With slow precision, Fiona took a seat and unzipped the backpack. She selected a notebook and slid it across the desk, nudging the other woman's papers out of the way. Still Shelagh refused to look up. Her slim fingers lay lightly on top of the jotter, partially obscuring her name written there in neat script on the blue cover.

Fiona moved her chair an inch forwards. 'The entry for 7th June is somewhat revealing.'

Silently, Shelagh flicked through the notebook, taking her time to read various pages before stopping at the entry Fiona had mentioned. Was there a faint trembling of her hands? Fiona was finding it hard to see. The only light in the room was the low-wattage desk lamp that uplit Shelagh's angular features, giving her strong face an eerie mask-like quality, the white clerical collar adding a handsome severity. Fiona glanced through the inner door that led to the main body of the church. It lay in darkness, and she felt as if the yawning black chasm was ready to engulf her should she cross the threshold. She turned back to Shelagh, who, to her surprise, was staring directly at her. For a fleeting moment she felt that the minister had read her thoughts.

Without warning, Shelagh pushed her chair away and sat back, legs crossed. Dangling the notebook between thumb and forefinger, she now looked the picture of relaxed elegance.

She gestured to the backpack. 'I assume your bag's full of these. Where did you get them?'

'Somewhere only you have access to.'

Shelagh tilted her head. 'Oh? Then that means trespass, theft or burglary.'

Fiona laughed. 'So you're going to report it. I don't think so. Not with evidence like this.'

'*Evidence!*'

Fiona jumped as Shelagh threw the notebook across the desk and into her lap.

Shelagh pointed at the bag. 'If the rest are like these then you're on a hiding to nothing. They're not mine and they're not in my handwriting. I can prove that since I still have various jottings from childhood.' She leaned forward, the light catching the muscle movements in her face as she spoke. 'Look, we both lost something precious in that fire.'

Fiona sat more upright to meet Shelagh's challenge. 'Yes, but your brother took all the limelight. My aunt was forgotten.'

The minister shook her head repeatedly. 'No, she wasn't. But the death of a young child will always lead to outpourings of grief. If it didn't, there would be something very wrong with our society.' Shelagh nodded at the bag. 'I don't know what kind of game you're playing, but I tell you, these are not mine. You'll find yourself very foolishly out on a limb if you try to do anything with them. A sad, lonely voice. I imagine it will cost you dear personally and professionally.'

She looked from the bag to Fiona. 'Is Murray Shaw involved in all this?'

Fiona lifted the notebook from her lap and slipped

it back inside the backpack. 'Let's just say he knows what I'm doing.' She tapped her hand on the bag. 'Oh, and by the way, I'm *not* out on a limb. I was guided to these. Somebody in your midst knows an awful lot about you.'

This time the flicker of fear was unmistakable; momentary but real. Fiona pressed her advantage. 'I'm going to see that you pay for what you did.'

Suddenly, Shelagh thrust her chair back and stood towering above her. 'Get out of here!'

Fiona held her breath as Shelagh moved round the desk towards her. For a second she thought the other woman was going to strike her. Instead, Shelagh swept past, the skirt of her cassock brushing Fiona's legs.

As Fiona collected up the backpack, she was aware of Shelagh opening the vestry door. A gust of cold wind invaded the small space, swirling the papers on her desk. Shelagh stood like a sentry, seeing her off the premises. Without a word, Fiona moved past her into the dim yellow light coming from the lamp above the door. Immediately the door was shut with a firm thud, a key rasping in the lock. Next, the outside light was extinguished. Fiona was momentarily disorientated. Standing stranded at the rear of the church, she was in complete darkness with only the wind rustling through the surrounding trees to navigate by. Above, the previously clear sky was black; cloud cover had obliterated all the stars.

Moving swiftly but carefully, she made for the

right-hand side of the church. Soon she was in the open. With a sigh of relief, she could see the manse, the office building and the street lights on the lane. She breathed deeply and began running across the graveyard, certain that from somewhere deep in the church, Shelagh was watching.

Shelagh stood in the vestibule tracking the retreating figure of Fiona until she was out of sight. Then she closed the front door of the church quietly and retreated back inside. She took her time in lighting a few candles by the altar and then walked back up the aisle. Choosing a pew on the left, she slid along it and fell to her knees, head bowed, resting on her tightly clasped hands, ready for prayer. Her dry lips began moving; the words, though whispered, seemed to echo around the cavernous, dimly lit space.

'Please, God, let it all stop. Take me from this earth if you so desire. I have done all I can to please you, to atone, to beg forgiveness. I know I still have darkness in my heart, but so do others. I have enemies. Seen and unseen. Known and unknown. There seems not enough light to extinguish the dark. Have you forsaken me? Have you? Will the dark pull me in?'

Slowly she lifted her head. The altar and pulpit were barely visible through the flickering candlelight. As she rose to make her way back down the aisle, she felt an overwhelming urge to run. A sob caught in her throat and halted her progress. Ahead, the golden cross set on the altar table reflected the wavering light of the candles. She looked upwards, turning through three hundred and sixty degrees, the vaulted ceiling high above seeming to spin. She began to weep freely. This church, once a place of salvation and sanctuary, now seemed to mock her. It had become a place of torment. A place of dread.

# Forty

Rowan tried one last time. 'Elliot. Why didn't you go on the trip? You deceived me. Don't you think I've got enough of that going on at the moment?' She kept the tears in check. The last thing she wanted was to break down in front of him. But she was nearing her emotional limits. If both her son and husband were going to deceive her, then what hope was there? She slumped back on the sofa and watched the flames flaring in the grate, though they offered precious little comfort. The windows rattled as the wind launched another attack. It was as if she was under siege from all sides. She shivered. *Alone. I'm all alone in this. Trapped here in this house, in a place I don't know, with no one to help me.*

'Mum?'

She looked up. He was sitting opposite, looking worn-out and tense. He still wasn't eating properly and she could smell the cigarette smoke on him.

'Mum, I'm sorry. When it came to it, I just didn't feel like going. I'm sorry about the phone, sorry about everything. Everything's so messed up at the moment. I didn't feel like doing anything. I'm sorry.'

*Yes*, she thought. *Everything was indeed messed up.*

He looked away from her and then back again. 'I'm sorry, really sorry to have worried you so much.'

Then, quite unexpectedly, he launched himself into her arms.

She hugged him tight. 'Okay, Elliot. Okay, darling.' That it had come to this – her son forced into running away for the day – left her reeling with guilt. She looked at him. It was obvious he wanted to go upstairs.

She too was exhausted. 'Let's leave it for now. I'll make something to eat and give you a shout when it's ready.'

She dragged herself to the kitchen and began hunting around in the fridge, barely hearing the knock on the front door above the noise of the rising wind. The last thing she wanted was any visitors tonight. As she approached, the knocker was rapped again, more violently this time.

'All right, just a moment.' She wrenched at the door and a gust of wind almost tugged it from her grasp. Standing, wind tearing at her cassock, was Shelagh Kerr, and a middle-aged man.

Rowan smiled. 'Oh, hello.'

Shelagh Kerr's face remained unsmiling. 'Is Murray in?'

'No ... he's away overnight.' Rowan caught the look that passed between the pair.

'That's a pity. Then may we come in, please? This is Gordon, my husband.' He too was unsmiling.

Rowan could sense the tension and felt anxious at what they wanted from her. 'Yes, come in.' She led them into the living area and showed them to the sofa facing the fire. 'Can I offer you a drink?'

'This is not a social call.' Gordon Kerr had spoken for the first time, and joined his wife positioned uncomfortably on the edge of the sofa. He looked not only stern but angry; quietly furious.

Rowan balanced on the arm of a nearby easy chair. She stifled a yawn. 'Look, I'm sorry, I've had a very long and tiring day. There's obviously something wrong. Can I help?'

Shelagh Kerr lifted her hand towards her husband. 'Let me, Gordon.' She paused and stared. Rowan began to feel even more uneasy.

Eventually, the other woman spoke. 'It's obvious you have no idea why we're here. We came to see your husband, but if he's away overnight then I feel we must talk to you, as ... indirectly it does, or it *will*, concern you.'

'What will?' Rowan could feel the anxiety taking hold now, the rush of adrenaline waking her up.

'Do you know a woman called Fiona Muir?'

Rowan shook her head. 'I'm afraid not.'

'I see.' Shelagh Kerr sighed. 'Fiona Muir is the head teacher of the local primary school. The one your husband attended. The one Angus attended. She was a pupil at the school at the same time as them, and she is the niece of the teacher who died with Angus. Your husband knows her. I ... I thought you might have been introduced by now, but evidently n–'

'Come on, Shelagh!' Gordon jumped to his feet. 'This is outrageous. Tell her!'

'Gordon, *sit down*.' Shelagh gave him a sharp look.

'Tell me what? *Please.*' Rowan could feel her heart rate rising. 'What *is* this?'

She watched as Shelagh waited until her husband had resumed his seat. 'Fiona Muir is accusing me of setting the fire that killed my little brother and her aunt. She has produced what she says is "proof". It is nothing of the sort. Furthermore, she has cited your husband in this. He has obviously been assisting her.'

Rowan gazed incredulously at the woman. 'I . . . I have never heard of this Fiona Muir, nor has Murray ever said anything of the kind about you to me. Are . . . are you sure?'

Shelagh offered a bitter smile in reply. 'Oh, yes. I wouldn't be here if I wasn't. Fiona Muir has in her possession some old school jotters. She claims that they are mine. They do indeed have my name written on the covers. The contents are . . . well, graphic. And one particular entry seems to be a confession, by me, to starting that fire. Others apparently go into greater detail of what I did and why.'

'My God.' Rowan slipped down into the seat, looking from husband to wife. 'I don't understand this.'

'Frankly, neither do we.' Gordon looked from her back to his wife. 'We, particularly Shelagh, have done nothing but reach out the hand of friendship to your husband. I admit, I was nothing short of . . . *astounded* and . . . furious when I discovered who was living here. It seemed utterly distasteful. But Shelagh talked me down. Could even see some benefit in it.'

Rowan felt Shelagh's close scrutiny again as her husband continued. 'Tell me, Mrs Shaw, when your husband told you about this house, how did you feel? Did you have no qualms in buying it, in moving in here?' He paused, his eyes narrowing. 'He *did* tell you?'

The unblinking stare of both pairs of eyes was almost unbearable. It was all she could do to stop herself from fleeing the room. Brushing her hair back from her face, she sat up.

'Of course he told me. Actually, we were sifting through so many property details that although we short-listed this place early on, Murray didn't even put two and two together. We were looking for somewhere in Corstorphine, preferably, and of a certain size. This one fitted the bill. But there were others we were looking at too, here and all over Edinburgh. It was only when Murray set up the first viewing that he twigged.'

Parroting Murray's own explanation was all she could come up with under such pressure. There was no question of her admitting the truth: that she was more in the dark than they were, that she'd thrown her husband out of the house, and that, ever so reluctantly, she was conducting her own investigation into his story.

Rowan continued, trying to keep her voice steady. 'Naturally, we discussed the matter. Murray explained very vividly how much he had cared for Angus and how he had enjoyed himself as a regular guest here. Honestly, after forty years, we didn't expect that anyone from Angus's family would still be here. For that, I'm sorry.'

She looked directly at Shelagh, who was listening intently, her face unreadable. 'All I can say to you both is that I'm puzzled about what you've said. I can't speak for this woman Fiona Muir. But until we actually hear from Murray himself, I think we should reserve judgement on him. That is what I intend to do.'

Had the plea fallen on deaf ears? She waited. Again, she caught a silent communication between the couple. It was Shelagh who spoke first. 'When will your husband be back?'

Rowan had dreaded the obvious question but had her lie ready. 'He's gone to visit a relative who is very unwell. It may be a few days.' She shook her head, pre-empting what would surely be the next question. 'What I'm *not* prepared to do is call him and discuss this over the phone. When he's back, I *will* talk to him and we'll be perfectly prepared to meet with you both. I'm sure there is an explanation.' Rowan prayed that would be enough.

Shelagh looked thoughtfully towards the fire. 'Very well. We will have to accept that. But when you do talk to him, I'd be grateful if you could convey the fact that the so-called "proof" produced by Fiona Muir is, quite simply, rubbish. The notebooks are not mine. She said they were found somewhere that only I would have regular access to, which suggests a private part of the church or the manse.' She looked back at Rowan. 'It implies that she has either trespassed or broken in.'

She paused and her husband took over. 'We are

seriously considering taking legal advice on the matter. Ms Muir has not, to our knowledge, discussed this with anyone other than your husband. During my wife's deeply unpleasant confrontation with her, it was suggested that she keep her ludicrous and deeply hurtful allegations to herself.' He stole a quick glance at Shelagh. 'My wife doesn't mind people knowing about her brother, about who she is. What she, what *we*, won't tolerate is this campaign of vilification.'

Rowan turned to the other woman. 'Tell me, why do you think Fiona Muir is doing this? I mean, she's a respectable member of the community. It seems strange. Why should she be your enemy?'

Shelagh's slim fingers began stroking the rim of her clerical collar. 'I have no idea. She was considerably younger than I was at the time. I was at secondary school, while she was below your husband by a year or two in primary. However, I was a friend of her older sister. I confided in her after Angus died and . . . and got a bit confused . . . and upset. Looking back, I probably needed professional help after such a shock – bereavement counselling or something. But in those days all we had were our friends. I recall that Fiona would tag along behind us when she could. I think she felt excluded.'

Shelagh raised a hand. 'I'm not suggesting she's harboured some petty hatred for forty years. No, but . . . I say this reluctantly and in confidence. What I do know about her recent life is somewhat sad. I have been told about it by a trusted parishioner who doesn't want to make trouble for Fiona as they consider her to be a very gifted teacher and good for the school.'

She was gazing back into the fire again, the light flickering off her lean face. Rowan recalled Viv Baxter's description of her as more than a pretty girl. Shelagh Kerr was still indeed a very handsome woman.

Eventually, she spoke up. 'Shortly before we arrived here a year ago, Fiona Muir had a very unhappy love affair. It was with the then head teacher of the school. She was his deputy. It was, by all accounts, serious. He was married with young children. Fiona wanted him to get a divorce and told his wife about the affair to force the issue. Then his wife killed herself with an overdose. He found her. Within a fortnight, he and his children were gone. The school knew nothing of the affair and thought Fiona the natural choice for head.'

Rowan shook her head. 'That is a horrible story.'

Shelagh looked at her. 'It is indeed. From what I can gather, she is now a bitter and damaged person. Fiona's former lover has never kept in touch with her and, it is assumed, blames her for what happened. Why exactly she has turned her ire on me, and where she got these fabricated notebooks from, is beyond me. Unless she faked them herself, as a way to damage me. However, I will not let that continue.'

Gordon stirred at last. 'Fiona Muir has been very clever to date. She chose her time to find Shelagh alone earlier this evening most carefully. But she would be ill advised to bring these allegations out into the open.' He stood up, offering a hand to his wife. 'If this small community is unable to sustain both Fiona Muir and us, then I will move heaven and earth to ensure that it is *she* who leaves.'

Rowan felt the full force of suppressed anger in his voice. She had no doubt that he meant every word.

# Forty-one

Rowan lay in bed, rigid, staring into blackness as the wind continued to rattle the windows. She felt the tears coming now, and ignored the warm trickles that made their way across her cheeks and on to the pillow. Why she'd even bothered going to bed, she didn't know. With a supreme effort of will, she had managed to make some supper and batted away Elliot's questions about the visitors, until he had gone back upstairs for the night. She was grateful that he'd been at the top of the house out of earshot during the visit, only realizing that she'd had visitors when he heard the door closing on their way out.

In the last few hours she had been dealt a double blow. Elliot's running away from Glasgow had left her feeling wounded and desperate; coming directly on the back of that, the Kerrs' news had been devastating. If what they had told her was true, then she and Murray were finished. Whatever else, they were most certainly finished with this house, this community. It was unthinkable that they should remain here, but she was due to start her new job in a matter of days and Elliot had to get back to school, a new school: a potentially traumatic experience in itself. She closed her eyes against the tears, wishing that she were back in her familiar flat in London, going back to her familiar job. Then she remembered that Ben was coming up at the weekend. *Thank God. An intelligent, caring friend that I can talk it all through with.*

Rowan sat up and reached for her dressing gown; she needed a hot drink. Padding towards the stairs, she paused by the landing window. Across the lane she saw two figures bent against the wind. Shelagh and Gordon Kerr were loading up the car with two holdalls. Moments later, she heard their front door close and the car headlights lit up the driveway of the manse. Sluggishly, the car made its way down the lane until it disappeared out of sight. Rowan continued her way down the stairs, thinking back to that awkward encounter earlier in the evening. As she'd seen the Kerrs out of the house, Shelagh had offered her a sympathetic farewell glance. Did she know or suspect the truth: that Murray had kept his own wife in the dark?

But the manner of her parting had left Rowan strangely relieved. It suggested that at least Shelagh wasn't blaming her. There was something else that had made her feel connected to the other woman. Shelagh had obviously been containing her upset, even if her husband couldn't. Her reserve had nearly fractured when she had said that they were going away for a couple of days to 'get over things'. Rowan could see then that Shelagh had been near to tears. She too had her limits and her pain, a pain that not even her faith could assuage.

*

The phone call from Viv Baxter had woken Rowan up around 8 a.m. She'd managed about three hours' sleep. He'd apologized for ringing so early but he wanted to let her know that the sweetshop owner was still alive and living up near Loch Long, a comfortable day trip from Edinburgh. He'd called her and she'd said that she would be happy to meet Rowan and talk about the fire – today if Rowan wanted to. Rowan had had barely a minute to worry if her monosyllabic response had come across as rude when she'd heard Elliot in the kitchen.

Now they were driving to Glasgow. She felt better but Elliot still looked tense, although there had been a flicker of relief when she'd told him that she was going to arrange for them to delay their new job and school start dates by a week. What she hadn't said was that maybe they would be delayed for ever. Perhaps Elliot already knew that. She felt the familiar pangs of guilt at the thought of his being destabilized even further. It was bitterly ironic; this move was supposed to have ended all that. Now look where they were.

She was driving them off the motorway and heading for an upmarket part of the city. One positive thing was going to happen today. Elliot *was* going to see his old school friend. Maybe that would perk him up. He'd been sitting huddled into his parka, even though the car was over-warm, listening to his iPod the entire journey. Now he switched it off and sat up, pulling the earphones away from his head.

'Mum, where are you going today? Is it to do with Murray?'

She was surprised – not by the question, but by how long it had taken him to ask it. 'Sort of. It's to do with the house *and* to do with Murray.'

'Are you leaving him?'

She said nothing for a moment, making a show of concentrating on getting off the slip road and on to the right route. The truthful answer ran through her mind. *I don't know what I'm doing. I don't know what's happening to us.*

Instead she told him, 'Murray's got some problems he needs to sort out. I'm sorry, Elliot. I know this is hard, really hard. But . . . it just has to be this way at the moment. Listen, don't think about it today. Promise me you'll have a great time.'

To her left lay the shores of Loch Long. She pulled up to check her directions. The weather had changed as she'd left Glasgow and headed north. Now, two hours later, the sky was grey and overcast. There had been snow here, though little more than a sprinkling was left now, but it highlighted perfectly the pleasing contours of this unspoilt and deserted landscape. She was glad to be away from humanity. Glad too for the past two hours of solitude, to think. Throughout the night and early morning she'd been plagued by morbid thoughts of the fire in the summerhouse and visions of Ruth Gillan dying there alone. *Enough.* Looking at the dashboard clock, she started the engine again and pulled out, driving slowly to take in the view.

Agnes Meade had sounded younger than Rowan had expected when she'd called her earlier in the day. Now, in the flesh, she certainly didn't look anything near her real age. Her skin was tanned but not weather-beaten, while her long hair, piled neatly on her head, was improbably dark, showing no grey except at the temples. She was thin but not skeletal and sat erect, poised to launch into conversation.

'I'm eighty-three but I keep fit. Plenty of walks by the loch. Then there's reading and crosswords to keep my mind fresh.' She stopped to pat her hair. 'And regular visits to the hairdressers for my tint. An indulgence. But you've got to look after yourself. Self-respect is important. Keeps you young.'

Rowan was beginning to worry. This woman was clever and astute, that was clear. Would she be able to see through her cover story? The lie had come to her easily enough. She was a journalist looking into the school fire for part of a historic review of unsolved Scottish crimes. It was a more convincing lie than she had initially given Viv Baxter.

Rowan shook her head at the offer of biscuits and watched the old woman opposite her. They had been talking for a few minutes, exchanging pleasantries while the tea was poured. Rowan tried to relax. The fact that she was deceiving a perfectly decent old woman left her feeling grubby. This crisis in her life had, in many ways, brought out the worst in her. She took a deep breath, looking over Agnes Meade's shoulder to the large bay window with its magnificent view of the loch, trying to set all thoughts of guilt and shame aside. She had skirted round her main reason for being here, but time was getting on and she needed some answers.

She focused her attention back on the old woman. 'Tell me, Mrs Meade. You were featured at the beginning of the case, from the bits and pieces I've read, as having seen a child around the school that day. How did you manage that?'

With great care the old woman placed her cup and saucer on to the low table between them. 'Well, my shop was next to the school's back entrance in those days. The shop's not there any more, I believe, and it's a sign of the times, that the place was turned into flats. Anyway, I never usually opened on the annual sports days. The children were my main customers and on sports day all the food, including some treats like sweets, were provided in the park, laid on by the school. The shop was mainly a hobby, to be frank. My late husband and I were very comfortably off, but I enjoyed the work. The shop was my sister's, but she gave it up when she had children. We bought it from her. I never had children, so it was a lovely way of being around them, you know, being the "sweetshop lady". I got to know them all, the teachers too.'

Rowan sensed that this could become a lengthy reminiscence. She drew the woman's attention back to the point of her visit. 'And that year's sports day? Why were you in the shop?'

'Ah, yes. I was behind with my stock-taking, so I thought it was the perfect thing to do that Friday. I'd just come from the back storeroom with some supplies to fill the sweetie jars, when I saw someone run past my shop window. It was a child. They had to have come from the school. That seemed odd, since I thought everyone was at the park. I actually walked to the front of the shop and saw the child some way away. He stopped briefly to turn round and then he was off.'

'He?'

'Oh yes, it was a boy. His hair was tousled and he looked out of breath as if he'd been running. Shortly after that I left the shop for the day and went home. I knew nothing of the fire until the next day. Anyway, I told the police what I'd seen. They were interested at first, but when the janitor came under suspicion they switched their focus to him. Quite right too, if you ask me.'

'Really?'

'Yes, indeed.' The old woman was adamant. 'He was a very strange man. Never said hello when you passed him in the street, and the teacher that died had lodged a formal complaint against him. He'd lost his temper when she asked him to fix the window in her classroom. She had apparently mentioned it to him *four* times. Well, apparently he ranted and raved about how busy he was, and swore away at her. It may be acceptable behaviour now, but in those days it just wasn't done.' The old woman shook her head. 'He was *very* lucky not to stand trial for the murders.'

Rowan felt deflated. It seemed she'd come a long way for very little. She reached for her bag and began readying herself to leave, but the old woman seemed in no hurry to see her off. 'It's funny. You see someone every day and think you know their face. I must have had most, if not all, of the children from that school in and out of the shop during the week. But nothing registered from my brief glimpse. I don't know what the lad was doing at the school that day. He wasn't in uniform. No, he was in shorts, and was holding something that looked like a cricket bat. For the sports day, surely? I couldn't see it very well, but I think that's what it was. Maybe he'd popped back into school to get it. Who knows? Maybe he was too scared to say he'd been there.'

Rowan rose from her chair. 'Yes. That would make sense'. She was only vaguely listening. Her thoughts had turned to Elliot, praying that he'd had a good day. She needed to get on the road and collect him.

The old woman got up with Rowan and guided her to the hallway. 'It was only a year later that I realized who I'd seen. I mentioned it to my husband but he said to leave it well alone. If the boy had seen anything he'd have come forward by then.'

Rowan was stopped in her tracks. She looked at the other woman. 'A year? Why did it take you a year to realize?'

'I'll show you.' Agnes Meade picked up a small

wooden box from the hallway table. 'I looked this out in case you were interested.' She opened the box and pulled out a bundle of old black-and-white photographs. 'They're the end-of-year class photos. The final-year class. I knew their teacher very well – she's dead now, bless her. She used to give me one each year to put up in the shop. Some of the children would come back after they'd gone up to the big school and have a look at them. Have a giggle.'

Rowan peered at the bundle as the woman began to leaf through it. She felt her breathing quicken as, eventually, Agnes stopped at one image. It was a classic school portrait of its era: the entire class in rows, some smiling, some frowning, others looking bored. Girls sat at the front on wooden gym benches while the boys at the back were standing. All were in school uniform. The smiling teacher stood to one side, clearly proud of her charges.

Rowan reached out for the photograph. 'May I?'

It was the beaming teacher's face that had caught her eye. She had seen this photograph before and very recently.

'That's the lad. There.' The old woman pointed a bony finger at the solemn-looking pupil fifth from the left. 'It's something to do with the tilt of his head and the way his hair flops over at the front. That's how I saw him, when he turned round that day. I remembered as soon as I saw the picture.'

Rowan stifled a gasp and the photograph fell from her trembling fingers, landing face down on the carpet. She had seen the very same picture a few days before while they had all been unpacking boxes. There had been laughter and jokes about it.

A photograph of her husband from forty years ago.

## Deceit

Deceit has always come easily to me.

Why? I'm not sure.

But since childhood I have been blessed with an easy
  charm.

My father was the same.

An outer face. An inner face.

A Janus face.

Charming on the outside.

Full of light.

Something quite other on the inside.

Darker than dark.

Darker than death.

# Forty-two

Murray stood staring at the scattered herd of deer: some with their heads down, picking at the grass; others looking up, eyeing him warily. He hadn't been to Edinburgh Zoo since childhood. Now the place was transformed. Scarce remained of the old-fashioned cages and compounds. But standing at the highest point of the zoo, where the land stretched out over Corstorphine Hill, he could almost imagine that nothing had altered, that here he was again, on a regular childhood trip. Not surprising since the zoo had been so close to their homes. They had been happy trips. He and his father and Angus and his mother. They'd all got on together well and he recalled much laughter and joking, Angus's mother seeming to enjoy herself even more than the rest of them. She'd always been so welcoming when he visited their house. She appeared to be, and presumably was, a different woman when her husband was away. Murray frowned. He saw the zoo trips through different eyes now. Not those of a child. Though he could still feel the happiness of those times. And what of Shelagh? Where had she been? He couldn't remember. She'd come on only one visit.

The afternoon was cold but bright with winter

sunshine and the familiar views across Edinburgh might almost have made him believe that he was still a ten-year-old child, enjoying a visit to the zoo. Almost. He headed for a wooden bench, Fiona Muir's backpack in his hands. Then he unzipped it and hauled the jotters out in one bulky handful. To say he now knew them off by heart would have been an exaggeration. But he had been up most of the night reading them, puzzling over their contents. This morning he had done the same as he stopped for coffee in the zoo restaurant.

He thought back to last night. There had been yet another visit from Fiona. This time she'd an air of triumph about her, swinging the bag of jotters like a schoolgirl. *'Here, keep them for a while. Read them. Interesting stuff.'* And then she'd dropped her bombshell. She had gone to the church and confronted Shelagh with them, who had denied ownership. Hardly surprising. He leafed through one of the notebooks. The entries seemed to have a pattern: a poem one day and then a straight-forward entry the next. Shelagh may have denied that they were hers, but some of the contents could only have been known by her and a very few others. Fiona wasn't aware of this since she'd had very limited access to the family all those years ago. Murray had been content to keep her in the dark about that.

He found the entry he wanted. It had been no coincidence, his decision to come to the zoo. The words in front of him had given him the idea.

*The visit to the zoo was dreary. So boooorrring. Mum likes it though. But then she likes animals. Shame Dad won't let us have a dog. 'Wretched, fawning beasts!' That's what he says about them. Suppose Mum can forget about Dad for a while when she's here. Angus and Murray and his nice dad like it too. They like the children's zoo bit. You can touch the sheep and donkeys and pigs there.*

*DAD IS A PIG. A BIG HORRIBLE PIG. HE SHOULD GO TO THE SLAUGHTERHOUSE.*

Murray closed the jotter and studied the crumpled cover. He remembered that day. Shelagh had been quiet all through the trip while he and Angus ran riot. If she didn't write this, who did? Who else would know about this unremarkable day? It was hardly something she would tell friends, surely? Still, if she could prove that the notebooks weren't hers, then that was a problem for Fiona certainly.

Rowan took a last glance at the peculiar yet striking architecture of the Scottish Parliament building and reluctantly turned away to walk up the Royal Mile, wondering if she would ever see the building again, let alone work there. She'd spent the morning trying to blot out the troubling thoughts that her meeting the day before with Agnes Meade had left her with.

Reaching the crossroads at the Tron Church, she saw the café where Murray had suggested they meet. When she'd called him earlier in the day, he had answered the phone immediately and eagerly. Had he been waiting for her to call all this time? He'd sounded as if he were standing in the middle of a field, his voice airy and distant.

Rowan ordered a coffee and checked her watch. She had aimed to arrive early and pick her territory. Selecting a quiet but well-lit corner table outside, under a heater, she checked her surroundings. The day was beginning to fade, car headlights flooded the street and shop windows twinkled, their seasonal wares reminding everyone that November had slipped into December. Christmas was on its way. A depressing thought. Where would she be by Christmas? She nudged the thought away, pulled out a spiral-bound reporter's notebook from her bag and glanced down the list.

- Redundancy
- Shelagh's visit
- Fiona Muir
- Jotters
- Agnes Meade's sighting
- Summerhouse fire/Ruth Gillan's death
- Cash withdrawals (explanation)

Was it mad having a written agenda for seeing her husband, as if she were at work attending an editorial meeting? She passed a pencil down the list, stopping at the bottom, and pressing the tip hard into the paper. *Husband*. She scribbled the word down the margin of her notebook, running over the lettering again and again until the pencilling was nearly black.

The word was beginning to feel alien. And then it hit her: the distance she had travelled from Murray in such a short time. *Nightmare*. She pencilled the word next to his name. That was what she was in, there was no escaping the truth.

Her hand hovered over the page and then she let it rest, laying the pencil to one side. Was Murray involved in Angus's death? Involved in what was going on now with Shelagh, with the fires in the back garden, at the school? Involved in something more?

She felt his arrival rather than saw it: the sensation of someone staring at her. Then his shadow, cast by the overhead lights, floated across the pages of her notebook. Hurriedly she closed it, placing both hands protectively on top.

'Rowan?' He pulled the chair opposite her towards him and sat down, dumping a backpack on to the ground.

She glanced back down to her coffee. But she'd seen enough. He looked pale and haggard, almost ill, as if he hadn't slept. He'd lost weight – she could see as much from his cheekbones, which strained at the drawn flesh of his face. Like Elliot, he wore a haunted look. Her family was literally fading away before her eyes.

He placed both palms face down on the table: a gesture of submission? Rapprochement? She could tell that he was waiting for at least one word of acknowledgement from her. Well, he was going to get more than that.

'I want you to listen to me, Murray. I feel like I'm in

a nightmare – a *nightmare*, do you realize that? And you've put me there. Worse than that, you've put *my* son there too.' She could see by the flicker of pain that passed across his eyes that her emphatic use of the possessive had hit home. 'Shelagh Kerr and her husband came to see me the night before last. They were looking for you. They told me about the jotters.' She caught his quick glance sideways at the ground. The jotters must be in the bag. 'I know about Fiona Muir,' she went on. 'The Kerrs say you've been "helping" her in these allegations against Shelagh. For Christ's sake, Murray, what are you doing? Are you having an affair with this woman?'

There. It was out. Her most deep-seated worry. That he might be deceiving her sexually, as well as in every other way, was an unbearable thought.

He leaned forwards. 'No, no, no. Absolutely not. I . . . I only met her recently. I went to look at the school again. But I've not been "helping" her with anything. She . . . she's got it in for Shelagh Kerr and thinks that she killed Angus. I don–'

Rowan cut in. 'And the "proof" is these jotters.' She pointed at the ground. 'Is that them?'

He shook his head. 'Well, it's not just them –'

She cut in again, spelling it out in short staccato bursts. '*Is. That. Them?*'

'Yes. Look, she gave me them to read last night. That's all. I had nothing to do with getting them.'

'Where did she get them from?'

Murray hesitated. She couldn't read his face. It had

closed down. Was he thinking of lying to her, saying he didn't know?

'She got them from the manse.' He avoided looking at her.

'She *stole* them from the manse.' It was a statement, not a question.

Murray met her eyes again and lifted his hands. 'Listen, I had nothing to do with it. But it's not just *her* – Fiona, I mean. Someone is helping her. Someone's been writing to her. Someone who knows the Kerrs, who must live or work nearby, probably in the church. They told her where to find the jotters, how she could get in. That the back door would be unlocked. The Kerrs have another enemy. And it's not me.'

'Are you telling me that you have not been involved in these allegations?'

'Of course not. And I'll tell you another thing. These notebooks contain information that only she and a very few others could know. For example, there's an entry about a visit that Dad and I made with Angus, his mother and Shelagh to the zoo. Everyone who was there that day is dead, except Shelagh.'

'And you.' The implication was clear. Rowan waited for an explosive denial.

Strangely, she picked up nothing sinister in his comment. 'Yeah and . . . I suppose her father would have known. But I don't see how that fits in . . .'

Rowan's thoughts drifted away to Viv Baxter's musings on Robert Gillan's potential guilt.

Murray's voice broke in: '. . . well, do you?'

She shook herself back to attention. 'Do I what?'

He was lifting the bag and thrusting it towards her. 'Do you want to read the jotters? Here, have a look.'

'Are you joking? Of course I don't want to read them. I want you to return them. *Today*. I mean it. I've told the Kerrs you would go and see them. I said you were away visiting a relative for a few days and that you'd go round when you got back. Just say you came home early.'

He dropped the bag, letting it thud to the ground. 'I'm not going.'

'What?'

'I'm not going to the Kerrs. You've obviously made a friend of her. *You* take the damn jotters back.'

'Stop being so childish, Murray. Have you heard a word I've said? What is happening to you? I need you to tell me why you gave up your job, why we came here, to Edinburgh, to the house. What have you done? You've been lying to me. I want to hear the truth, no matter what. And I want you to stop this vilification of Shelagh Kerr.'

He slumped back into his chair. 'I have not been involved in that, I'm telling you!'

'I don't believe you.'

'Rowan, do you love me?'

The unexpected question almost knocked the breath out of her.

'Do you love me?'

Her head snapped up. '*Stop it, Murray. Stop it!* This isn't fair, I'm trying to find out what's going on with you and . . . *you can't do this to me*!'

Suddenly Murray pushed his seat back. The scraping of the aluminium chair on the pavement was deafening as he got to his feet. 'Stop what, Rowan, stop what? What's more important than us? If you love me then trust me.'

He could see that she had no response. He kicked the bag towards her. 'Take the fucking jotters. Give them to bloody Shelagh Kerr. You're obviously taking her side over mine. I haven't done anything wrong. I haven't!' He turned to go. 'You're not on my side. And that's unacceptable. It's disloyal!'

She tried to stand up but her legs buckled. 'Don't go, Murray. Tell me what's going on.' As he began to walk away, she shouted after him, 'I'll find out one way or another! I'm finding out something new about you every day. Like the fact that you were there at the school the day Angus died. You were seen. By the sweetshop owner. I've spoken to her.'

He stopped abruptly, his back still to her, and then turned his head. 'Oh, really? Well, she's mistaken.' Without warning, he turned fully and walked back to the table, his voice rising. 'You know, instead of behaving like the journalist you *once were* and *investigating* me, you should try *trusting* me. I've said I'm sorry. Why can't things be as they were?'

Once again a confusion of anger and pain gripped

her. She kept her voice low. 'I'm leaving if you don't tell me the whole truth.' She stifled a sob. 'Or maybe I've already left.'

He looked as if she'd just struck him. Wordlessly, he turned for the final time and began marching down the street. She wondered if he could feel her eyes burning into his back as he walked away into the darkness of the early evening.

Wiping at her tears with one hand, slowly she opened her notebook. The word stared back at her. *Husband.* With deliberate care, she tore the page from its spiral binding, hole by hole, and then crumpled it in her saucer.

# Forty-three

Elliot pulled the earphones away from his head, the music sounding suddenly tinny as he threw the iPod on the table and moved to the door of his attic room.

'Mum?'

He heard her footsteps on the stairs and walked down quickly to the first landing. She was standing at her bedroom door, her coat still on, clutching a backpack he'd never seen before. Her smile was forced. 'Hi, darling. I've a bit of a headache – I'm going to lie down. You okay to make something to eat for yourself?'

She looked terrible. He pretended not to notice. 'Yeah, of course. I'll raid the freezer.'

'Okay then. See you later.' With that, she disappeared into her room and gently closed the door.

Elliot remained standing on the landing. He couldn't remember when he'd last seen her so ... so vulnerable. Of course it must have been to do with that visit from the Kerrs. *Mind-blowing!* He'd heard just about every word of it, perched on the stairs. He'd even sneaked a peek at the couple as they'd left. During the visit, part of him had wanted to rush in and say, 'Yes, it's true! Murray has been up to something. With that woman, and other things besides.' But he'd managed to fight the urge. He couldn't help smiling

265

when the minister's husband had lost it. Yes, he could see him giving Murray a hiding. Though older, the man looked fit, as if he could take care of himself. Murray wouldn't stand a chance against him.

Quietly, Elliot made his way downstairs and headed for the kitchen. Ignoring the freezer, he unlocked the patio doors, gently slid them open and stepped into the night. He wandered across the lawn towards the burnt patch of ground where the summerhouse had once stood, pulling out his cigarettes and lighter. Taking slow deep draws, he circled the area, clouds of exhaled smoke and breath mingling in the wintry air.

He heard a rustling near the back wall and stopped dead, holding his breath. Nothing. He shivered, threw the glowing, half-smoked cigarette end towards the trees, following its orange arc until it landed, and then turned away, his footsteps picking up speed as he headed for the kitchen.

In the hallway he hesitated at the coat rack, one hand hovering over his parka. A minute later he was out in the lane and making for the main road. At the hotel reception he was relieved to see a middle-aged man was on duty, not the nosy girl from before. The receptionist answered his query politely.

'I'm very sorry. You've just missed Mr Shaw. He checked out about half an hour ago.'

Elliot offered his thanks and walked out into the street. He felt the first flakes of snow as he cut down a side road. He paused to light another cigarette; it would help him think more clearly. Then he moved on, his pace brisk. He knew where he was going. By the time he'd reached the row of cottages, the snowfall had increased and the rising wind was turning it into a near blizzard. He pulled the drawstrings on his fur-lined hood as tight as they would go. The snow gave him one advantage though: no one was venturing out tonight on foot or by car. He moved slowly into the small cul-de-sac. Three cottages were lit up: the first, second and last – Fiona Muir's. Elliot bent down as he approached her door, but he needn't have bothered. Each cottage, lit or unlit, had curtains or blinds drawn. Elliot had little doubt: if Murray had checked out of the hotel, this was the place to find him.

He felt almost sick at the thought of what it would do to his mother if she found out Murray was having an affair. Elliot shook his head at the very idea. Murray was good-looking for his age. Maybe this wasn't the first time he had cheated on his mother. He sucked at his cigarette, feeling the anger rising. *It would destroy Mum and then I'd destroy him.* It was bad enough that the Kerrs had told her that Murray and Fiona Muir knew each other. Elliot thought back to that moment last night. He'd been relieved that his mother had sounded only puzzled rather than suspicious.

As Elliot had hoped, down the side of the cottage there was a path to the back garden. He dropped the half-smoked cigarette and ground it out underfoot. Then, inching his way round, he listened for any sign of life. At the back a rectangle of yellow light shone on to the snowy expanse of what he presumed was the lawn of her small garden. That meant the window was uncurtained. Crouching right down he slid underneath the window, still listening. There was no double glazing and he could hear a mumbling female voice.

The mumbling was getting louder; he could now pick up fragments of sentences. Then, without warning, the back door was flung open. He froze. Fiona Muir was standing looking out at the snow, a mobile phone clamped to her cheek.

'Okay. I'll be there. Five, ten minutes maybe. The weather's filthy.'

Elliot watched as she ended the call and cradled the now silent phone. He pressed himself into the shadows. If she turned round to her left, she might see him. The light didn't reach as far as his hiding place, but if her eyes adjusted to the darkness, he was done for. What was she up to? She was just standing there, in the doorway, no coat on and staring down at the phone, preoccupied. He couldn't see her face since her back was turned towards him, but moments later she sighed, her voice a near whisper.

'*Okay. This is it!*'

He watched as she walked over to the small garden shed to her right and stepped inside. In a minute she had emerged, black Wellington boots in her hand. Still seeming preoccupied, she re-entered the cottage. Next moment, the rectangle of light shining on the snow was extinguished. Elliot rose stiffly, his legs aching from the cold and the stress of the position he'd had to hold for the last few minutes.

He heard her at the front door; the jangle of keys told him that she was locking up. Peering down the pathway, he could see her. Wrapped in a long, thick coat and with the boots on, she paused at a car. He held his breath. If she chose to drive now, he'd had it. If she was going to meet Murray, and he was convinced she was, then he would never find their rendezvous, no matter how near it was. She looked upwards; the snow was falling as heavily as ever. With relief, he watched her walk away from the car, head bent against the blizzard.

As Elliot moved out from the shelter of the side path, he now realized that the weather was a major disadvantage. With no one else about, could he follow her without being spotted? She turned right out of the cul-de-sac – his signal to go. Keeping as far back as visibility would allow – too close and he'd be seen, too distant and he'd lose her – he saw with relief that it was going to be easier than he'd anticipated. She was practically on automatic pilot. Head still bent firmly against the driving snow, she clearly knew where she was going, almost without looking.

Six minutes later, he could see where she was headed. The outline of the school appeared and he watched her stop to look up at the fire-ravaged skeleton of the east wing. Through the deadening silence of the snow, he heard the main gate creak as she shoved it open, followed by the metallic click of its closing.

As the building swallowed her up, Elliot moved to the gate, keeping in the shadows. He surveyed the playground, scanning her line of fresh footprints. That was interesting. There were no others. If she was keeping a rendezvous, where were her companion's footprints? Had they been obliterated by the falling snow? Or had whoever she was meeting – surely Murray – not arrived yet? And why were they meeting here?

Inching the gate open, keeping the creaking to a minimum, Elliot eased his way through. As he padded across the playground, the fresh snow squeaking under his feet, he made sure to walk only in her footprints.


Fiona cursed silently as she slipped on a pile of stray scaffolding poles lying on the ground, hidden by the snow.

'Up here!'

She swivelled round. A silhouetted figure, torch in hand to light the way, stood one storey above her. She cursed again and shouted, 'Why the hell up there?'

'Just come up. Quickly!'

Fiona approached the smoke-stained entrance to the stairwell and made her way gingerly up each step. Patches of ice had formed on almost every one.

At the top, the figure moved forwards. Fiona felt her temper near to breaking. 'Look, I thought we were meeting in the main school. It's one thing to be away from prying eyes. But why the hell have you brought me up here? I th–'

Before she had time to finish, her body shuddered as a blow struck her head. Stunned, she could do nothing as she felt herself being dragged to a broken-down wall. Her final sensation was of falling through the air, snowflakes caressing her face as she fell to the ground, her spine shattering on the pile of poles.

# Forty-four

Shelagh Kerr sat staring at the flames in the grate. The entire day had been spent listening to parishioners gossiping about the terrible accident Fiona Muir had suffered at the school the night before. Contractors had found her early in the morning. She was apparently near to death.

Shelagh stared at the mess around her. The living-room floor in front of her was strewn with CDs. She had been trying desperately to find some music that suited her mood. But these past two hours that mood had seemed to change almost by the minute. She had begun with some light jazz and had eventually settled for some gentle plainchant. But now even this was unsettling her, the haunting notes setting off a feeling of impending doom.

She stood up and began clearing away the CD cases, putting them in the tall rack in alphabetical order. She thought back to the short break at her favourite hotel in St Andrews and her spirits lifted momentarily. It had been wonderful: the food, drink and service were superb as ever; the long walks along that most beautiful of Scottish beaches, invigorating. Gordon had designed their time well: a perfect balance of physical activity and self-indulgent pampering.

Slotting the last CD into place, she moved back to the sofa and sat down, drawing a comforting cushion to her stomach. She felt relieved that Gordon had gone to his monthly wine club. Although he'd seemed tired and a bit distracted after the drive home, she knew he'd go. Wild horses wouldn't stop him from taking part in that jamboree, which provided him with the perfect excuse to drink himself silly on the finest wines while pretending that the exercise was all about 'educating the palate'. No doubt he'd return in the early hours – in a state she'd not have to witness since she would be in bed pretending to sleep.

Still feeling restless, she stood up and crossed the room to hit the off switch on the CD player, finally silencing the mournful voices. As she did so, the doorbell rang. For a moment she had half a mind to ignore it. But the visitor would have seen the lamp on and probably heard the music. She marched down the hallway, stopping briefly to check her appearance in the mirror.

Standing on the front step, looking behind him nervously and illuminated by the outside light, was David Menteith. She hadn't seen him since the funeral of the child. As the minister of a neighbouring parish she talked to him on the phone fairly regularly, but to have him turn up on her doorstep at night, unannounced, was unheard of.

'David? Hello.'

Unsmiling, he began walking towards her. 'Shelagh,

I'm sorry for dropping by like this but we need to talk.'

His face was grave and, feeling the tension gripping her more powerfully than ever, she allowed him to walk past her, into the hallway. She led him into the living room and he sat down on a sofa, not bothering to unbutton his overcoat. He peered across the low-lit room at her as she chose an armchair by the fire.

'Can I get you anything to drink?' she asked.

'No, thank you. Shelagh, when did you last speak to Sandy?'

'We . . . we've been away for a short break. I spoke to him yesterday, on the phone. Why?'

She watched as her visitor, suddenly feeling the heat of the room, began to unbutton his heavy coat. 'It's difficult. It's about the fire at your local school, the body they've found, all that. And you've heard about the teacher who's been injured?'

'Of course. Everyone's talking about it.'

'You worked in prison chaplaincy with Sandy, didn't you? Wasn't he an assistant?'

'Yes, David. Look, what's this about?'

He sighed heavily. 'Well, they've identified the body. I think it's someone you used to know.'

She remained absolutely still. 'Really? Who?'

'Someone called Matthew Docherty. An ex-life prisoner. Do you remember him?'

She nodded, not daring to speak.

'Right.' David looked at her quizzically. 'Do you recall much detail about him?'

'Remind me.' She waited for him to go on, keeping both hands tightly clasped in her lap.

David continued in a low voice. 'Docherty was in his forties, recently released after serving nineteen years for the rape and murder of two young Aberdeen women. He became something of a celebrity in prison. Gained degrees in both theology and art, even went on to sell some of his work through the country's top galleries. Since his release he'd apparently been working on major exhibitions in London and New York. Do you remember now?'

'Yes, he was a high-profile prisoner.'

David went on. 'He was also a cause célèbre among miscarriage of justice campaigners, including prominent lawyers, journalists and some Church people. There was persistent talk of police corruption in the case. Apparently Sandy had a lot to do with him and added his voice to the campaign. I take it you were aware of all that?'

She had managed to steady herself, answering with deliberate slowness and precision. 'Sandy took a special interest in a few prisoners. I think he was keen to help Docherty because he seemed to have had genuine faith. But it was more than that, you're right. Docherty's conviction was thought in many quarters to be unsafe. Sandy supported him, was very moved by how he had overcome this injustice.' The feeling of sick dread inside her was intensifying with every glance at his tense face. '*Please*, David, what's wrong?'

David sat forwards. 'Sandy's been arrested. I've just

been at the police station talking with his solicitor.'

'*What?*'

'They're saying it was a lovers' quarrel.'

'What was?' She stood up. The room was too hot. She needed to open a window.

Her visitor stood as well. 'I realize this must be a shock, but you need to know.' He moved towards her, clearly concerned. 'Sandy was having an affair with Matthew Docherty.'

# Forty-five

David was leaning over her, trying to read her expression. 'Drink this.' He waited a moment. 'Is that better? Are you sure you don't want me to call Gordon?'

Shelagh drank greedily at the whisky. The last person she wanted here was Gordon, half-cut and full of concern for her. 'No, no, David. Please. Sit down. I want you to tell me what ... what did the solicitor say? Can we go and see Sandy? I ... I just can't believe it. They must have made a mistake. Surely?'

David retreated to the sofa, clearly anxious to give her some breathing space. His face had lost its look of deep concern. Now he seemed sad. 'I don't think so. Shelagh, I know this is difficult. You mentored him so carefully and were so generous with your time, bringing him on.' He paused, obviously trying to work out what to say next. 'The solicitor agreed to tell me what the police had found. Sandy said that he could. He's denying any involvement in the killing. Apparently, this Matt Docherty had been living in Glasgow since his release. After they identified him through DNA, the police went to his flat. They found letters from Sandy. Love letters.'

He dropped his head. 'I don't care about Sandy being gay. This is the modern world, Shelagh. I know you think like me. But it was what they found in the letters. It became clear that Docherty had ended the relationship some time before he was released. Meaning that they had . . . that their relationship had been going on for some time while in prison.'

Shelagh cleared her throat. The whisky had raced to her head and she had trouble formulating her question. But she had to ask it. 'But . . . how could it happen? In a prison?'

'Oh, come on now, Shelagh. Don't be naive. Let's not kid ourselves. Prisoners have affairs with other prisoners; prison officers and prisoners have affairs. It goes on all the time. Think about it. Why not a chaplain? A prisoner requests private time to worship, to be counselled or t–'

'Okay, David, okay. Stop it. I get the picture.' She breathed deeply. 'So what evidence have they found? And why the school?'

At last he shrugged off his coat and sat back, looking more composed. 'They're not sure, except that at night-time it made for a deserted rendezvous. They also think that Sandy may have been trying to divert police attention by making it look as if there were a random arsonist on the loose. Apparently there was another fire in the area – a minor one – recently. They think that was Sandy.'

'There was a fire right across the road. Vandalism they thought, initially.'

David frowned, obviously thinking through what he was going to say. 'As to other evidence? The solicitor says it's circumstantial but strong. The police found letters in both Docherty's *and* Sandy's homes. But it's the letters from Sandy that are the problem. They're pretty grim, it seems. First pleading and then threatening.'

'How could they be threatening? Surely Sandy was the one vulnerable to threats?' She was surprised at how controlled she could appear.

Her visitor was looking tense again. 'It gets worse. The letters show that ... well, it would seem that Docherty, despite all the fuss, the campaigns, *did* commit the two murders and rapes he was convicted for. He admitted as much in letters to Sandy. He may have been convicted through corrupt police practice, but he was guilty. It must have been a double blow to Sandy. The loss of love and the loss of ... well, what he thought was truth, justice. It must have been appalling for him.' David was staring at her, clearly looking for some form of sympathetic reaction.

'Of course,' she replied.

'You know, Shelagh, this Docherty sounds like a thoroughly dreadful creature. The textbook psychopath. Charming, charismatic, brilliant and ... *evil*. I'm not ashamed to use the word. You and I may run modern ministries in a modern world, but let's acknowledge evil when we encounter it. This man was a monster.'

She couldn't take much more of this. *Keep it factual, keep it away from evil, away from emotions. Focus on Sandy.*

'The evidence, David. What else?'

'Right. The solicitor said that they're still trying to link Sandy to the fire. Forensically, I mean. At the moment it's the letters and Sandy's admission about the affair, *and* that he had met Docherty since his release. There was a very public row at Glasgow Central station some time back. The solicitor is sure members of the public who witnessed it will come forward when there's a police appeal. And there are two other problems.' David Menteith shook his head pityingly. 'Sandy has absolutely no alibi for the night of the fire. He's claiming that he was at home, alone. But there's nothing to verify that. All the other lodgers in his place were out. He didn't make or receive any calls on mobile or landline. He didn't use his PC or go online. And speaking of his PC . . . they found some gay pornography. He'd also been accessing gay chatrooms and has admitted to "cruising" on Calton Hill. It's all very sad.'

He leaned forward. 'There's one final thing. The woman who's been injured at the school. You must know her?'

'Yes.'

'Well, the police think Sandy is responsible for that too. They're wondering if she saw him around the school the day or evening of the fire but only came to the conclusion later that he had something to do with it. Perhaps initially she just didn't believe that he could have been involved. Sandy denies he was there. Says he was out cruising but came home early – alone – because of the weather.'

She looked on dumbly as her visitor stared back in disbelief. 'It's an unlikely explanation though, Shelagh. Given that the weather was so appalling, it seems unimaginable that anyone would even *think* of going looking for outdoor sex. The solicitor says they've got something from CCTV in the area. They've got a back view of a tall, male figure, like Sandy, dressed in a parka, one of those long fish-tailed ones with fur round the hood.'

'A parka?'

'Yes, and they're tearing Sandy's place apart trying to find it, although Sandy denies owning one. Still, I suppose if they can't make out the face of the person, they're going to have a hell of a job proving it's him. The solicitor says they're trawling through any available CCTV in the area to see what they can find. But it's not well covered. After all, it's a safe residential area. Well, it was until recently.'

He stood up. 'There's an emergency meeting at the presbytery office in the morning to discuss it all. Ten o'clock. I'll pick you up. They're arranging cover for our morning services, so don't worry about that. Just be ready.' He reached for his coat and she tried to get up. 'No, Shelagh. Stay. This has been more of a shock than you realize. Take it easy.'

She ignored his plea and got to her feet unsteadily. 'We have to help Sandy.'

'We'll talk about it in the morning.' Buttoning his coat, her visitor turned to go.

At the front door, he tried to smile but she didn't

return it. 'You don't think he did it, David – surely not?'

He paused, hand on the door knob. 'Look, the stance the solicitor is taking is that Docherty probably had many enemies. He probably had other love affairs that had gone sour. That may all be true. It's certainly the route he wants to pursue. In any event, Sandy is, of course, innocent until proven guilty. I . . . I'm just very, *very* surprised at what I've heard about his other life. As I say, it's sad, so sad. He sounds as if he was lonely. That can be a very destructive state.'

Shelagh followed her visitor's progress as he made a quick dash through the cold night to his car, and then she closed the door slowly. She leaned against it, her head back and eyes shut tight. Slowly, she made her way to the living room and switched on the CD player, rekindling the mournful tones of plainchant. Extinguishing the lamps, leaving only the fire embers for light, she lay down on a sofa. With a terrifying sense of inevitability, she now knew that it was time to plan her endgame.

## Justice

Justice doesn't really exist, does it?
Not as an actual, external reality.
The law doesn't deliver it.
Not police, not courts, not judges.
Nor God?
There is no God.
There is the devil though.
The devil lives inside us.
Not God, the devil.
Understand?
Good.
For, once you know that, once you *feel* that,
Then you know that's what justice is.
It's the hell inside.
The eternal hell.

# Forty-six

Rowan stopped outside the front door of St Margaret's House and stared across to the church. The graveyard was covered in a fresh sprinkling of snow, glittering eye-wateringly white in the morning's winter sunshine. The view, which had for such a very short time seduced her into believing she had found a perfect new home, now seemed to mock her. The words of the Gillans' friend, quoted in one of the old newspaper reports, came back to her: 'St Margaret's House, once the home of a fine and decent family, has become tainted by tragedy.' She smiled bitterly. *And it's not only this house.* The beauty of the view across the road was deceptive; the cold reality – that there were scores of the dead's bones lying beneath the surface – seemed more in keeping with how she felt.

She assumed working ministers must rise early; yes, the main door to the church was open. Wearily, she swung the backpack over one shoulder and crossed the lane. A further mockery of beauty – the sweet-smelling vase of fresh flowers – greeted her as she entered the vestibule. The exceptional brightness of the outside made for a shock when she stepped into the body of the church. For a moment the darkness seemed absolute, and she heard the sound of a human presence before she saw it. Down the central aisle, towards the altar, Rowan could make out the scraping of shoes on the stone floor, accompanied by a faint series of rhythmic thuds. Warily, she approached the source of the noise. As she did so, it stopped.

'Hello, Rowan.'

Rowan paused until her eyes adjusted to the darkness. Back-lit by the faintest of wall lights and a handful of flickering candles stood Shelagh Kerr in flowing cassock, the clerical collar whiter than white around her thin neck. The light thudding resumed as the minister moved slowly along the front row of pews, throwing down hymn books at regular intervals.

She looked up again. 'What brings you here?'

Silently, Rowan continued approaching until she was a few steps away. 'These.' She eased off the backpack and lifted it with one hand. 'The jotters. I've brought them back.'

Shelagh paused mid-throw, a hymn book held halfway between the pile in her hand and the pew. After a few seconds she let the book fall with a final thud. She gestured for Rowan to join her. They sat on the neighbouring pew, a comfortable distance between them.

Shelagh pointed at the bag. 'They're from your husband?'

Rowan tilted her head in acknowledgement as she took her seat. 'How did you know?'

'Because if they had been found with Fiona Muir, I imagine the police would be here right now instead of you.'

'The police?'

Carefully, Shelagh placed the pile of hymn books to one side and then accepted the bag of jotters. She laid that to one side too, apparently uninterested in it.

Staring at the altar, she began to speak, her voice low and steady. 'I thought you'd know. Fiona Muir was critically injured the night before last, the night of the bad snow. She was apparently in the ruined part of the school and fell.'

Rowan shook her head, staring at the other woman. 'No, I know nothing about this. How did it happen? What was she doing there?'

Without answering, Shelagh stood up, collecting the backpack as she rose. Then she turned to face Rowan. 'Come on. I've finished in here. I need to go soon. Let's get out in the air.'

The two women walked in silence until they were halfway across the graveyard. Near the far wall, Rowan could make out faint wisps of smoke.

Shelagh followed her eye line. 'Don't worry. It's nothing sinister. The gardener's been doing some tidying up. Let's see if he's still there.'

An elderly man, his bent back towards them, was stirring the well-controlled bonfire with a long stick.

'Peter?'

The man, a roll-up cigarette between his teeth, turned around slowly. 'Shelagh, hello. I've got rid of most of the dried branches, leaves, all that. I'm just settling the fire down now.'

Shelagh made no attempt to introduce Rowan. 'That's okay, Peter. I'll put the fire out. Go and have a cuppa. It's freezing out here.'

The old man obviously didn't need any further encouragement and, with a wave, disappeared behind a tall tombstone, on his way to the church office.

Rowan watched Shelagh unzip the backpack and empty the jotters on to the ground, their bright blue covers contrasting starkly with the glistening white snow. Unhurried, she knelt down and began flicking through them, then paused to look up.

'Have you read these?'

Rowan shook her head emphatically. 'Of course not. But what's this about Fiona Muir? Murray said he got these from her . . .' A spike of anxiety hit her as she worked out the date. 'He said she gave them to him two nights ago. The night you say she was injured.'

Shelagh eased herself to her feet. 'Is that so?' Holding the stick in one hand and a couple of jotters in the other, she began poking the fire until flames were visible. Carefully, she threw the first one on and waited as, slowly, it began to ignite.

She turned from the fire to face Rowan. 'These aren't mine, you know. You only have my word, but please believe me.' She fed more notebooks to the fire. 'What has your husband said about them?'

'Not a lot. He did say something about an entry that described a visit to the zoo.' Rowan thought she detected a flicker of anxiety in Shelagh's eyes. Then it was gone.

The minister tossed another jotter on to the fire. 'I'm afraid I can't explain that. Whoever wrote these has clearly got inside information about me.'

Rowan backed away to a nearby bench and sat down, watching the flames take hold.

Shelagh kept throwing more notebooks on to the fire. For a few moments she seemed mesmerized by the flames and then she began talking again, her eyes staying on the fire. 'You want to know about what happened to Fiona Muir? Your husband doesn't know yet?'

Rowan, not daring to speak, shook her head.

'That's funny, I thought he'd have seen it on the news or been trying to get in touch with her.' Shelagh resumed feeding the bonfire. 'Anyway, it's complicated. The police have arrested my assistant, Sandy. Have you met him?'

'Yes ... briefly ... but arrested him? Why, for goodness sake?'

Jotter after jotter was piling up on the bonfire. Suddenly, Shelagh stopped, leaned on the long stick and faced Rowan. 'The body found in the school fire has been identified as that of a former prisoner, Matthew Docherty. Sandy used to work in prison chaplaincy with me, and Matthew was one of the inmates.' She looked downwards and began poking the stick into the snowy ground. 'The police have found evidence of a love affair between Sandy and this man. An affair that went wrong. Docherty ended it some time ago when still in prison. He was released recently. It's being suggested that Sandy was having trouble accepting the break-up, and so lured him to the school and killed him.'

Shelagh looked up. Rowan thought she was near to tears but clearly determined to go on. 'Worse, they're accusing Sandy of attacking Fiona Muir. They think she saw him around there the night of the fire and had begun to wonder if he could be to blame. The affair between him and Docherty is true, Sandy has admitted that. But I don't believe anything else, and Sandy is denying the allegations, of course. His solicitor is concerned. He says it's a strong circum-stantial case. Not good. Also, they've got some CCTV pictures. A tall male in a long parka. They can't see his face, but they're apparently moving heaven and earth to find the coat – one of those fish-tail ones with a fur hood. I've never seen Sandy in anything like that. Not his style. So I think they're on a hiding to nothing.' She looked at her watch. 'I'm going to a church meeting soon to discuss what we can do for him.'

She turned back to the fire and Rowan watched every last ember being flattened and extinguished by the stick. The news was astonishing, whether Shelagh's assistant was guilty or not. Did Murray really have no idea what had happened to Fiona the evening before last? Maybe they hadn't kept as close company as she had thought. If there was no affair going on, that could be true. Then Rowan felt a jolt within her. What if Murray *had* been having an affair with her? Could it have gone wrong? Somehow led to this woman's terrible injuries? *No, please, not that.*

Unwelcome questions forced their way into her mind. Murray had his flaws, his emotional imbalances. But how bad were they? What had really happened with his first wife? Was the injunction just the beginning of a much more worrying story that he'd never admitted to her? Suddenly she wanted to be away from this place, to be alone. She felt the other woman's stare.

'Something's wrong, Rowan.' Shelagh began moving forwards, a hand outstretched. 'It's to do with Murray, isn't it?'

Rowan felt the beginnings of tears. The temptation to offload her worries was almost irresistible. But somehow she had to fight it. She wanted, *needed*, to keep the veneer of a solid family unit intact. To give in now would be to admit the collapse of everything. If it came to it, she could face the worst privately, but she was not yet ready to own up to her fears publicly.

So, it was with a wave of relief that she saw the figure of Gordon Kerr approaching from the manse.

# Forty-seven

Shelagh watched the slim figure of Rowan disappear up the steps and through the front door of her house. She turned to face her husband.

'I feel sorry for her. There's something wrong, very wrong. I think it's to do with Murray. I'm wondering if they've split up. I think she told us a lie before, about him being away.'

'Can't say I'm surprised.' Gordon scowled. 'Wouldn't trust him one bit. God knows what she sees in him.'

'Well, his looks for one. He can also be charming when he wants. He tried it with me the first night I met him.' She caught a trace of pain – or perhaps jealousy – cross Gordon's face. She hadn't intended to cause that reaction, but it left her feeling strangely satisfied. She went on. 'But you're right. I think she *is* unsuited to him. She did a very decent thing in getting the jotters back.' She nodded to the fire. 'That's all that's left.'

Gordon looked at her. 'I know. I saw you from the window.' He passed a hand over his shaven scalp, a gesture he made whenever he was worried. He glanced at the fire. 'I know you don't want to hear it, but given what's happened to Fiona Muir, it's just as well you got rid of them.'

Absent-mindedly he took the stick from his wife,

patting down the embers and kicking over the traces with his boots. 'I've been thinking over what you told me this morning about Sandy. I'm sorry for him, but I want you to promise me something.' He looked up at her, his face serious. 'I want you *not* to get over-involved. You've got the meeting this morning and the Church will look after Sandy, so please, take a step back. You just can't take much more pressure. What with your father, all the demands of here and . . . well, the reminders of Angus, thanks to that sod Murray. It's too much.'

She backed away from the dying fire and eased herself down on to the bench. 'I don't think the Church *will* stand by Sandy.'

He twisted round to look at her. 'Why on earth not? He's innocent until proven otherwise. Surely his employers owe him a duty of care?'

She shook her head. 'I think the general view will be that there have been too many "transgressions". There is no doubt about one thing: Sandy abused his position in the chaplaincy. Not intentionally. I'm assuming he couldn't help himself, but the charge will stand. To have had a sexual relationship, let alone a *homosexual* relationship, with one of his prison congregation is an utter breach of trust, an abuse of position, and breaks every ethical tenet we swear to when we are ordained. Some of the Church elders will see his behaviour as just one notch down from paedophilia.'

'The hypocrisy!' Gordon threw the stick down. 'The Church is full of gay men. Closeted ones. Some of those who are going to sit in judgement on him this morning probably fit that category. Anyway, this man Docherty was a psychopath. It was *he* who was abusing his power. You know how irritated Sandy can make me. He's so feckless at times ... and pedantic and ponderous at others.'

Steeling herself to maintain her composure, she watched in silence as her husband toed clumps of snow over the last embers and then turned back to her. 'But Sandy's harmless. Isn't he?'

Four hours later Gordon stood at his bedroom window. Below, his wife was heading towards the churchyard. He knew she was going to Angus's grave. It was going to be one of those rare visits. She'd sit out there for ages. At least he'd persuaded her to wear a coat. After that, she was off to see her father, alone. He shook his head pityingly. *What a masochistic day. She's really putting herself through it.*

Predictably, she'd returned from the presbytery meeting depressed. Only she, David Menteith and one other had spoken up for Sandy. The mood of the meeting had been clear: they were cutting him loose. So much for the loving, caring ethos of the Church. *Sickening.* He turned from the window and began to make his way downstairs.

He thought back to his earlier exchange with Shelagh at the bonfire. It had been very quick thinking on her part to get rid of the jotters. Presumably she must trust Rowan Shaw if she had done that in front of her. Yes, they seemed to get on well, despite or perhaps *because of* that wretch Murray. His wife had now disappeared behind a bush. He envisaged her, head bowed, at the grave of her brother. What on earth was going through her mind? She was now under intolerable stress but hiding it very effectively. That was one of her great skills, a skill learned all those years ago when she had coped with the very worst traumas that life could throw at a teenage girl. But now, despite the brave, at times even cold, demeanour, he judged that his wife was reaching the end. At least he'd convinced her to cancel the evening service so that she could visit her father. She'd seemed relieved at his suggestion and soon had her band of trusty volunteers ringing round the parish advising those who wanted to worship to attend David Menteith's Sunday evening service instead. Gordon sighed. It was for the best; she was in no fit state to fulfil her church duties at the moment.

As he headed down to the wine cellar, he wondered if her faith would help her stay the course. If not, would she find life unlivable? And would she take her own steps to end it very soon? Perhaps, among other things, she feared the mental disintegration that would turn her into her father.


'Mr Gillan, Shelagh's here to see you.' The nurse bent down to look into his patient's eyes. 'Mr Gillan. It's Nurse Terry. Your daughter's waiting to see you.' As expected, there was no response. The nurse turned and saw a colleague poke her head round the door.

'What's up, Rebecca?'

'There's a phone call for Mr Gillan. It's family. Might as well see if it'll make him talk. By the way, I've asked his daughter to go and get coffee, then come back and wait outside here. Just so we can get him ready to see her. I've got the phone, he can take it in here.'

She offered her colleague the handset and was gone, closing the door of the small room behind her. Nurse Terry turned to his patient. 'Mr Gillan, there's a phone call for you. After that we'll get your daughter in here, okay?' Slowly, the nurse lifted the old man's left hand and wrapped his gnarled fingers around the phone. 'There you go.'

Suddenly the phone fell from his grasp and hit the floor. Nurse Terry held up a hand. 'It's okay, Mr Gillan. I'll get it.' As he lifted it up, he heard the voice.

*'Dad? Dad?'*

The nurse cursed under his breath. The phone must have gone on to hands-free. As he tried to work out how to turn off the function, he felt the old man stir. The voice at the other end of the phone spoke again.

*'Dad? Dad? Are you there? I'm coming to see you soon.'*

As the nurse was about to put the handset back on to normal setting, the voice rang out once more.

*'Dad. It's Angus.'*

# Forty-eight

In one swift movement, Robert Gillan lashed out at the phone, smashing the nurse's hand with his own. The handset flew from his grasp, hitting the nearby wall. Then the old man jumped unsteadily to his feet. *'No, no, no! Stay away, stay away!'*

Halfway down the corridor, Shelagh heard her father's voice. She began running, the takeaway coffee slopping over the cardboard cup's sides and scalding her hand. She hurled the cup to the ground and raced towards the pale blue door through which she could hear his screams. But another sound had joined her father's: an alarm bell. From an opening on her left came three figures, all sprinting towards the door. As she reached the room, she could see four nurses and one doctor crowding around the crazed figure of her father as he repeatedly hammered the telephone handset against the wall, leaving a small crater in the plaster.

Ten minutes later Shelagh was sitting facing her father's psychiatrist. Also in the room was the nurse who attended her father and, standing beside him, the colleague who had handed him the telephone.

Nurse Terry was holding his ground. 'There is absolutely no mistake. The caller said, "Dad, it's Angus."'

Shelagh looked at him. The trembling inside would not stop, and she held her hands tightly clasped in her lap to hide any sign of shaking. She could feel the psychiatrist's scrutiny and knew he wasn't missing anything. Eventually, he turned to the nurse. 'That's fine, Terry. On you go and thank you. And you, Rebecca.' He waited until his office door was closed. Then he pushed his chair back, trying to adopt a more informal pose.

Shelagh sat up even straighter. 'Don't your staff read their patients' files? The nurse who took the call said the person on the line identified himself as a member of Mr Gillan's family. He even said yes when she asked him, "Are you his son?" I can't believe this. There *is* no son. *The only son he ever had is lying in my graveyard!*' She felt the blood rush to her face and held up a hand. 'I'm sorry. But I was here, on the premises. Someone could have asked me to take the phone to my father. If they'd told me who claimed to be on the line, I would have known. It was cruel ... a *terrible* trick to play. It's ju–'

Anger and fear were building inside her. She couldn't trust herself to say any more for a moment. The psychiatrist took his chance.

'I agree. It is utterly reprehensible. Have you any idea who would do such a thing? You heard Terry say the voice sounded like an adult male. But he couldn't be sure.'

Shelagh shook her head. 'Of course I don't have any idea. He's a mentally ill old man. He doesn't have enemies. Just the demons inside himself. It could have been anyone who knows about my father's case. Another patient, perhaps? But you've still not addressed my last point. How did the call get through in the first place?'

'I will investigate that, Reverend Kerr. We're short-staffed here, so people move around more than they used to. Neither of the nurses would have had the opportunity to familiarize themselves with the details of your father's case.' He stood up, indicating that the meeting was over. 'Please, come back tomorrow. See your father then. I hope he will be calmer. It'll be good for him to see you.'

She remained sitting. 'Has anyone visited my father of late? You must, at least, have some control over that.'

The psychiatrist shook his head. 'There have been no visitors. Would you have expected there to be any?'

'No. I'm ... I'm just looking for some kind of explanation.'

As she left the claustrophobic atmosphere of the office and looked down yet another endless corridor, she had to face the truth. Someone outside these four walls was terrorizing her father. And in turn, perhaps intentionally, they were tormenting her.

# Forty-nine

Rowan turned her head and shouted towards the open living-room door, hoping that her voice would carry upstairs. 'Elliot, can you bring that other suitcase, the one with the wheels, down from the attic, please?'

She heard his muffled shout of acknowledgement and continued packing. The living room was strewn with her clothes and Elliot's CDs. They needed to hurry. She wanted them to have an early night. She'd planned the drive to London carefully, so that they could have plenty of rest breaks. If they left at six in the morning when the roads were clearer, they should make it to Ben's house in Camden for a late lunch. Once again, he'd come up with the goods when help was needed. When she'd rung him and, in a tearful voice, told him that rather than him visiting them, she and Elliot needed to get away, he hadn't asked her why. Instead, he had calmly offered her the unused flat at the top of his house for as long as they needed it.

She checked the clock on the mantelpiece. It was getting on for 7 p.m. She looked through the front windows and saw with dismay that the snow had started again. If it fell as it had done a few days ago then they couldn't drive tomorrow. They'd just have to sit it out. That was the last thing she wanted to do.

She'd talked matters through with Elliot but had given him nothing near the truth. She'd said that she wanted to get away from the house for a while, to 'take stock'. A few days with Ben seemed the best solution. Elliot had jumped at the chance and was cheerier than he'd been for ages.

She turned around, scanning the room for what to pack next, and then she saw it: Elliot's parka, thrown across the back of the sofa. Slowly, Rowan picked it up, running a hand along the soft fake fur of the hood. She eased herself down on to the edge of the sofa, examining the coat. It hadn't occurred to her at the time – perhaps because she had been so astonished by the news of Shelagh's assistant – but the description of the parka Shelagh had given matched this. Exactly.

She let it drop in her lap and cast her mind back. The evening Fiona Muir was injured ... *that's right, I went to bed early after that awful meeting with Murray. I saw Elliot on the landing. He was going to make himself something to eat. Could he have gone out? But he knew nothing of Fiona Muir. No, it was all right. What a silly, illogical thought. I'm seeing demons everywhere. Just shows how badly I need to get away.*

She was about to throw the parka back on the sofa when she noticed the tear, under the left armpit. Lifting up the sleeve she saw that the torn area had something black on it. She peered more closely and sniffed: it smelled of something burnt. Like charred wood.

'Mum? I've got the case. Sorry to take so lo–' He stood in the doorway to the living room, both arms around the massive case. 'What are you doing with my parka?'

Despite the open fire and the central heating on high, she felt cold. 'Elliot, sit down please.'

She followed his movements as he put the case down and then walked slowly to the chair opposite. 'What is it, Mum?'

'Do you know who Fiona Muir is?' Her diction was deliberately slow and ponderous, but she wanted him to listen, really listen to her. 'I need you to tell me the truth.'

Nothing.

She tried again. 'Tell me. Please.'

'Yes. I know who she is.'

She shivered. 'Do you know what's happened to her?' He was staring at the fire. 'Elliot, look at me.'

His face remained blank, but he answered her. 'What do you mean, what happened to her? I don't know what you're talking about.'

'She's in hospital, Elliot. It sounds like she might die.'

This time he looked at her but said nothing.

'How do you know her? Tell me.'

He gazed at the fire once more. 'I saw her at Murray's hotel one night recently, after you threw him out. And . . . and I wanted to find out who she was.' He stopped.

She prompted him, dreading his reply. 'You went out the other night, didn't you? The night of the heavy snow. Why?'

He began biting at his lower lip, a habit she had hoped was long gone as it always signalled that he was feeling a deep anxiety.

'You don't know this, but Murray stayed at that hotel up the road much longer than he said. I went up there to confront him about it and about Fiona Muir.' He flicked a lightning quick glance at her and then looked back at the fire. 'That night the Kerrs came round, I heard everything they said to you. I wanted to run down and say, yes, I know Murray and that Fiona woman are up to something.'

He stopped to glance at her again and Rowan's heart turned over to see the frightened, vulnerable look she remembered from his childhood. *Oh God, Elliot, whatever you've done, I'll be with you, get you through it.* She waited for him to go on.

'I wanted to see Murray again, to have it out with him. If he was hurting you by being with that woman, I was going to . . . I don't know. Anyway, I'd missed him. He'd checked out. I thought he must have gone to Fiona Muir's. I was convinced they'd be together. I knew where she lived. I was going there.' He paused to take a deep breath. His look was far away, as if he was back in that empty, snowy street. 'He wasn't at hers, but I heard her talking on the phone. She was going to meet someone. I followed her to the school.'

Rowan felt sick. 'What happened?'

He said nothing. She tried again. 'Whatever you did, I'll help you.'

This time his head snapped up and he looked

directly at her. 'I didn't *do* anything. I'm telling you. I *did* follow her in, but I lost her. She went into the main part of the school. I trailed her through the building and then I saw her going out the other end. I ran to catch up. I couldn't see her outside, but then I noticed her footprints leading to the burnt-out wing.' He stopped to look at her again. 'I heard them.'

'Them?'

'Yes, her voice and another's. I couldn't make it out. Then I . . . I heard what I thought was a scream. I was scared then, so I turned and ran away. That's what happened. You have to believe me.'

*I want to believe you. I do, I do.* She held up the parka. 'The police are looking for a tall male dressed in a parka like this. The CCTV must have caught you. Your parka smells of burnt wood and you have a new tear under the armpit. I want to believe you, but you lied to me just now.'

She threw the coat to one side. 'You *did* know that something had happened to Fiona Muir, didn't you? Why did you deny it? Why didn't you tell me you had been there?'

He jumped to his feet. 'All I've done since coming here is to try and protect you from *him*.' He snatched up the parka. 'And I've been trying to protect you again over all this. It's not me you should be worrying about.'

He dragged the coat on, a twisted sneer on his face. 'It's Murray. I think *he's* the one who attacked Fiona Muir.'

# Fifty

She heard Elliot's angry slam of the front door and felt the tears start. The room appeared to be closing in on her. If only she could fly away and change time. She visualized herself, like Superman, spinning around the globe backwards. But where would she stop? Two weeks ago? A month? A year? To a time before she had met Murray? To before her career had taken precious time away from her and Elliot?

But that was all bitter fantasy. Now was now. Her family had imploded; she could trust neither son nor husband. Elliot may well have been speaking the truth when he said that he'd been protecting her, but how far would he go to do so? Did he want to extinguish Fiona Muir as her love rival? A simple equation: remove Fiona Muir – make Mum happy. Or, and this was the more sinister option, had he removed Fiona Muir and, by doing so, deliberately implicated Murray? Both her husband and son could get angry; she had seen it. But could they get angry enough to do that?

Whatever the truth, one thing was clear. When it came to it, she put Elliot above all else. She scrabbled about in the pocket of her jeans for a paper tissue and wiped at her eyes. There was an inescapable dilemma arising from all this: what should she do about Shelagh Kerr's assistant? Rowan felt sick at the thought. The information that the figure the police were looking for was in fact Elliot would help Sandy. But could she turn in her own son? Suddenly she heard the click of the front door.

'Elliot?' She stood up, listening for his reply, relieved that he'd come back so soon.

The heavy footsteps paused for a moment and then continued. Murray stood framed in the living-room doorway. Rowan, still choking from another onslaught of tears, could say nothing as her emotions turned from pain to fear, the adrenaline pumping through her body. Still she could say nothing. He stared silently at her for what seemed like an age. Then he took one step into the room. Instinctively, she took a step back.

'You've been crying.' He moved no further.

She found her voice. 'Why are you here?'

'I need to talk to you. Properly.' He looked around the room. 'You're packing. Where are you going?'

'Elliot and I are going away for a few days.'

He moved fully into the room, looking again at the mess of clothes and CDs. 'You're leaving. Why would you take so much stuff? What about your job, Elliot's school?'

Rowan stepped forward, quickly assessing if she could make it past him and into the hallway for a dash to the front door. But, even if she could, she knew she wouldn't. Elliot could return at any time. If Murray stayed in the house, who knows what might happen.

She repeated the lie. 'It's just a short break. We both need it.'

Murray looked even worse than last time: drawn, thin, pale and unshaven. 'You're going to Ben's, aren't you?'

Her face gave her away. Although, in truth, Ben was the only friend she had right at this moment and Murray knew that. She stood her ground and watched as he dragged both hands through his tangled hair.

'I can't believe this. *Fucking Ben!*' He kicked a pile of CDs out of his way and moved to the centre of the room.

Rowan edged away. 'Yes, we *are* going to visit Ben. Elliot's been missing London. A few days should be good for him.' She needed to calm Murray down, get him off the subject of Ben. 'So, why did you come here?'

But he seemed not to have heard her. He walked over to the fire. 'I don't want you to leave me, but I don't blame you if you do,' he said quietly. Uninvited, he sat down in exactly the same place that Elliot had occupied minutes earlier and began dragging at his hair again. 'Everything's fucked up. I'm fucked up.'

Rowan moved slowly to her previous position but didn't sit, merely perched on the arm of the sofa. That way she had the slight advantage of height over him and, more importantly, she was nearer the door. *Yes, that's right. Admit it for what it is. You're scared of your own husband.* She glanced out of the front window. The reassuring glow of lights from the manse offered her a heartening thought. She wasn't trapped here until Elliot came back. If she had to, she could run for help across the road and watch for his return.

Keeping her eyes averted from Murray's, she continued staring at the lights opposite. 'Fiona Muir has been attacked.'

He didn't reply immediately. Moments later she felt him look at her. 'I know. God knows what she was doing there at night in a building so unsafe and in a snowstorm. It's been all over the local news – as has the latest about the body in the fire. They've arrested someone for that, apparently.' He looked bleakly around the room. 'I need to talk to you. About this house.'

'Oh, really?' Her tone was glacial. Still she refused to meet his eye.

'Rowan? Please, look at me. I want to explain.'

She swivelled her head and offered him an icy glare. 'Do you? Well, don't bother.' She stiffened her legs, ready to move for the door if she had to. 'I told you before. I know you were there the day Angus died. The sweetshop owner saw you.'

'And I told you she was mistaken.'

She shook her head. 'Don't lie to me any more, Murray. I've been to see her. She's got an old class photo of you. She identified you. *You were there.* I don't know why you came back here or dragged us with you, but what I *do* know is that you're hiding something about that time. About Angus. And God knows what you did to Fiona Muir or why.'

He slumped back into the sofa. Slowly, Rowan stood up, watching the flutter of emotions cross his features. Eventually, he stood up too, but moved away from her towards the windows, turning his back to her. 'Go if you want,' he told her. 'Go on.'

They stood in silence. She could leave now, without fear. Make it across the road. But she was rooted to the spot. She had to hear what he was going to say.

Suddenly, he spun round. 'Unbelievable! Tracking down bloody witnesses and fuck knows what else. Investigating *me*.'

Then, just as unexpectedly, his features relaxed and his expression became unreadable. 'This is all my fault, I know.' His voice was surprisingly steady. 'I should have been honest with you from the start. But . . . going behind my back, th–'

She cut across him. '*Your* back. That's outrageous! You haven't been truthful with me or Elliot about anything.' She gestured to the doorway. 'I don't know you, Murray. I want you to leave. *Now*.' She pounced for the mobile lying on the coffee table. 'Or I'll call the police.'

He moved forwards. 'You mean it, don't you? You would call the police. You are wrong, so wrong.' She moved aside as he brushed past her and then, with lightning speed, he swung round, snatched the phone from her grasp and tossed it over her head to land on the sofa. Both of his hands gripped her upper arms as he held her rigid, forcing her to look at him, his face close enough to kiss her.

'I am not leaving. Yet.' He released his grip and stood back. 'I can't go on with this, Rowan. It's . . . it's ruining . . . it's *ruined* my life.'

'Then tell me. Just tell. What is it?'

He looked up, his face crumpling with pain.

'Angus was my brother. And . . . and I think I helped kill him.'

# Fifty-one

Rowan watched as he dropped his head in his hands, his body trembling. Slowly, he shuffled towards the sofa and lowered himself on to it. She followed him and sat opposite. 'How can Angus be your brother? What are you talking about?'

He said nothing for a long time. Then he raised his head, his face pale. He looked like he was going to faint. 'Half-brother. My father had an affair with Ruth Gillan. For years. They met through the church. Before he died, Dad told me so much. Said that he had to. He wrote to me and he talked to me about it all during the last few weeks of his life.'

He looked away from her. 'I couldn't tell you. You can't begin to know what I've been though. The hurt. It's strange – once you know something, even if it's a lifetime ago, the memories return but in a different way. Dad seemed so quiet after Angus's death. Mum was shocked, yes, but not in the same way. And . . . and we used to go to the zoo. Angus, me, Dad and Ruth Gillan. I see why they were happy times now. *God!*'

Rowan leaned towards him, trying to make sense of what he'd said. 'But . . . what do you mean you *think* you helped kill him? What happened that day?'

He glanced briefly at her and then looked away again. 'I sneaked away from the sports day that afternoon. I wanted to see how Angus was and take him some sweets. I'd won some chocolate at rounders. We were using my cricket bat. I still had it in my hand as I ran from the park across to the school. I assumed he'd be in room fourteen in the north wing. That room was always used for detention. I went into the school through a side door on the ground floor and, just as I reached the stairs, something hit me on the head.'

Tentatively, he touched the back of his head and went on. 'I woke up outside again, by the side door. I couldn't remember anything. I had absolutely no idea what had happened to me. I was confused. Had I tripped? Had something fallen on my head? Then I smelled it. Petrol. It made me scared. I wanted to get back to the park as quickly as possible. I didn't know what was going on, but . . . some instinct told me to run.'

Rowan studied his face. He seemed distant and shut off, as if he were back there in the school, forty years ago. 'As I got up to go, I saw my bat. It had blood on it. I picked it up and ran for it. Then, just past the sweetshop, I stopped. I knew something was wrong, but I panicked. I thought I'd get into trouble. The bat had my name etched into it. I ran behind the sweetshop and back into the school.'

'You went back?' Rowan asked.

'Yes. By then the fire had taken hold, even in the corridor. I threw the bat into the flames and ran away again, back to the sports day. My parents and the teachers didn't seem to notice anything strange about me. It was a busy, chaotic day.'

'You never told anyone about this?'

'No. I was scared. I didn't see anyone. Whoever attacked me was behind me.' He tugged anxiously at his hair. 'I've been living with this for ever. I've tried to forget about it over the years. Then . . . then Dad brought it all back. Told me things I never knew. Asked me things I wish he never had.'

'Asked what?'

He looked away again, staring at the floor. 'Ruth Gillan contacted Dad when she came back here, just before she died. She said that there was something in the house that would help . . . help explain why Angus died.'

'But why didn't she go to the police?' Rowan asked.

Murray shook his head. 'She didn't want to, or for my dad to go either. She said that if what she'd put in the house was found sooner rather than later, then it was meant to be. If not, then so be it. She said that the longer it was left, the longer the guilty would suffer. She said it was up to God. She wasn't very coherent. My dad said that she'd just about lost all reason.'

'And that's why you came here?'

Suddenly he stood up. She watched as he began pacing the room, constantly looking out towards the church. 'Dad was obviously in love with her. Her pain, his pain, over Angus must have been appalling. Worse for him, since he couldn't admit to it. It would have meant the end of his marriage. And he wanted to stay married to my mother. He cared about her. And for my sake, he said. But . . . but he asked me to look into the house if I could, to get to know it. Get to the truth. But I've found nothing. Maybe there is nothing to find.' He stopped pacing and turned to her.

'You see, Ian, the estate agent, was an old university friend of mine. He got in touch with the owners of this place, who didn't want to sell. But . . . well, that was what all that money was used for, all Dad's money. I paid way over the odds.'

Rowan scowled. 'So all this getting stuff from estate agents about other properties was all show?'

He dropped his head. 'Yes, and the sales pitch I showed you for this house was a mock-up. It was a private sale between me and the buyers. I . . . I couldn't tell y–'

She cut in. 'And you deliberately gave up your job to do all this?' With increasing disbelief, she tried to make sense of what he was telling her.

He glanced at her before looking away again. 'Yes. I wanted to be up here . . . and there was voluntary redundancy on offer. On lucrative terms. I needed the money.'

Rowan stood up, trying to process the scale of the deceit. There had been so many lies. Could he still be lying to her? Could he have killed Angus and the teacher? No, surely not without help. But why? What else didn't she know?

She looked up at him. Had he been reading the

doubt on her face? His eyes narrowed. 'You don't believe me. I promise you, I did nothing to Angus, *or* to Fiona Muir. And I was *not* having an affair with her. I don't want anyone else. Only you. I love you.'

He was looking for something from her. Understanding? Approval? Sympathy? But she had nothing for him, only the suspicions, fears and awful truths that had been swirling round her head for days.

'I don't know what to believe. I do believe that Angus was your father's son. I've been told that Ruth Gillan had an affair. But I don't think that is all that's eating you up. I think you did something much worse that day than you've admitted to me. Maybe it was a bit of bullying that got out of hand and became something far more sinister. I think you and Fiona Muir and maybe others were involved. Or maybe she knew something of what you did. I don't know all the reasons that brought you back, but you must have got the shock of your life to find her *and* Shelagh Kerr here.'

'No, no. It wasn't like that! Just listen. There's more, much more I need to tell you.'

She held up her hands. The anxiety and anger she'd felt over the last few days was at last being unleashed. 'Shut up, Murray. I think you and Fiona Muir maliciously tried to get rid of Shelagh, starting with your stupid trick with the jotters. But you had a falling out and now you've half killed her.' She dropped her hands. 'The guilt's written all over your face.' Rowan stood back. 'Leave.'

He didn't move.

*'I said, "Leave"! Fucking leave, you bastard!'*

Wordlessly he marched forwards, pausing to look at her. She turned her head away and felt the air shift as he brushed past. The slam of the front door told her that she was, again, alone. For a moment she felt nothing, unable to move.

Eventually, she caught sight of the mobile phone lying on the sofa where he had thrown it. *Elliot*. She had to find out where he was. Everyone she had once loved and still did love had left her this night. A dizzying sensation of loneliness and isolation gripped her, almost doubling her over as an uncontrollable sob burst forth. She looked around. She didn't want to spend another night here. Hurriedly, she moved across the room, picked up the phone and with shaking hands called Elliot's number. Straight to voicemail. She tried again but the same thing happened. He must have switched the phone off. Twice more she tried. Twice more there was no answer.

She was fumbling with the phone to try yet again, when the landline rang out. Her heart leapt and she ran over to the extension in the kitchen.

'Elliot?'

'Is that Rowan?'

'Yes. Who's—'

'It's . . . it's Gordon Kerr. I'm sorry to call you at night but . . . have you seen Shelagh? She's not . . . not with you, is she?'

She could feel her anxiety levels rocketing. 'No, why? What's wrong?'

'Could you come over here? Now, please.' His voice was strained and urgent. 'Of course.' Racing down the hallway, mobile still clutched in her hand, she called Elliot's voicemail, urging him to get in touch immediately. As she jumped down the front steps, she looked warily from left to right. No. Murray would be long gone. She reached the graveyard in seconds, but the nearest gate was closed and locked. Grasping the low wall she began to scramble over it. Ahead, the church lay in darkness. Even the outside light was off and the front door shut. But the manse showed signs of life. The porch was aglow and she could make out light coming from the rear of the ground floor. Having cleared the wall, she jogged across the graveyard, leaping over a low, ancient tombstone. But as she landed on the snowy grass she slipped, her right ankle twisting awkwardly.

'*No!*'

She ignored the burning pain and raced towards the manse. Without knocking, she fell into the vast hallway.

'Gordon? Gordon!'

She followed the flow of light all the way to the kitchen area: deserted. Then she heard a sound from behind. In the living room, lit only by the flames of the fire, sat Gordon Kerr. Around him a trail of paper lay scattered, extending as far as the fireplace, where some lay half burnt. He looked utterly dejected as he slumped on a sofa staring blankly at the mess.

She moved towards him and, ignoring the pain in

317

her ankle, crouched down at his level, forcing him to look at her. 'Gordon, it's Rowan. What happened?'

His eyes slewed from side to side until he managed to focus on her. 'It's . . . it's okay, I'm okay now. But . . . but I'm worried.' Suddenly, he went rigid and glanced manically around the room as if he'd just realized where he was. 'Are you sure you haven't seen Shelagh? I thought she might be with you. She . . . she likes you. Respects you.'

Rowan stretched to switch on a lamp. She needed to see more clearly what had gone on here. Painfully crouching back down, she looked at him. 'No, I've not seen Shelagh. Look, Gordon, what's happened? Has there been a break-in? I'll call the police.'

Her fingers searched for the mobile that she had thrust into the back pocket of her jeans as she'd raced across the churchyard. But he grabbed her sleeve.

'No, no. Nothing like that.' A shaking finger pointed to the other side of the room. 'Please, there's a bottle of brandy in that cabinet over there. Could you get me some?'

She hobbled over, grabbed the bottle along with a glass and returned. As she stooped down, her swelling ankle caused her foot to slip on the papers lying around. She glanced at them. They were pages from letters – handwritten letters – and what looked like lines of poetry. Greedily, Gordon snatched at the brandy and, with an unsteady hand, clinking bottle against glass, poured out the liquid. He drank it down in one and then picked something up from the floor.

He handed her two crumpled and part-torn pages of one of the letters.

'Please, look at this.'

With a growing sense of dread, Rowan began to read.

# Fifty-two

*Shelagh*

*What more is there to be said, you might ask? I am sorry for your transgressions. Or rather, I am sorry that your beliefs make you feel that you have committed the most heinous of sins. But as you said repeatedly during our hours of pleasure, you simply could not help yourself. You were 'powerless'. Yes, that's how you put it. I too was powerless to resist your charms, more breathtaking since they were hidden beneath both that seductive cassock and your respectable exterior. But I broke through, didn't I? That first illicit coupling I will always remember. I have had many sexual encounters, but to have trespassed beyond those holy robes was beyond fantasy. You took me inside you so willingly, gratefully, desperately. You whispered how long you had been secretly watching, admiring me, imagining this moment. Now, there you were, having me in a place of holiness where you preached the word of God! I couldn't have written a better script.*

*The support you have given me I can never repay. Please do not feel any guilt about what has happened between us. You say that it has been the most exciting experience of your life since you were called to the cloth. That is quite a comparison! Me and God!*

*I said earlier that the support you have given me I can never repay. But in one way I can. I can repay you with the truth. I* *hope that it will bring us even closer. Especially as you plan for the rest of our lives together. When you hear it, you may think I have deceived you. But it is better to have no secrets. I only lied to you so that I could get near to you. So that you would see the <u>real</u> me. Not the one of all those years ago.*

*As you know, I have written poetry for some time. It has been of great benefit to me – a kind of cathartic outpouring. I haven't shown you it all. But I show you this, my last poem. I have no need for any more.*

*Now that I have you.*

### Truth

Lies. No more.
Guilt. No more.
Sin. No more.
Secrets. No more.
Truth:
I do not believe in God.
I do believe in hell.
I have lived there.
Truth:
I have had many sexual obsessions.
Not love though.
Truth:
I have taken life.
Truth:
Guilty.
As sin.

# Fifty-three

Gordon Kerr's light touch to her hand brought Rowan back to reality. For a frozen moment the room had seemed to stand still in time. Images of Murray had come into her mind. Murray and Shelagh Kerr. Not Murray and Fiona Muir . . .

With a trembling hand, she held up the letter. 'I . . . I . . .' But her voice gave out.

Gordon gripped her hand more tightly and then let go. 'Do you see who it's from?' He tapped the page. 'Do you understand? Look at the top. Of the letter. *Look*.'

She lowered the two pages and studied the first one. The top was still crumpled over and torn. She brushed the side of her hand across it. Then she saw.

```
HM Prison Peterhead. Prisoner number PH
36453. DOCHERTY, Matthew.
```

She was having difficulty absorbing the information. 'But, bu–'

She felt Gordon gently remove the letter from her fingers. Then he reached for the glass and poured another brandy. He held it out to her but she shook her head. He downed it in one. She saw that his face was getting some colour back.

He turned to look at her. 'Shelagh thought that I was out tonight. But I came home early. I found her trying to burn these.' He nodded once towards the fire. 'They're a . . . a horrible mixture of stuff like that and some . . . verse, I suppose you'd say. Poetry. He seems to have been able to get them out of prison through one of his legal people. I assume they didn't know what was in them. Shelagh seemed calm when I discovered her. As if she wanted me to find her. I think she did.' He paused but shook his head when Rowan tried to speak. 'We had drifted apart some time ago, but I had no idea why. I . . . I didn't think for one minute there was anybody else. And when we moved here, I thought . . . well, being close to Angus was affecting her, making her strange.'

She frowned down at the letter. 'But I don't understand. *Sandy* had a relationship with this man Docherty too.'

She watched Gordon wince with pain and saw the beginning of tears in his bloodshot eyes. 'Yes. They *both* did. This . . . this *animal* Docherty obviously targeted them both. By all accounts he was the classic, seductive psychopath. Shelagh said . . .'

He tailed off and suddenly his body began shaking with silent sobs. Rowan moved closer and laid a hand on his cold arm. 'Okay, Gordon, okay.'

Just as suddenly the sobbing stopped and he swallowed hard. 'Shelagh said that she couldn't help herself. She explained it all. How . . . how they planned to make a life together when he got out. She said it was a sort of insanity.' His breathing was slowing. 'He wrote this letter to her before his release. A kind of baring of the soul before they were going to be together.' He stopped to swallow back a sob. 'At the same time he told her about his guilt. The allegations against the police were true. Docherty was, in effect, fitted up. But' – Gordon stopped and, half sobbing, half laughing, waved the letter in the air – 'they got the right man!' He lowered the letter into his lap. Rowan studied his face. He seemed more composed now after his outburst of emotion.

She put a comforting hand on his shoulder. 'Okay, Gordon. What else did Shelagh say?'

He sat up straighter, inhaling a deep breath before answering. 'Shelagh said that she had suddenly woken up, and saw that she'd been seduced by a devil. But . . . she woke up too late. I suppose it all had to catch up with her eventually.'

Rowan looked around the room. 'What happened tonight?'

He kept staring at the floor and began talking, more to himself than to her. 'I . . . I think it's because we'd drifted apart. I haven't been picking up on things about her.' He looked ready to cry again. 'And I drink too much. I'm not always on the ball. But I think Shelagh became overwhelmed by everything tonight. I said I'd forgive her for whatever she did with Docherty, and I meant it.' He paused; a flicker of hurt crossed his eyes. 'Though it's very, *very* hard to read that stuff about the woman that I love. Docherty's admissions of guilt were devastating to her, but somehow she managed to struggle on. But the news that Sandy had been Docherty's lover too. Well, I think that finished her off.'

'She had no idea?' Rowan asked softly.

He looked away. 'No. And now Sandy is in the most serious trouble imaginable. She said that she wanted to help him. And to do so she had to come forward. Yes, ruin her life. Reveal the letters. They would be relevant to any investigation into Docherty's murder. They were a strong motive, and here she was, destroying the incriminating evidence against her.'

He took the crumpled pages from his lap and smoothed his palm over them. 'Oh, God. You must understand. Part – *most* – of me wanted to help her. I'd been burying my worries about what had happened to Fiona Muir. Tonight, though, I had to ask Shelagh. About the fire that killed Docherty. About Fiona Muir.'

'And what did she say?'

He didn't answer, just dropped his head.

'Gordon?'

Slowly, he touched his face and drew the fingers downwards in a gesture of utter despair. 'Shelagh broke down. She was full of hate for Doherty, for Fiona Muir. I think she killed him and attacked Fiona. I tried to calm her but she became hysterical . . . ' He touched his scalp. 'She did this.'

Rowan could see the traces of a cut, coated with dried blood, just under his hairline. He held up his other hand. 'It's a very slight wound. I'm okay. Shelagh was like a demon. Full of anger, self-hatred. She kept saying that God had tested her and she had failed. That he was getting his own back. I tried to calm her down.' Another flicker of pain crossed his face. 'I shouldn't have tried to touch her, to embrace her. She shoved me into the fireplace and I hit the corner tiles.'

Rowan stared down at the crumpled letter in his lap, her mind whirling. 'What did she mean, God was getting his own back?'

He gave a bitter laugh. 'When you think about it now, how could she ever have escaped it? Inside she's been slowly killing herself every day. Maybe her beliefs helped for a while – years even. Self-delusion can be a powerful force. And coming back here was meant to be an act of atonement, a seeking of forgiveness. But it was doomed to failure.'

The tears began to slide down his cheeks again but he seemed oblivious. 'Tell me' – he turned to Rowan, his face ashen – 'how do you seek forgiveness for a little brother you battered and burnt to death?'

# Fifty-four

Rowan seemed to shrink into herself. The dark room, lit only by the fire and one solitary lamp, was hemming her in. She steadied herself as Gordon shifted beside her and she saw his strained face.

'Are you *sure* that's what she did to her own brother?'

'I'm as sure as anyone can be,' Gordon replied. 'She's never told me outright, but I know she's lived with it all her life, as I have lived with it all my life.'

'All *your* life?'

He tried to smile, but there was no joy there. 'I was Shelagh's teenage lover. Shelagh and I met in Corstorphine Park one day and that was it.' He let the crumpled letter fall to the floor. 'It's easy to mock teenage love, but I knew I'd found someone very special. It was to be taken away from us. Her father split us up. He never knew who I was. Shelagh had confided in Angus that she had a boyfriend and sworn him to secrecy, but the father got it out of him. He kept her in the house for weeks, claiming that she had glandular fever. But worse was to come. She was pregnant. He procured an abortion for her that left her sterile.'

'My God. That is appalling.' Rowan felt chilled; the

327

news left her reeling. But had this really driven Shelagh to murder?

'Surely she couldn't blame a young child like Angus?'

'She had to blame someone and, perversely, I think she loved her father. She certainly wanted to be loved *by* him. It was easier to blame her little brother. Imagine her state of mind. If it had happened today, I'm certain she would be excused on mental health grounds.'

He nodded sharply, as if convincing himself. 'You know, I think she spent her whole life trying to make amends. That's why I'm certain.' He closed his eyes, clearly trying to staunch the tears, and then opened them to look directly at Rowan.

'Shelagh and I saw each other only once again at that time, shortly before the family left the area. We met in the park. She didn't say much. Never admitted it. But I . . . I just knew what she had done. And when I met her again just a few years ago, I wasn't entirely surprised she had taken to religion in the way she did. If I believed in a higher being, I would have said that we were fated to be together again and that I was destined to be her saviour. I found her through the Internet and got in touch. I couldn't believe it. She still wanted to be with me. Maybe for a while I was her saviour.' He looked away again. 'But I failed her.'

Rowan shook her head in confusion. 'But why did she . . . why did you both come back here?'

'I went where she went. She said that she wanted to be near Angus. What could I do? She squared it with the Church. They knew that her brother had died here . . . And we decided to tell people that she and I only met for the first time later in life. It . . . it was just easier that way. '

'It must have been difficult when Murray came back,' Rowan said.

'I was furious. It was an added complication that Shelagh didn't need. I thought that whatever she had done, she had paid for it. When I thought he and Fiona Muir were out to get her, my instinct was to protect her.'

Suddenly, he stopped and stood up. 'I've got to find Shelagh. I thought, I *hoped*, she might have run over to you in her panic.' He glanced at the clock on the mantelpiece and then looked pleadingly at Rowan. 'She's been gone for ages. I'm worried.'

Rowan shook her head at the irony. All this while she had been looking to this place as a sanctuary, a place of refuge. 'She hasn't taken her car. I saw it in the driveway as I came over. Have you tried phoning her?'

'No point. Her mobile's in the kitchen.'

Yet again she thought of Elliot. 'Listen, it's complicated, but my son walked out this evening after a row. I need to find him. And my husband's not around either. Let's go back to my house. We'll think about what to do from there.'

She stood up and immediately the pain from her right ankle brought her up short.

'What's wrong?'

'I hurt my ankle running over here. Never mind that. Come on, hold my arm.'

His large hand gripped her firmly and she struggled to put her other arm round his thick torso. He was a well-built, muscular man, but she knew the journey was going to be painful. Rowan grabbed hold of his shirt and they began making their way down the hall to the front door. Rowan opened it. It had begun to snow heavily and the cold air roused them both.

She felt him nudge her gently. 'Okay, Rowan. Let's stick to the path and get over to your house as quickly as possible. *But watch your step.*'

They set off. Once out into the open, the wind and snow began their assault and she repeatedly had to spit snowflakes from her mouth and wipe them from her eyes. Twice he slipped and her ankle ached as she braced herself to catch him. Halfway across the graveyard he stopped, rubbing the snow from his face with the back of his hand. He was shivering violently and seemed to be faring worse than she was. She had to get him into the warmth, and tugged at his waist, but he wouldn't move.

'Someone's in the church,' he said. He was peering over at the building, its silhouette still visible despite the growing blizzard. He pointed through the snow. 'Look! There's a light on!'

Pulling away from Rowan, he staggered towards the church. 'It's Shelagh! It must be Shelagh! She'll be praying! Go back to the manse. I'll go and see.'

She watched as he moved further away into the blizzard, and felt the first pricklings of unease. In the immediate crisis her fear had vanished, but now it was back. Squinting through the snow across to the bright lights of her house, it seemed the most welcoming of refuges. She turned away and saw Gordon Kerr fading into the blizzard. Reluctantly, she bent towards the wind and limped after him, aware that the church, with its dark, threatening silhouette, was drawing them both away from sanctuary.

# Fifty-five

She caught up with him as he was rattling the front door. The outside light was off, the door firmly shut and locked. He tried again, wrestling with the circular cast iron handle, twisting it clockwise.

'Come on. *Come on!*'

Rowan eased his hand from the door. 'Gordon, it's locked.'

He snatched his hand away and began hammering at the ancient wooden door. She tried again to reason with him. 'Gordon, you know there's another inner door, just as thick as this. In this weather, with the wind, no one will hear you. Please. Let's go over to my house.'

He spun round, swaying slightly, and peered across to the manse. 'There may be spare keys there. I have to go back.' He took one step forward and slumped back against the door.

'Gordon, stop this. We're not even sure anyone is in there. Look at me. You're not dressed for this.' Neither was she, and she fought hopelessly to control her shivering. 'Stay out here much longer and you'll get hypothermia. I mean it. *Now come on!*'

He allowed her to take his arm and begin guiding him across the graveyard. But three steps later he stiffened and wrenched himself from her grasp.

'*The vestry door!* There's an entrance round the back that leads into the church through the vestry. I must try it!' With a surprising burst of energy he turned from her and began shuffling away through the snow.

'Gordon! Come back!'

Her voice couldn't compete with the rising wind, and the snow was swirling everywhere, whiting out visibility. Already she had lost sight of him. Cursing the pain in her ankle, she began heading down the side of the church, one hand touching its ice-encrusted wall to keep her on track. Drift upon drift of snow had collected where the wall met the ground, and she repeatedly had to step around them. She could just about keep up with his footprints before they were filled in.

'Gordon! Gordon, please wait. I'm coming!'

She made slow progress, staying as close to the church wall as possible, then stopped. Ahead was the silhouette of someone. For a millisecond she had the presentiment of danger. Then it passed as she saw Gordon emerge, a finger on his lips.

He staggered towards her. 'Ssh. The vestry door's unlocked. But something's wrong. I thought that I heard voices but the lights are all off again. I'm certain I saw one on earlier. I'm going in anyway, just to check. You go back to your house if you want. I can make it over in a minute.'

She shook her head. 'Absolutely not. I'll come with you. Go on, you lead the way.'

Tentatively, Rowan followed him. Moments later they were standing at the vestry door. Raising a finger to his lips again to ensure her silence, he slowly turned the handle. She detected the softest of creaks and then they were in. As she stepped into the dark, silent room, closing the door gently against the elements, she felt another stirring of unease.

'Gordon, be careful,' she whispered through the silence. 'Wait until your eyes get accustomed to the dark. It can take a couple of minutes. But don't put a light on.'

'Okay. Stay close.' His voice was rough but steady.

She could make out the bright white of his shirt and hear his slightly laboured breathing. The two minutes seemed like hours and then he spoke. 'Okay. I can see the door that lets us into the main part of the church.'

Inching forwards behind him, she heard the click of the door. They padded across the stone flagging together and moments later they were inside. Gordon had been right. There was a light on: a faint glow directed at just one spot and illuminating all its horror.

Hanging from the high pulpit, a church bell rope around her neck, Shelagh Kerr's long, robed body was swinging slowly in thin air. Beneath her, lying like a fallen halo, lay the brilliant-white clerical collar, beaconing out into the darkness.

# Fifty-six

Rowan stumbled forwards, overtaking Gordon and grabbed the swinging legs.

'Quickly, help me! Get that chair! One of those collapsible ones stacked against the wall! I need to get up higher.' She watched in frustration as, in a daze, he turned round and round before seeing what she meant.

Moments later he was back. 'Is she . . .'

Rowan shook her head, struggling to keep hold of the legs and simultaneously step up on to the flimsy wooden chair. 'I don't know –' Suddenly, her ankle gave way, nearly tipping her over on to the stone floor. She turned to Gordon. 'Look, can you get up here and keep hold of her legs? I need to get to the pulpit.'

He didn't reply immediately, just kept staring at the inert body of his wife, her face turned away from them at an odd angle.

Rowan tried again, her voice rising with tension and frustration. 'Gordon, I need your help. *Please*. Can you stand up here? *Now*.'

He tore his gaze away and looked dumbly at her. She was doubtful if he would manage it in his shocked state, but she had no choice. Scuffing the clerical collar away with his foot, he staggered over to her. Carefully, Rowan passed the legs over to him. 'Hold tight. I'll just be a second.'

Ensuring that he was as steady as could be expected, Rowan limped round him as quickly as she could and made for the pulpit steps. Something had caught her eye: lying on the floor was one of Shelagh Kerr's black shoes. The other was jammed in a crevice of the intricately carved wooden pulpit. That could only mean one thing: she had changed her mind once she'd let herself fall and had been holding on with her feet until her strength gave out. Rowan shivered at the image and scrambled up the steps. Now in the centre of the high pulpit, floating above the church, her ankle burning with pain, she felt suddenly light-headed. *Keep control. You have to be in charge. Gordon can't be. Keep control.*

Immediately she could see how Shelagh had done it. The brightly coloured sally had been wound round the other side of the pulpit and the thinner part of the bell-rope threaded through various crevices in the carved woodwork.

'I'm going to untie the rope from up here. You just be ready to take her full weight. Okay?'

She heard a mumble of assent and began to untie the sally. But it was going to be difficult: the entire rope was pulled taut.

'Gordon? I need to reduce the tension in the rope. Can you lift her up a bit?'

There was no answer, but in a moment she saw the rope slacken slightly, just enough for her to begin to loosen the sally's knots. Thankfully, the rope looked brand new, making the knots larger and more easily manageable than those in a well-worn rope. Working at frantic speed with cold, trembling fingers, she began to see the knots unravel. This was it.

'Hold on tight, Gordon. It's coming away . . . *now!*'

She heard his grunt, followed by the clatter of the wooden chair. Limping to the other side of the pulpit she peered over. Below, she could see Gordon laying out the body on the cold flagging, the chair upturned nearby. Rowan edged down the pulpit stairs and hobbled over to help him. She bent down and put her face close to Shelagh's.

Immediately she felt it: the warm breath of life.

# Fifty-seven

Rowan tore off her pullover and rapidly tried to wrap it around Shelagh's torso. Next, she grabbed the nearest hassock, propping the unconscious woman's head and shoulders against it. She fumbled in the back pocket of her jeans. 'We need to get help now.' The mobile wasn't there. She checked her other pockets. Nothing. 'My phone! I must have dropped it on the way over here.'

Gordon stood up. 'It's okay. I've got mine. I'll call an ambulance.'

'And the police.' She looked at him and saw a flicker of pain. 'I'm sorry, we have to. You know why. It's not just about Angus. It's Docherty and Fiona Muir.'

'I know.' He wandered a few feet away and began mumbling into his phone.

Rowan shivered. The flimsy T-shirt that she was left with offered no protection in the ice-cold church. She bent down again. Shelagh's breathing was shallow but steady. A scraping of feet on the stone floor made Rowan look up. Gordon was coming out of the shadows.

'They're coming, but it might be a while. The roads are clogging up because of the snow. We've to keep her warm and not move her.' He looked over to the vestry. 'I'm going to see if I can find something else to keep her warm. She keeps blankets there for wheelchair users and elderly parishioners. I won't be long.'

Rowan waved an acknowledgement. Stroking the unconscious woman's cold forehead, she began talking in a low voice.

'Shelagh, why? There must have been some other way. What drove you to it? Were you so lonely, so afraid, so desperate that there was no other solution?' Rowan wiped back a tear. She might as well have been talking to herself: lonely, afraid, desperate.

She shivered again and glanced round the darkened church. The blackness seemed to be closing in on her and the silence was complete; an eerie effect of the thick walls, as outside she knew the blizzard was raging. She bent to check on Shelagh once more, but the scrape of footsteps made her head snap up. She was confused. Gordon was on the other side of the church in the vestry, wasn't he?

She stood up. 'Gordon? Is that you? Gordon?'

Suddenly she heard the faintest of groans. Down on the ground, eyelids fluttering, Shelagh was trying to move her head. Rowan crouched, bending over her face.

'Shelagh. Shelagh. It's Rowan. It's okay, help is on its way. Gordon's here. You'll be all right.'

She watched as Shelagh's eyelids fluttered again. For a moment her eyes fully opened, stared wildly at Rowan and then closed again. She seemed to have drifted back into unconsciousness.

Rowan twisted round, peering through the darkness. 'Gordon! Come here! Please!' But her voice seemed to ring out into nothingness.

Once again Shelagh stirred, her mouth trying to form words. 'Help me. I . . . I nee–' Her voice gave out and then Rowan heard it: the now-familiar scrape of footsteps.

'Gordon? Gordon?' No answer. 'Who *is* that?' The sense of unease that had unsettled her on reaching the vestry was back. She felt Shelagh stir again. Glancing back and forth between Shelagh and towards where the footsteps were approaching from the shadows, Rowan watched as a figure emerged slowly from the darkness.

Moments later, Murray stopped at the edge of the shadows, his face distorted and strange in the low light.

# Fifty-eight

Rowan pulled herself away from Shelagh. The latter's eyes were closed and she was mumbling low incoherencies. Slowly, Rowan approached her husband as Gordon appeared with a pile of blankets.

He looked hostilely at Murray. 'What's *he* doing here?' Gordon didn't wait for an answer but moved swiftly over to his wife and bent down, placing blankets around her.

'Is she okay?' Rowan asked.

Gordon gave her a firm nod and then walked towards Murray. He seemed to be only inches away from losing control. 'I'll ask you again. Why are you here?'

Murray ignored him and looked at Rowan. 'What's happened to Shelagh?'

'She tried to hang herself tonight.'

His expression was cold. 'Well, if you'd let us finish our conversation earlier, she might not have. You might have been able to stop her.'

Gordon was moving closer to Murray, and she held up a hand to stop him. She addressed Murray. 'What are you talking about?'

He moved past her towards the pulpit, glancing down at Shelagh, who was now conscious and trying to sit up. He picked up a collapsible chair from a stack nearby, unfolded it and sat down.

Rowan had no time to work out what he meant and went to help Shelagh. 'Please, don't try to move. An ambulance is on its way. Look, lean against here.' Rowan grabbed two more hassocks and made a make-shift bed for her against the base of the pulpit.

Gordon was hovering by her side. He looked again at Murray, who raised his hand. 'Please. Both of you. Get some chairs and sit down. I've something to tell you.'

They stared at Murray and then reluctantly obeyed, watching him as he brought out a stained foolscap envelope and drew out two sheets of paper from it. Once again, Shelagh stirred. He ignored her and Gordon, looking briefly at Rowan.

'I came back to the house recently when you were out. I found this. It's a note left by Ruth Gillan up in our attic shortly before she died.' Without further explanation he began reading in a soft clear voice, his words echoing faintly around the church.

'"I am reluctant to leave an explanation but, at the same time, feel that I must. I have been living with the knowledge that I believe will help to solve the murder of my beloved son, Angus, for over five years.

'"A few weeks before his death we discovered that my teenage daughter had a boyfriend. This had been forbidden by my husband, who ran our house like a tyrant, particularly when it came to moral matters. My husband made the discovery by tricking Angus, who knew about the boyfriend. Matters grew worse when we found out that Shelagh had become pregnant. No amount of threats or pressure could make her reveal her lover's identity. My husband's fury knew no bounds. He effectively kept her prisoner for weeks and made her have an abortion. It was botched and has left her sterile. My daughter's fury, too, was incalculable. She had lost her sweetheart, her child and any chance of future motherhood.

"'During the many rows that my husband and I had over Shelagh's predicament, I deliberately and cruelly let it be known that Angus was not his son. He never found out who the father was. I aim to keep that secret. But two people certainly hated Angus at the time of his death: his father and his half-sister – although I know her hatred was short-lived and a result of trauma. And neither of them had alibis that day.

"'I have been driven mad these past years as I watched them both. At times I see my dutiful daughter, who still lives with us, looking at her father with such hatred that I'm sure she knows that he killed Angus. At other times I am convinced that my daughter, in a moment of blind fury, is guilty.

"'I can never be sure, but I am certain of something. One of them did it. And I cannot go on living because of that.'"

Slowly Murray lifted his head and, at the same time, the church was filled with Shelagh's hoarse, anguished cry.

'No! No!'

Rowan rushed to her side. 'It's okay, Shelagh. Please, don't talk yet.' She glanced behind her and saw a confused-looking Gordon.

'Can you get me some water? Her throat will be swollen.'

He nodded an acknowledgement and disappeared into the darkness, his footsteps heading for the vestry. Rowan turned her attention back to Shelagh. She was now emitting hoarse, throaty growls that must have been acutely painful, and was trying to ease herself up. Both her eyes were fully open and she was propped up on a forearm, the woollen blankets tangled around her body.

'Rowan . . . hel-help . . . me. It's no–'

Rowan squeezed her hand. 'Ssh. Please don't talk. Wait until help comes.' She cursed herself for losing her phone. Gordon would have to ring the emergency services again. How much longer were they going to be? The weather must have deteriorated significantly since they had entered the church. But the police would have taken his number. If they were going to be much longer, surely they'd ring back. She felt Shelagh's body relax. She had obviously run out of what little energy she had. She slumped back, her eyes closed. Rowan peered over at Murray, her mind numb. *Focus on the now, on who needs you most. On Shelagh and Gordon.* In the momentary lull, she thought of Elliot. Where was he? At home? Safe? In the warm?

Shelagh croaked again, now clawing at her neck as

if still choking. Rowan squinted into the darkness. 'Gordon! Have you got the water? Quickly, please!'

It seemed like an age, but eventually he was on his way back. As he reached the outer limits of the light's glow, she could see that he was brandishing a large plastic bottle of mineral water in each hand. A second later the sound of a mobile phone rang out and rang once more. Then it stopped. Moments later it rang again. Gordon stopped short, fumbling with his trouser pocket while trying to hold both water bottles in one hand.

Rowan exhaled loudly. 'At last. That must be the emergency services ringing back. Ask them how much long—'

As the phone continued to ring out, she heard another set of footsteps. Gordon froze and looked over his shoulder. Rowan stood up.

Out of the shadows, a tall, hooded, snow-covered figure appeared, a mobile phone held to its ear. The deep hood obscured the face. Then, with a deliberate slowness, the figure swivelled its body from side to side, taking in the entire scene, and removed the phone from its ear. As the figure ended the call, Gordon's phone went quiet.

The figure took a step towards Rowan. 'The call wasn't for him. It was for you.'

He turned, pointing at Gordon.

'That's not *his* phone. It's *yours*.'

# Fifty-nine

The silence was absolute. Then the figure tugged down the hood and Rowan could see Elliot's pale, taut face as he shook the snow from his parka. She rushed towards him, the remaining snowflakes on his clothes melting against her as she embraced him.

'Elliot, wha—'

But he pulled away from her. 'Wait, Mum.'

They heard a loud splatter as both water bottles fell to the ground, one splitting. The liquid seeped through a large gash in the plastic and pooled in a dip on the ancient stone flagging. Gordon was running away into the darkness. The sound of his footsteps quickly faded, and was followed by the distant slam of a door.

'*Gordon!*' Shelagh's attempt at shouting after her husband had left her coughing painfully.

Rowan spun round. Murray was still clutching the letter, while Shelagh was gesturing to the bottle of water that remained intact. Quickly, Rowan scooped it up, unscrewed the top and held it to Shelagh's lips. With surprising strength, she grasped the bottle and began gulping noisily.

Rowan turned to Elliot. 'What's going on? What's all that about my phone?'

He didn't answer immediately. Instead, he stood

staring at the vacant spot of light and shadow where Gordon had been standing moments earlier. When eventually he spoke, his eyes remained fixed on the darkness. 'I got home. You weren't in. Then I saw Murray, out in the snow, heading for the back door of the church. I had to come over. It took ages. It's a white-out. I've had my phone off, but as soon as I saw Murray I got really worried. As I was coming into the church, I started calling you. I saw Gordon Kerr leaving the vestry and his phone began ringing as I called you. I thought it was odd and tried again. It *had* to be your phone.'

They heard a faint moan. Shelagh's eyes were bright and she had pulled down the collar of her cassock, presumably to ease the discomfort. For the first time Rowan could see the garish red weal along the side of her neck. Shelagh signalled for more water. She rubbed at the delicate flesh as she gulped at the bottle. Then eyes blazing, she looked away into the darkness.

'Gordon did this to me! And he killed Angus! He told me so tonight!'

Rowan gasped. 'Gordon? But why–'

They all turned at the sound of scraping footsteps. Gordon stepped out of the shadows and into the pool of light flooding the altar and pulpit. 'Oh yes, Shelagh. You've spent your life wondering if your wretched father was a killer. I can see why you might have thought that. And he was, in a way. If he hadn't treated you the way he did, hadn't got that stupid little bastard Angus to shop us, then we wouldn't be here now!'

347

He turned slowly, taking in the entire group. 'But Robert Gillan has got what he deserved. You know what, Shelagh? I've broken his mind at last. Tormenting him. I've been calling him, even managed to see him when he was in the grounds of that bloody nursing home, drugged up to the eyeballs. By that stage he'd have believed anyone was Angus come back to haunt him! Who do you think set the fire in the nursing home garden? Who do you think told him about the fire at the school?'

Gradually he began backing into the shadows. 'There's been justice all right. And there will be more.' Moments later he disappeared. They heard his running footsteps and the slam of the vestry door.

Rowan dropped from a crouch into a sitting position on the floor. She felt cold, weak and dizzy. She was finding it difficult to keep a grip on reality. Shelagh's icy hand gripped her arm.

'Rowan?' Her voice was hoarse but clear. Shock had rallied her. 'You can't be expected to understand.'

Rowan shivered and tugged one of the spare blankets around her. 'But . . . but Gordon called me. Explained that you'd been teenage lovers . . . and said you'd run off, showed me letters from that prisoner who died in the fire in the school. Matthew Docherty. And . . .' She felt herself on the verge of hyperventilating.

Shelagh put a protective arm round her as Elliot moved towards Murray. He in turn slouched down on one of the chairs, head back, eyes closed. Shelagh

348

looked back at Rowan. 'It's true. I had an affair with a prisoner, a murderer. But I thought he was innocent.'

Her voice was growing in strength, although her face was still drained. She went on, staring ahead into the darkness. 'Somehow Gordon found out about it. It put him over the edge. He's been planning his revenge for a long time. Tonight he cracked, forced me over here and ... and did this to me. I think he was trying to use you as an alibi of some sort. He thought he'd left me long enough and that I would have ... would have died.'

Rowan took hold of her hand. 'It's okay, Shelagh. You don't have to say any more. We need to get out of here.'

But Shelagh seemed impelled to talk, despite the obvious pain in her throat. 'I didn't actually hang. I caught my weight with my feet, against the pulpit. I'm stronger than you might think. And my collar protected my neck until it came off with the pressure of the rope. But after that . . .' She swallowed repeatedly and looked back at Rowan. 'I couldn't have lasted much longer. You caught me just in time.'

She closed her eyes. 'Believe me, I have tried to pay for my part in Angus's death by giving my life to the Church. But I failed. I thought coming back here would help. Then I ran into Fiona Muir. I think Gordon dealt with her as he did with Matthew Docherty.'

Rowan shook her heard in bewilderment. 'Gordon was very, very convincing. But ... but how was he able to hide so much from you? I mean ...' The naivety of the question was obvious. 'I'm sorry . . . of course anyone can hide anything if they want to.' She glanced up at her husband. 'I of all people should know that.'

Murray looked up. 'Listen, I'm so sorry. Sorry for everything. But . . . I really think we should get out of here. Gordon never called any ambulance. You need to be checked out by a doctor, Shelagh. I think we should try to get back to the house and call one from there.' He stood up and moved towards her. 'This is going to come as a shock, but . . . my father was your mother's lover. I'm Angus's half-brother.'

'*No!*'

He smiled. 'I couldn't tell you before.' He looked round at Rowan and to a puzzled Elliot. 'I couldn't tell *anyone*. And . . . I was at the school when Angus died. If I'd known then what I . . . ' He looked at Rowan and then back to Shelagh, holding up his hand. 'Don't say anything. We can talk later.'

Shelagh nodded repeatedly, amazement and confusion creasing her features.

The group got to their feet in the low light, feeling as if they were in a dream. Each remained in their own silent world until it was time to go. Elliot was the first to move down the central aisle, his footsteps loud as he strolled to the vestry door. Helping Shelagh to her feet, Rowan discarded the blanket. Murray threw it over the back of a pew before bringing up the rear of the ragged group.

In the background, Rowan heard the rattle of the

vestry door handle. 'Put the lights on, Elliot! There must be a switch somewhere!' She knew it would do them all good to get out of the gloom. The group waited but there was no answer.

Moments later, Rowan heard his footsteps. But something was different. This time he was running down the aisle, towards them. Elliot leapt back into the light, his gaunt features taut with fear. 'It's locked. And there's something else.'

But he didn't have to tell them. They all picked up the odour simultaneously.

Petrol.

# Sixty

The church was filled with an explosion of noise. Rowan moved towards the centre of the group, shouting. 'Phones! Phones! Elliot, Murray. Come on! Christ, why didn't we call the police as soon as he ran off?'

Murray shook his head. 'No good. My battery's down, the phone's fucked!'

Shelagh looked back into the darkness. 'Elliot, you've got a phone. *Quickly!*'

Suddenly, another pool of light appeared to their left. A lamp in a corner by the altar had been switched on. There Gordon stood, hands by his sides. 'You either give me that phone or I'll start the fires.'

Looking at each of the group in turn, he threw up the two polished chrome Zippo lighters as if he was about to start a juggling act. As he caught them, his eyes stopped on Shelagh. 'I mean it. I've rigged the place. Pretty rudimentary, but if the fires start, this place will go up like a handful of straw, believe me.' He switched his attention to Elliot. 'The wonderful windproof Zippo. Practically impossible to blow out, even if flying through the air. Imagine. Now slide that phone across the floor to me. *Now, damn you!*'

Shelagh moved forwards, grabbed the phone from

Elliot and skittered it across the floor. She touched his shoulder lightly. 'He means it.'

Next, she turned to face her husband. 'Gordon. Please, stop this. At least let *them* go. You hate me, I know, but they've done nothing wrong. Please.' She began to step forward, but Rowan dragged at her sleeve to stop her as Gordon raised one glinting lighter and flipped it open, the metallic click echoing round the walls of the church.

Slowly, he lowered his arm and flipped the lighter shut again. He stepped back into the shadows, his disembodied voice a low hiss. 'I *hate* you, do I, Shelagh? Well, let's just look at that, shall we? Look at the causes of that and the nightmare you've brought on me, on yourself, on everyone. You ... you transgressed all right. On the most sacred ground of all. Forget your God, your religion. It's all meaningless hypocrisy. You committed an unforgivable, evil deed. You took my love and you tore it to shreds.'

'I know, Gordon, I know and I'm sorr–' Rowan tugged at her sleeve again to stop her.

'Shut up!' Gordon's voice echoed round the building. 'Fucking shut up!' They heard the metallic sound of the lighters being repeatedly opened and closed. 'Do you know how much I loved you? I hoped – yearned – to find you again one day. And, like a miracle, I did. I found your name on the Internet. I had been searching for so long. I discovered what you now were: a woman of the cloth. It was no accident that we met.

353

I engineered it. Call that obsession if you like. I call it pure, devoted love. I was so scared. I didn't know if you'd still feel the same. But you said that you did and we . . . we seemed to have a happy time. At first.' The metallic clickings of the lighter tops resumed.

Rowan looked at each of them, almost imperceptibly shaking her head. She began to take deep breaths to quell the sense of rising panic. Standing up for so long was making her ankle throb, and she grasped the side of a pew for support. She waited for her captor to explode with rage at her movement, but heard nothing.

He stepped back into the spotlight. He was like a star turn, holding the stage, and they, the adoring audience, hanging on his every word or action. He seemed to be working out what to do next. Throwing a contemptuous glance at Murray, he said, 'So you were the little fool with the cricket bat that day. You almost wrecked my plan.' He looked at Shelagh. 'You had no idea what I felt when we had one of our illicit phone calls and you told me that your little brother was to miss sports day because he was going to be on detention. It was a prize! I knew how to get to him, knew what I was going to do to him.' He glanced back at Murray. 'But *you* almost fucked it up. Never mind, your bat came in useful. And, after all, didn't I let you live that day?' He clicked the lighters open and shut. 'But not today, perhaps!'

Rowan watched in sick apprehension as Murray said softly, 'Don't, Gordon . . . don't do any more. There's been enough.'

Gordon sneered contemptuously at him. 'Coming back here was the biggest mistake of your life. You weren't welcome, not by me or by my wife. I thought that little offering of fire I gave you in your back garden might have you thinking again. But no. Too bad. You deserve to be here.'

Shelagh spoke. 'Gordon. *Please*. Leave him.'

He ignored her and turned to Rowan. 'Is your husband a liar?'

She knew there was only one answer. 'Yes.'

Murray looked away from her.

Gordon moved one step forwards. 'What does he lie about?'

Without asking permission, Rowan took a seat in the pew that had been supporting her weight. 'I'm not sure of everything he lies about. But . . . he's lied to me and my son about the house. We knew nothing of its history until I found out by accident from your wife.' She acknowledged Shelagh's look of sympathy and went on. 'He lied about not being at the school the day Angus died.'

Rowan noticed Gordon turn towards Murray. 'You *do* deserve to be here.' He turned back to her. 'What else does he lie about?'

She knew she had to play for time, and went on. 'And I thought he lied to me about Fiona Muir. I *thought* he was having an affair with her.' She watched Murray shake his head but he kept silent.

'Do you think he attacked Fiona Muir?' Their captor's voice was taking on an even harder edge.

Rowan shook her head once. 'I thought he might have done. But I don't now. My son believed that they were having an affair. He was following her the night she was attacked. But now I think *you* attacked her.'

He didn't answer immediately but looked at them all one by one. 'I didn't attack her. I had been . . . well, playing with her. Sending her notes, pretending to be a knowledgeable local, someone who could prove that Shelagh had killed her little brother. The jotters were my work, among other things.' He turned to his wife. 'I knew about the nauseating letters and poetry he'd been sending you. I knew where you hid them. That was one of your greatest errors, Shelagh. God, I'd have loved to have seen your face when that bitch Fiona showed them to you. You must have been terrified. How had his verse got there? Did you think you were going mad? Did you think God was punishing you? Oh yes, I've been planning my revenge for a very long time.'

They all watched as he waved a hand at them in a carefree gesture. 'But whoever dealt with Fiona Muir did me a favour. I did wish her ill and she would have got worse from me than she ended up with, I assure you. She was scum and I had finished with her.' He turned, grimacing at Rowan. 'You don't think your son was being a bit . . . over-protective of you that night, do you?'

Before Rowan could shout a denial of her deepest, buried fear, Elliot leapt forward and Shelagh caught his sleeve. 'Don't. He's just playing with you, trying to provoke you.' She glared at her husband. 'Stop it! We know *you* did it.'

Now it was Rowan's turn to shoot her a warning look. They could not afford to anger him any further. They heard a single, threatening click of a lighter, but he stood stock-still, staring at his wife. Rowan stood up and pulled Shelagh back, turning her away from Gordon and whispering in her ear. 'He wants to needle you. Just wait. I'm trying to work out what to do.'

She felt the other woman relax and released her. As they turned to sit down again, Rowan noticed that the puddle of water from the split bottle seemed to have grown. How? She looked upwards. Was there a leak in the roof? Her gaze fell back to the floor and then the realization hit her. During the last few minutes the smell of petrol had been getting stronger. *Oh God, no. No.* Somehow he had doused the floor and the fuel was slowly creeping its way to the altar end of the church.

Elliot had caught on to what she was looking at and, wide-eyed, glanced frantically from the pooling liquid to her. She closed her eyes at him once, in a silent attempt to reassure and calm him. Murray, too, had seen what was under his feet.

Back in the shadows, Gordon's voice rang out. 'I see that you've just noticed what's beneath you. You know, kept in a sealed container, petrol is perfectly safe. But once mixed with the air? Well.' There was a short burst of metallic clickings and then silence. 'That's why it's one of the most commonly used accelerants in cases of arson.'

Rowan felt Shelagh stiffen and look down. Then she lifted her still unshod feet. Her stockinged soles were soaked in petrol. Rowan reached out and grabbed her hand, pulling her close. She kept a reassuring hand on top of hers and nodded to Elliot, who moved to sit beside Murray again.

She cleared her throat in an attempt to keep her voice under control. 'Gordon? If you burn this place down, and us with it, it will be obvious that it's arson. Don't . . . don't you think that you will be the chief suspect? Husbands of murdered wives usually are, aren't they?'

'Oh, thank you for your concern, Rowan.' His tone had changed to one of mock politeness. 'But this . . . this *outcome* is one of several I had planned. Any one of them would have done me just fine.'

He stepped back into the light, both hands in his trouser pockets. Then he brought them out, a Zippo glinting in each. He looked directly at Shelagh and then moved back into the shadows. As he spoke, Rowan gripped her hand, warning her not to react.

'So there you have it, Shelagh.' His voice had turned softer. 'Our final chapter.'

Rowan registered the significance of his last words a second too late. *He's going to burn us all. Himself too. He wants to die.*

'Run!'

Two metallic clicks and then, out of the darkness, she saw the twin lighters aflame, arcing high though the air in opposite directions, one aimed directly at their ragged little group.

# Sixty-one

With an agonizing heave, Rowan managed to push Shelagh to her feet and then bundled past her.

'Elliot! Run!'

To her relief, she saw that he had already leapt to his feet. She limped towards him, arms outstretched, just as he ran towards her, his arms mirroring hers. But, to her horror, as she reached him he dodged sideways and ran past. Spinning round, she saw him, as if in slow motion, his long, leggy stride taking him into the direct line of the blazing, falling lighter.

'*Elliot, no!*'

Suddenly he stopped and, like a cricketer waiting for the catch, stood, legs apart, both hands cupped, tracking the approach. But, as he adjusted his position, it happened: the slippery amalgam of petrol and water on the smooth stone floor beneath his feet had him tumbling backwards.

'*Elliot!*' Rowan ran as quickly as she could, arms still outstretched towards him. *If he dies, I want to die with him.*

As he continued falling backwards, his long right arm shot out, his slim fingers grappling for the burning lighter before it fell to earth. She reached out for the hand that contained the lighter, throwing her body on top of his and bracing herself for the impending fireball. Next she heard his explosive breath of relief as he pocketed the closed lighter in his parka. 'It's okay, Mum. It's okay!'

But as she rolled off him, she felt Elliot stiffen. '*Mum! Look!*'

The second lighter had done its work. Ahead of them, the entire central aisle was a line of fire. Rows of pews either side had ignited, and the noise of splintering wood rang round the blazing church.

Elliot shouted into her ear as he scrabbled to get up. '*Where are they?*'

Rowan pulled herself up, peering into the flames. 'I don't know! We have to find a way through!'

'But, Mum. The doors are locked, the windows are too high.'

She placed a damp palm to his cheek. 'Let's try the left aisle. There's still a way through there. They must have gone to the front door. Maybe we can break through it.' She grasped his hand and, as she pulled him with her, noticed the blanket hanging over the back of a pew alongside the half-full bottle of water. Pouring out the contents, she shoved the now-soaked blanket at Elliot. 'Take that. We may need it.' Looking back, she saw that Shelagh's clerical collar, that once brilliant-white halo, had been transformed into a ring of fire.

She tugged at Elliot and they moved forward. The noise of splintering wood was now thunderous in the high, echoing space. Halfway up the left aisle, as she dodged the attacking flames, she realized they had another problem. The smoke was thickening, obscuring vision and catching at her throat. 'Elliot. Put that blanket over us. Keep your head down and keep hold of my hand. I'm using the wall to my left as a guide. Stay with me.'

A few stumbling steps on and she could hear voices. Momentarily, the smoke cleared and she could see what was happening. On the ground by the front door, Gordon and Murray, his left sleeve in flames, were locked in combat. Standing over them, Shelagh was repeatedly screaming something incomprehensible. As Rowan pulled Elliot nearer to where Shelagh stood, she could hear what she was shouting.

'*Keys! Keys! He must have some on him! Get them!*'

Rowan pulled the blanket from their heads and approached the tangle of bodies. She threw the blanket over Murray's burning sleeve. Elliot tore off his still damp parka. Shelagh grabbed it from him and began patting out the flames. Suddenly, Murray flung out his other arm and something metallic landed at Rowan's feet.

'*Keys!*'

She hurled the bunch at Shelagh. '*Quickly!* You know which is which.'

Fumbling with the parka for what seemed like a lifetime, Shelagh threw it back at Elliot. 'Keep at it!'

In seconds, the inner front door was open. Rowan tugged at Elliot and pointed to the open door, pushing him towards it. Next, she dragged at Murray. But he pulled away as both men staggered to their feet and disappeared back down the left aisle.

She felt a tug. Behind her, Shelagh was shouting. 'Come on! Let's get out. We need to call for help.' Passing through the vestibule, the sight and scent of fresh flowers stopped Rowan short. *Reality. Another reality. A better reality.* Moments later, the three of them fell on all fours, coughing into the deep, fresh snow and gulping greedily at the welcome bracing air. Rowan looked upwards. The sky was dark but clear: the blizzard was spent.

Shelagh stood up. She was shivering violently. Her stockinged feet had disappeared into the snow, but her face was determined. She threw the heavy bunch of keys at Elliot. 'Take your mother to the manse. It's nearer. Call for help. There's a first-aid cupboard in the utility room. The smallest key will unlock it.' Rowan watched as Shelagh made her way back into the vestibule and turned. '*Go on!* I'll see if I can help Murray.'

Suddenly, Elliot was dragging her up. 'Come on, Mum.' He snatched up his parka and wrapped it round her.

With renewed energy, she took his hand and began wading through the snow, the scent of fresh flowers still with her, bringing tears of survivor's joy to her eyes.

# Sixty-two

*St Margaret's House, two weeks later*

Rowan stood at the living-room window, watching as the last box was loaded on to the removal van. She turned round to see Elliot shoving too much into a backpack.

'Hi, darling. Let me just see Viv off and then we'll go. I want to get back to London before nine. Ben rises early and it's not fair to keep him up waiting for us.'

She moved into the hallway. Viv Baxter walked towards her, a hand outstretched. 'I can't thank you enough for letting me look round this place before you go. In the circumstances it was very generous of you.'

Rowan took his hand and returned the warm handshake. 'Let's keep in touch.'

At the front door, he paused. 'I don't want to pry any more, but how is your husband?'

Part of her wanted to tell him that he wasn't going to be her husband for much longer. But that was private information. 'It's not prying. He's okay. He escaped with a badly burnt arm. He needed some skin grafts. He's still in hospital, but he'll be fine.'

'What actually happened? I mean, how did he get out of the church alive?'

'Through luck and courage. He showed considerable bravery in turning on Kerr in the first place. Once he'd managed to prise the door keys away from him, the rest of us ran out. Shelagh, to her credit, went back in for Murray. But he had already run down the other end of the church, away from Kerr. He's not sure why. A panic reaction. He just wanted to get away from him. Anyway, the next thing Murray knew, Kerr suddenly burst into flames. They had both been rolling about on the floor and were saturated in petrol. A spark or flame must have ignited him. Murray managed to run past him and out through the front door. Shelagh had already been beaten back by the flames and was lying in the snow outside. The two of them staggered over to us at the manse. Help was on its way.'

'I see. Can you tell me more about Gordon Kerr? Do you remember when I said that if a young boy had killed Angus, I wouldn't want to meet them today?' He shook his head in wonderment. 'And you did.'

Rowan sighed. She had been far from truthful in what she had told him during the morning's visit. Yet again she was going to have to lie. 'It's really a case of a lifetime of mental illness and obsession. The police have unearthed some adverse psychiatric reports from Gordon's Army days, which are really the only indication that something was wrong. But, given that he hunted Shelagh down in adulthood through the Internet and refound his true love, his insane jealousy isn't that surprising. Obsession and jealousy go hand in hand, don't they? He adored his wife, he hated his wife.'

She looked at him to see if she could detect any doubt about her simplistic explanation, but there was none. She went on. 'Gordon took a far greater interest in what Shelagh did in her job, and who she had contact with, than anyone knew. He was convinced that she was having an affair with this life prisoner Matthew Docherty, whom she had contact with during her chaplaincy.'

Viv Baxter gave a small laugh. 'Absurd, of course.'

Rowan tried to return the laugh. 'Of course. Anyway, they don't know how Gordon contacted him but he did and lured him to that awful death in the school. He told us that much. He denied the attack on the local head teacher, Fiona Muir, but we still think he did it. He was conflicted. Angry at his wife for supposedly cheating, but even more furious at Fiona Muir for vilifying his wife. And as for poor Shelagh? Well, she was very, very lucky. Perhaps Gordon's mistake was trying to use me as a witness. He'd miscalculated how long it would take her to hang, simply because he could never have guessed that she'd use her feet to cling on to the pulpit. That, and her clerical collar, saved her life.'

Rowan shrugged. 'And of course Murray and Elliot's arrival really made it all too much for him to control. Though he would have burnt us all alive if he'd had his way.' She hunched her shoulders at the thought. 'He tried and almost succeeded.'

Her visitor shook his head pityingly and stepped back to take a final look at the house. 'I'm glad you're okay. I'll keep in touch. Take care of yourself.'

Rowan watched Viv stride down the lane and then waved to the driver of the removal van, whose head was thrust out of the cab, waiting for her instruction to go. With a judder, the van pulled away from the house.

'Rowan!'

Shelagh was hurrying across the lane, elegant as ever in what looked like a new cassock. As she trotted up the stairs, Rowan was relieved to see that the woman appeared rested and refreshed. They had enjoyed a farewell dinner at the manse the night before, but both of them were still exhausted and had retired early. It seemed as if Shelagh had caught up on her sleep.

She put her arms around Rowan. 'Have you heard about Fiona? She didn't make it. I talked to the police first thing. They definitely think Gordon did it.'

Rowan returned the hug. 'Yes, I know about her. I heard it on the radio. It's appalling.'

Shelagh smiled, obviously trying to lighten the mood. 'You weren't going to run off without a final, *final* farewell?'

'Oh, no. I had a last-minute visitor. I was going to pop over. You're looking well today.'

Shelagh lowered herself on to the narrow wall that bordered the steps and Rowan did the same on the other side. The action reminded her of two gossipy schoolgirls whispering their secrets.

'I'm very well, Rowan. This morning I seemed to have turned a corner. I think it was getting Gordon's funeral out of the way. It was yesterday afternoon.'

Rowan was surprised at the news. 'Why didn't you tell me? You didn't go, did you?'

Shelagh looked over to the manse. 'I wanted to get through the day on my own. Of course I didn't go, but it . . . it's just knowing that the funeral's over. It's a relief.' Her eyes narrowed. 'He got his divine retribution.' She seemed to drift away for a moment and then looked back at Rowan.

'You know, I have so much to be thankful for. I've found a specialist unit that will take Dad. It's on the shores of Loch Lomond, a bit of a trek but it's a good place. The restoration of the church interior began today. I'm just about to go in and have a look at what's going on. Oh, and my new assistant's starting today, too.'

'I meant to ask you last night. How is Sandy?'

Shelagh looked back over to the manse. 'He's working for a charity in London. He knows the Church can't accommodate him, but I think he's going to be happy. He wants to come and visit me soon.' She lowered her voice. 'It is . . . *beyond* kindness for you and Murray and Elliot to respect my privacy about Matthew Docherty and to . . . well, to square your stories about everything. I know it's lying. Let's call it for what it is. I'm worse. I've lied *and* destroyed evidence. The letters are all burnt. And you–' She hesitated. 'You know what? I never sent him one letter back, ever. Not one. I wonder if, somewhere inside, I knew he was dangerous . . .' She let the word slide into silence before looking up again at Rowan. 'I can never repay you for all you've done and for saving me.'

Rowan moved to sit beside her and put an arm round her thin shoulders. 'Look, Shelagh. I'll only say this once more. Your private life is yours to live with. It is none of our business. We are not moral judges. Also, you went back for Murray and put yourself in great danger.'

Shelagh lifted a hand in protest. 'Yes, but Elliot put himself in worse danger. When I saw him run for that lighter, I thought he was going to go up in flames. He is an exceptional young man, thanks to you.'

Rowan felt the beginning of tears. 'Yes, he is exceptional. Now, listen to me, Shelagh. Gordon was either very ill or evil. I'm not sure I believe in the latter, bu–'

'I do.' She felt Shelagh stiffen. The two words had been whispered, as if to herself. Now she had fallen silent.

Rowan squeezed her shoulders gently. 'Okay. But either way, you and others have suffered for long enough. The police have accepted that Gordon was responsible for killing Angus and Matthew Docherty, and for almost killing you. And who knows about Fiona Muir.'

Shelagh whispered, 'Yes, she has suffered retribution too.'

'Maybe so. But listen, let's just leave it all now. You will never be able to live with yourself or . . . or with God if you don't let it rest now.' Rowan waited. Had she gone too far by presuming to speak about her faith, something she knew nothing about and certainly didn't share?

Eventually, Shelagh answered. 'You're right. It's that age-old thing. Moving on. Angus has been laid to rest now.' She stood up and placed a hand softly on Rowan's. 'You didn't talk about Murray last night. Is the situation still the same as a few days ago? You're still splitting up?'

'It's over, Shelagh. He accepts it. Has to. There have been too many lies. I think he needs some help. Therapeutic help. He's a bit of a lost soul really. We just don't fit. And Elliot comes first. He'll never accept Murray again.'

Shelagh squeezed her hand gently. 'You must be relieved, though, that all your worries about him having an affair with her, and maybe attacking her, are unfounded.'

Rowan lied for the second time that morning. 'I'm not even thinking about that now.' *And I'm trying so hard not to think about Elliot that night either. He told me the truth. Didn't he? Now, leave it be.*

She embraced Shelagh for the last time and felt a shudder go through her thin frame as she spoke. 'It's funny knowing that Angus had a half-brother. Maybe, if Murray sorts himself out, I'll see him again. Anyway, say goodbye to Elliot for me. And keep in touch. You're welcome to visit any time. Look after yourself.' She stepped back. 'And, Rowan? Be happy.'

Back inside the house, Elliot was waiting, backpack in one hand and parka hanging from his head by its hood. 'Is this it, then?'

Rowan grinned broadly and picked up her handbag.

'Oh yes, my darling. This is it. London here we come.'

Without a backward glance, they marched slowly in single file down the empty hallway. Once on the front step, Rowan locked the door and took one final look up at the house. *You have a life of your own, don't you? A life of love and hate. You're alive.*

# Sixty-three

Rowan stared in dismay at the back of the car. It would need rearranging. Elliot had stuffed the luggage in any old way. She watched him, slumped in the passenger seat. She couldn't scold him. Like her, he just wanted to be on his way as quickly as possible.

She began unpacking everything and laying it out on the driveway, her thoughts turning back to Fiona Muir. How the police would prove that Gordon was responsible she didn't know. Maybe they never would. It was odd, though. He had been adamant that he hadn't attacked Fiona Muir. If he was responsible, why not admit it, as he had with everything else he had done?

As she loaded the last bag, Rowan felt the release of tension. Slamming the tailgate shut, she made her way to the driver's seat.

'Right, let's go. Got everything you need?'

'Yeah.'

She turned on the engine and began inching out into the lane. Opposite, she saw Shelagh crossing the churchyard with a striking young man, dressed, like her, in a dark cassock. She looked up and waved, her face beaming. Rowan waved back and turned into the lane.

Beside her, Elliot was leaning over into the back seat struggling to get his parka. She braked as he fumbled in the pockets, eventually pulling out his iPod from the breast pocket. As he teased out the earphones he paused, parka on his lap.

'Mum? You know when you took my parka in to be cleaned and mended? Did you empty the pockets?'

'Yes, of course.'

He frowned. 'Oh, okay. It's just that . . . I forgot until now. The lighter, the Zippo. Was it there, in the front top pocket?'

She looked at him. 'No. Why?'

He looked confused. 'It must have fallen out when we were putting out the fire on Murray's arm.'

As Rowan moved the car forward again, she caught sight of Shelagh in the rear-view mirror, her hand raised in a final farewell. Then Shelagh turned and placed her hand gently on the young man's shoulder, inviting him to enter the church ahead of her.

Suddenly Rowan braked again and the car jolted as her thoughts drifted back to what Shelagh had just said. *Retribution. For Gordon. For Fiona. Divine retribution.*

She thought back to that night as she'd tumbled out of the blazing church into the snow, gasping for breath. Through eyes stinging with smoke, she recalled Shelagh's tall figure moving slowly back towards the church door, something silver glinting in her hand. What? The bunch of keys that Murray had wrested from Gordon? Momentarily she closed her eyes, trying to conjure up the scene again as if it were a film rolling by in slow motion. She opened them again. *She'd remembered.* Shelagh threw the keys to Elliot. Now Rowan saw it clearly in her mind's eye. *Silver. Glinting. The Zippo! Stolen by Shelagh out of the parka. And tossed into the church at her husband.*

*Retribution. Delivered by a woman of the cloth.*

'Mum? You okay? It doesn't matter about the lighter. It must have fallen out.'

She turned to Elliot, trying to smile, and then looked away, edging the car down the lane as her hands began to tremble on the steering wheel.

Rowan risked a final glance in the rear-view mirror just as Shelagh's tall, elegant figure turned one final time to look at her, before being swallowed up into the darkness of the church.

# CARO RAMSAY

**SINGING TO THE DEAD**

Two seven-year-old boys have been abducted from the streets of
Glasgow. Both had already endured years of neglect and betrayal - but
for Detective Inspector Colin Anderson the case is especially disturbing,
because the boys look so much like his own son Peter . . .

Then, with police resources stretched to breaking point, a simple house
fire turns into a full-scale murder hunt. An invisible killer is picking off
victims at random and, if DS Costello's hunch is correct, committing an
ingenious deception.

As his squad struggles to work both cases, DI Anderson learns that
deception and betrayal come in many guises. For while the boys'
abductor is still out there no child is safe - as young Peter Anderson is
about to find out . . .

'A cracker . . . many shivers in store' *The Times* (for *Absolution*)

# DAN WADDELL

**THE BLOOD DETECTIVE**

**From the author of the bestselling *Who Do You Think You Are?*
comes a haunting crime novel of blood-stained family histories and
gruesome secrets ...**

*'The past isn't like that; you can't just bury it, mark it down as history.
It's taken more than 125 years, but the events of 1879 have finally
washed up ...'*

As dawn breaks over London, the body of a young man is discovered in
a windswept Notting Hill churchyard. The killer has left Detective Chief
Inspector Grant Foster and his team a grisly, cryptic clue ...

However it's not until the clue is handed to Nigel Barnes, a specialist in
compiling family trees, that the full message becomes spine-chillingly
clear. For it leads Barnes back more than one hundred years - to the
victim of a demented Victorian serial killer ...

When a second body is discovered Foster needs Barnes's skills more
than ever. Because the murderer's clues appear to run along the tangled
bloodlines that lie between 1879 and now. And if Barnes is right about
his blood-history, the killing spree has only just begun ...

'There's panache a-plenty in this intriguing tale...Sharp plotting,
elegant writing, engaging characters, a cracking climax. A series is
promised. Bring it on!' Reginald Hill

'A fascinating and original investigation into the dark roots of our
family trees' Val McDermid

# He just wanted a decent book to read ...

Not too much to ask, is it? It was in 1935 when Allen Lane, Managing Director of Bodley Head Publishers, stood on a platform at Exeter railway station looking for something good to read on his journey back to London. His choice was limited to popular magazines and poor-quality paperbacks – the same choice faced every day by the vast majority of readers, few of whom could afford hardbacks. Lane's disappointment and subsequent anger at the range of books generally available led him to found a company – and change the world.

*'We believed in the existence in this country of a vast reading public for intelligent books at a low price, and staked everything on it'*
**Sir Allen Lane, 1902–1970, founder of Penguin Books**

The quality paperback had arrived – and not just in bookshops. Lane was adamant that his Penguins should appear in chain stores and tobacconists, and should cost no more than a packet of cigarettes.

Reading habits (and cigarette prices) have changed since 1935, but Penguin still believes in publishing the best books for everybody to enjoy. We still believe that good design costs no more than bad design, and we still believe that quality books published passionately and responsibly make the world a better place.

So wherever you see the little bird – whether it's on a piece of prize-winning literary fiction or a celebrity autobiography, political tour de force or historical masterpiece, a serial-killer thriller, reference book, world classic or a piece of pure escapism – you can bet that it represents the very best that the genre has to offer.

**Whatever you like to read – trust Penguin.**